OCCIPITAL CIRCUS

& Other Stories
Regarding Phrenology

By

Anders M. Svenning

A HellBound Books Publishing LLC Book
Houston TX

Anders M. Svenning

A HellBound Books LLC
Publication

www.hellboundbookspublishing.com

Printed in the United States of America

Preface

You are reading *Occipital Circus & Other Stories Regarding Phrenology*. In the late eighteenth century, phrenology became a foremost science of the personality. Some even considered it a religion. The premise of phrenology is composed of six basic tenets.

1. The brain is the organ of the mind.
2. The mind is composed of multiple, distinct, innate faculties.
3. Because they are distinct, each faculty must have a separate seat or "organ" in the brain.
4. The size of an organ, other things being equal, is a measure of its power.
5. The shape of the brain is determined by the development of the various organs.
6. As the skull takes its shape from the brain, the surface of the skull can be read as an accurate index of psychological aptitudes and tendencies.

The stories contained in this collection regard the face or cranium. Going into this project, I had the intention of reinventing horror. Horror too often is based on the supernatural. Within many horror stories, the characters undergo experiences that are unexplainable or paranormal. The stories contained herein are not this type of horror. The stories and the horrors contained herein take place within the characters' minds. Some of the stories contained within this book achieve this effect more so than others. It is cerebral horror which takes place every day. A fear becomes manifest and projects itself onto the world at large and develops into a bigger and heightened fear.

Phrenology, too, has developed. Phrenology has transformed into contemporary nanoscience. Phrenology is extinct, for the most part. People, scientists and commoners alike, question phrenology's validity. The examination of the skull to determine human aptitudes has been replaced by the nanoscientific study of the brain.

In 2006, a theory called grounded, or embodied cognition, surfaced in the scientific thought pool. The premise of grounded, or embodied cognition, regards the correlation between fiction and actuality—that is, the reading of fiction and the internal performance which takes place within the brain. Subjects, in 2006, were hooked up to a Magnetic Resonance Imagine (fMRI) Machine and told to read a book. When subjects read words like "Lavender," "Cinnamon," and "Soap" not only was the temporal cortex (the language center of the brain) activated, but the olfactory (smell) cortex, too, was activated. When subjects read words like "Perfume" and "Coffee" the olfactory cortex lit up. The olfactory cortex was activated when reading words conveying a sense of smell. The sensory cortex acted similar. When a subject read phrases or metaphors like "Velvet voice" and "Leathery hands" their sensory cortex was stimulated, as if the velvet voice were heard in actuality and as if the leathery hands were touched in actuality. The same occurred when subjects read phrases like "John grasped the object" and "Pablo kicked the ball." The motor cortex became activated, as if the readers were moving in actuality, grasping the object, and kicking the ball.

Many discoveries have been made since the surfacing of phrenology. The above theory, grounded, or embodied cognition, is one of them. Reading Occipital Circus & Other Stories Regarding Phrenology, your brain will be stimulated and will be emulating the characters' actions. Phrenology has developed into nanoscience, and horror has developed into grounded reality. This book is the conduit and you are the subject.

Anders M. Svenning
Tampa, Florida
Spring 2017

Anders M. Svenning

Table of Contents:

OCCIPITAL CIRCUS

& Other Stories

Regarding Phrenology

Anders M. Svenning

Charlie

The mysterious occurrences, which followed the events six months ago, could not have left me in any more a taciturn state. Many times, as a psychologist, I have wondered about the contents of the human mind—that is to say, the physicality of that device, which beings know and operate.

It has been said by colleagues, professors, and revolutionaries in the field, the human mind is a manifestation of the brain. Still do I believe this; and yet my mind conceives an ill- regarded poise. Learned have I of the theory of sensation and perception. The mind senses certain cues in the world, and the mind processes these perceptions into what is real or believable. The truth is that all we know is what has been shown to us by a greater, macrocosmic entity, who reigns supreme in a setting of the dogmatic human mind.

I know many have been put in homes for the demented as a result of what I have experienced; and yet, I seem to have presided as triumphant, regarding phantasmagoric hallucination. Have they been hallucinations, which have resided in my eye and ear over the past six months? Any such answer does not state Charlie is a false being, for he has shown me the unseeable and the forsaken world of the supernatural.

Many with whom I have spoken say this is a symptom of mental illness or madness. It is not the case, as I have interacted with, since then, the supernatural. It was incomprehensible, at first, and, because I was delirious, I thought not of analyzing the visions, which were presenting themselves to me as dark orbs, flashes of light, and absolute feelings of euphoria and dysphoria and paranoia. The tale begins on the way home from work. I had had a headache, and it seemed to be reproaching.

As I got into my car, at about 6 o'clock p.m., I yearned for my returning home and having a proper sleep. Driving down the interstate highway and without my seatbelt fastened, a truck slammed on its brakes, and I collided with the rear end of the truck and was thrown through the windshield; I had shattered it with my skull. I woke in the hospital later, after having fallen into a coma for three dreadful days. Upon waking, I heard the crackling of fire between my ears, and a purple cloud of paranoia was all but present; I did feel the urge to tear the IV from my arm and run into the streets, but the doctor had come in and had begun to state I had suffered from a blow to my head and that my brain had been bleeding and that my temporal lobe was quite swollen. He said it would take weeks for me to become full in my functionality.

I was sent home hours later; and upon my homecoming, I fell into the deepest, darkest sleep of which I had ever been a part, for during that sleep, I was tormented with visions of black entities walking hither and thither, a hoarse voice called to me from within the bathroom, lampshades spoke in whispers, an apparition was sobbing in the mirror, phantoms strode in and out of my bedroom, to and from my bedside, with hooded raiment and cowls covering their faces in darkness, cats clung to the walls, with their claws, and hissed at my seeing them, hairy hands stroked my forehead, and my imagination was taken to a new heightened level, as if my walls and ceiling gave way and my nights were spent in an open breeze, underneath a tarp, beneath which was being performed empirical Babylonian ritual; for the grave sounds of monkish basso were heard, and the tenements were no longer mine, but were for the passage of dæmonic spirits. Fevers took me, and cold sweats accumulated on my brow and I howled in pain at the throbbing of my head, constellations lending care, asteroids bounding and fighting off the shadows. Hallucinations of fire licked my forehead and mists soothed me, simultaneous. Deep in a state of torment I resided for the following week, after my release. I did relinquish my will to live, for the hallucinations and the visions were growing in darkness. Words were spoken to me and my emotions were tumultuous. Pain, as well as fear and agony, were omnipresent. Days and nights passed until the episode receded and I was able to get out of bed and walk and get bread from the kitchen. It was then the hallucinatory phenomena started taking a more physical form. I know not whether my fiancé had heard it, for she stayed asleep, but as I approached the living area with concerned steps, I saw what was occurring. A schizophrenic split tore my apartment in two; and a large, purple orb, which was in the middle of my apartment, gave way to whence the beast came. He was small, three feet in height at most, and malicious and temperamental. Hoarse croaking emanated from the center of that abyss. I was paralyzed; and the croaking and coughing of the animal, whom I was to name Charlie, came out from the orb in a greenish-black smoke. The feline eyes captivated me. The beast had teeth like that of a wolf. It occurred to me, for the space was from then on cursed, the exchange was not of Earthy descent. He had come from the abyss and the dark recesses of the human.

I uttered not a word and hoped no other would ever see him. I hoped whatever this was should be a mere hallucination. This was the first time I saw Charlie, but it was, with certainty, not the last. The being, as fast as it had appeared, had vanished, and left me in bleary-eyed wonderment, as I, trembling, took to my bedroom, where my fiancé was asleep. She had not heard what had occurred in the other room. I would tell her when I felt it most appropriate. I was sick. The headache had not subsided, and I lay down in my bed for a short sleep.

The visions and chilling pains subsided, and I had a dull headache with which to contend, and then I slept, however frightful I may have been; for Charlie had entered my life, and he would never leave.

***

To this day, the darkness that filled my living area that night takes residence in my heart and mind, for nothing, as horrid as it had been, could have been more beautiful. I decided, the following day, what I had witnessed was paranormal in nature. My mind was captivated by the occurrence. Days passed. I thought, with frequency, of the happenings of nights prior, and, slow, the headache did recede, and I started taking walks with the dog we had in the apartment, a small Beagle, who was to learn of the certain wrath of the paranormal, first hand. Doctor appointments, MRIs, and pain pills were the common successors of brain trauma, and yet, there were still the uncommon ones—I told nobody of what had occurred, neither the sleepy visions, nor Charlie's manifestation—and nothing had occurred for some time, until I decided I was not going to speak of it to anybody. It was when walking our dog and returning home from another paranormal sight one night I told my fiancé what I had experienced.

Walking in the rural parks of south Florida, the dog and I came upon a particular ill-lit stretch of sidewalk. The trees whispered foul thoughts in the air and the sick, green moon shined downwards, and squawks and calls of crows were heard from the path, which narrowed out into the ill-lit area, and when the dog approached to sniff a bush, the shadows of the bush feigned and gave way and came alive into the shadows, which twisted and turned and formed the small mass that was he—the bush no longer had a shadow—Charlie, who had consumed the shadow, in whole, and who then sank his teeth into the small Beagle, and the Beagle leaped back and squealed, and I blinked and the bush was normal. I looked, and the dog had four holes in its hide, which told me what I had seen was not an hallucination, but a reality. I carried the dog back into the apartment, where we dressed the wounds, and my fiancé said she would bring the dog to the veterinarian the following day.

Upon lying down at night, I, as a learned psychologist, understood the matters of hallucinations, but I no longer believed what I was experiencing were hallucinations. What I was having was called, by the professionals, a psychotic break from reality; but I knew what I saw was real and not fabricated. I contemplated the fruition of these circumstances. The mind was a manifestation of the brain, yes. The brain was composed of gray matter and white matter, the physical brain and the dream essences, respectively. I thought what I was seeing was black matter, the very source of mental illness and depravity. Paranoia, euphoria, and all detrimental states of being must have been associated with this black matter and what I was seeing was none other than this, and I knew I was not the first to witness it, nor the last, because people experienced this on a daily basis, clairvoyants, spirit sensitives. I decided this was what I had become, in some peculiar and partial way, and I realized the scenario, and I was not going to let this entity take violent to the innocent, nor was I to let it get out into the public. I feared hospitalization. I did not want to be a victim of the very field in which I studied. It was daybreak by the time my thoughts settled, and I had gotten very little sleep. I decided I was going to wait for something to happen, and when it did I was going to be ready.

***

I walked to the grocery store one afternoon, while my fiancé was at work. The dog lay in its crate, and I took to fancy steps to and from the grocery store, ambivalent and feeling much better, following the recent few days. Climbing the steps to my front door, I realized I had forgotten the key and I was locked out! I stood for many seconds, outside my apartment door, and when the phenomenon—Charlie, the supernatural—surfaced in my mind, like it always did in the recent few days, I heard a crack in the door and a click. The lock had been thrown open, and I entered my apartment building. I know not how or why that lock was thrown. Nobody stood opposite the door when I opened it.

Nobody but Charlie could have opened the lock. I thought of luck. Perhaps this paranormal entity could help me in some ways. A peculiar sensation had been felt, upon stepping into my apartment; and I knew Charlie had been the one who had opened the front door. It made too much sense in my mind; and as I put away the groceries, a thought pulled me into the bathroom. I looked into the mirror for a time, contemplative. The hair was growing back, above my ear. The stitches were still present. I turned around and went into the living area, where the torment had vanquished my skepticism. The front door opened, and I jumped in shock. My fiancé was home for lunch.

Over lunch, we discussed our marriage. We had set a date, months prior, and she was excited, thinking about the planning of the ceremony. Over the past few months, many of the chores, which preceded marriage had been delivered, the flowers, the church, and the reception. She asked me if I wanted to move up the wedding to a closer date, perhaps in two weeks. I agreed, just as well excited as nervous. I was undergoing an intense feeling of nostalgia, and I was a part of something, which was out of my control. Nevertheless, I agreed to move the wedding up to a closer date, and I hoped all would be cordial.

The day of our wedding was lavish and set with ornaments of flowers and eucalyptus. The soft scents of frankincense eased my wary head into reverie. The people were gathered in seeming groups, on the pews. We had walked down the aisle, irreversible—the ceremony was said to be eternal—and eternity filled my thoughts, for in this state, when death did do us part, was he, too, going to be there, the havoc-ridden entity of my imagination and fears, as an essential periphery?

Would he not be there, to bark into my ears? I mused yes; and when I threw the veil, I felt descend upon me the realization he was watching—I felt the urge to spin around and search for him, up and down throughout that hall and underneath the pews, nervous twitches rendering my lips incapable of speech—and I uttered my vows, upon finishing which, I heard the church settle, and I pulled my lips from hers, and I heard the stark barks of a dog outside the church and the applause of the people and the laughter of the priest—and the howls of Charlie.

Theories upon theories—mind manifestation, sensation and perception, hallucination, the normal and the paranormal, the natural and the supernatural—were at hand, and what came first, it was apparent, was the brain, and then came the developed mind, i.e., theology.

It dawned on me these occurrences were not a shade apart from religion. For if there was a god, there must have been the opposite end of the spectrum, and Charlie was not a deity, or was he? Was he, Charlie, the anti-deity of whom so many tales have spoken? I knew not. I knew only that in two weeks' time, we would be off to Marrakesh, Morocco, for our honeymoon.

***

Arriving in Morocco, I was greeted with the sweet scents of spices and lavender. The

climate was so hot I broke out in beads of sweat, and a thrumming resounded in my chest. Here, I would learn more of him, in the mysterious settings of Africa, where superstition reigned true and supreme, and where ancient secrets lay waiting.

On the first night, I looked into the starry night's expanse. The Moroccan night was adorned with constellations and arduous zeal. The blazing sun had set, and the moon was gazing, picturesque, to the right, as the waning moon gave way to a shooting star and soothing aromas. I felt confident under its Neolithic eye, which looked upon me with radiance; the great city ochre, the square of Jemaa el-Fnaa rich, the Saadian sultans pure, the fortified Gueliz—all watched over me on their own accounts, and the only thing that would take me higher in thought was mounting a Berber carpet and flying into the cosmos, dipping wholesome into the Menara Gardens and perhaps touching the silken stratosphere. The Palace of El Badi called me, and there the magic carpet flew. Jocular festivities lit brazen fires in my mind; and I thought I must learn of him. I decided, on the morrow, I would visit the fountains of Gueliz plaza, and learn of my certain fate. Poppy and gold embraced my eyes. The liquid riches of the city trickled over the pupils, which had seen the incomprehensible. I dreamed of the belly dancers of traditional Morocco. I saw with my inner eye the callings of knowledge; and therein did I wake and hike into the city.

I was to call him, while in the square of Jemaa el-Fnaa. I, with my wife, strode into the square, and I found a bench on which to sit. I was approached by many people, selling their goods, but I dismissed them with a sure wave of my hand. She was perusing the shops when I closed my eyes and went deep into a trance. The headache was not so much present, but there was a hollow pressure above my ear. I focused on the pressure for many seconds, until I said to myself his name, and then I opened my eyes.

He was standing in a dark aura before me. Nobody saw him; and people walked through

him, as if he held no substantiality. He growled at me, and I heard the growl not from where his body was, but within my head. I felt again the purple cloud of paranoia descend. The hollow, dull feeling in my head tingled with sensitivity; and I was sure this was the time in which I was to see his true nature. The greenish-black smoke in which he was shimmered. A scream was heard, and he threw his head around and looked at the young girl who had spotted this devastating and fearful entity.

So, somebody else had seen him. When the young girl's mother asked what was the matter, the young girl cried and said no words in return. Charlie was still there, breathing fumes of hatred and abhorrence. I thought, within myself, and asked him what he was. He breathed out the fumes of wrath, spoke in a hoarse voice, "DJINN."

I had heard of the word. It was the darker side of genii. They were innate in their evil, and when compelled they did works for the host. Upon cracking my skull, I had awoken a dark recess of my brain, where the djinn were housed. Charlie was one of the disturbed masses, which once roamed the deserts and tormented nomads of the Sahara. In Jemaa el-Fnaa was the only time I saw Charlie in Morocco; and there I sat, on the bench, watching Charlie dematerialize and planning my literature. My bride stated she wanted to bring home a rug, on which I would put a coffee table, and on the coffee tables I would light candles, to encourage reality. Charlie was all my fears and all my insecurities and all my quirks and ticks, embodied as one man and as one person; and as I write, benevolence is needed, because I do not see myself succumbing to Charlie's darkness and turning to a darker form of Henry Gaudreau. It writes my tale. Not many people have tested my faith. I have triumphed. I shall take residence in the triumph.

Malorana

Before the team embarked on the expedition, they had gotten vaccinated for the mumps, West Nile Virus, scarlet fever, yellow fever, cholera, and half a dozen other diseases—all of which circled pinpricks behind fleshy legs, sensitive and heavy, and the trip had been launched in early autumn, when the diseases would be less rampant and when the bugs would be less fierce, to avoid any viral encounters. The team had taken its precautions; the excursion, which was to delve into the colors of mysticism and time, had been organized by a man, Dr. Reid Phillips. "Six weeks in the bush," it was said by Dr. Phillips, "would be an incredible experience in your lives." Dr. Phillips, with good fortune, possessed a boundless and, it almost seemed, unquenchable sense of yearning, an outstanding force, distinct, since his childhood, to understand the lost knowledge of man; and many of his students shared this same wonderment, Dr. Reid Phillips's white eyebrows jumping at the thought of Man's reconciliation. "Needless to say," said Dr. Phillips, "you will have participated in perhaps the grandest discovery in all of history, a truth belonging to the gods," Dr. Phillips, with a head full of advantageous ideas and with his chosen students, the biologist, the psychologist, the geologist, and the photographer in front of he, Dr. Phillips, as the head archeologist in the team, which had been found.

***

Lloyd Caston had ordered a chunk of amethyst prior to the meeting held by Dr. Reid Phillips, and he was to miss the delivery of the amethyst. The expedition to the Peruvian rainforest was to encompass weeks, and the amethyst was to be delivered in the weeks he was in the Amazon, with the excavation team. Missing the amethyst did not faze him. The amethyst was something to which to look forward, upon returning from the trip to the Peruvian rainforest.

Lloyd Caston was studying amethyst, as well as many other crystals, which held a degree of spiritual gravity, to many peoples around the world. Amethyst, tiger's eye, and emerald were only a few crystals of which Lloyd Caston was studying, and the crystals were worshiped as gifts from the gods, by people around the Earth, and the crystals were said to hold mystical qualities in their compositions—natural anomalies, which were said to be compositions of living creatures, living animals, and with thoughts and ideas. Lloyd Caston had started to believe in the once-foolish notion that crystals had thoughts and ideas. He, in all of actuality, found himself, with interest and even on a spiritual level, compelled to study the crystals and the stones, which held this mystery. The excavation, however, took precedence. Lloyd Caston was excited about the excavation, and he was excited in that the

Amazon rainforest and the pyramid, which they were to excavate, held spiritual matters; and he had been quite compelled to join the team, because of those stones and the pyramid—all the minerals of which were transported from far reaches of South America and of rarity. Lloyd Caston, the geologist, was thus a part of the team, and he packed his bag for the Peruvian rainforest, upon reaching home from the initial meeting, organized by Dr. Reid Phillips, in his incredulity.

Bridget Alcoy had been studying Rodentia and their dependence on cocaine in a social setting, with peers and proximity. She was fascinated by the similarities between the human and the rat, and in the especial circumstances of addiction and social action. The Rodentia, as she observed, were much like humans. The psychologist, in her laboratory, had laced a pool of water with cocaine, and she watched as the rats, with repetition, went back to the cocaine-laced water when thirsty. The Rodentia did grow sick. They did overdose on the laced water, and when they did recuperate they avoided the laced water from then on forward, because they learned from their mistakes, the results of all of which the perquisite to a second study, which proved the two groups of Rodentia—one group with fresh water and one group with laced water—did avoid the laced water and did even take care of one another's sicknesses, which had been brought on by the laced water. This was an extraordinary discovery, as far as social cohabitation was concerned—compassion was innate—and Bridget Alcoy wanted to go into clinical psychology, practicing with the ill the works and wonders of compassion, for the reason of and importance of the human and innate faculties in the human being. Bridget Alcoy had a knack for compassion and being that the trip down to the Amazon was to be trying upon the psyche and well-being of the team members, in entirety, she was asked to join the team and selected by Dr. Reid Phillips to be a lead psychological means in order to keep morale high, should a worst-case scenario occur in the rainforests of Peru, towards which the team was bound.

It had been guaranteed the team, by Gus Reichen, they would find at least three new species of bugs while on the expedition, and he did extend a bet, which nobody dared accept. The ant farm, as a child, was the beginning of the compartmented Gus Reichen, who did have an ant farm, and not of regular Insecta, but of Solenopsis, or fire ants, because he lived in the state of Florida as a child, and because the Solenopsis, or fire ants did have awesome poisons, with which they fascinated many an individual.

Becca Holmvik was the photographer. She had taken incredible stills of Iranian cave drawings, depicting horses and war and rare Hindu rituals—all of which had landed her with countless job offers before she reached the age of twenty-five, a certain prodigy.

The plane swept through the clouds, with fluidity, its breadth of wings, the sleekness and slenderness of its fuselage divine. Flying into Iquitos, Peru, Dr. Phillips perused over the team's personal profiles. Dr. Phillips had a still of Becca Holmvik's in her profile. It was the cave drawing, and he took it out and admired it, and then he turned it in his hands and looked at Becca, who was sitting beside him, in the window seat, and looking out at the stratocumulus formations. "Becca," he said. "These are incredible photos."

She turned to him, coy, and replied, "It was lucky I got there before anyone else. Many photographers were en route." She chuckled. "We were not permitted into the country."

Phillips laughed, "A risk taker—"

Becca Holmvik said, "Probably, we would have been held hostage or deported, depending on who caught us. It's where the good stuff is, Doctor. You know that." She smiled and turned back to the window and the stratocumulus formations, and Dr. Reid Phillips watched her for a second, not long before the clear Peruvian city came into view and all the blue world became people and limits.

***

Sparkling diamonds, citrine, and amethyst, sunshine refracted through the foliage, pierced the membrane of the virile and exotic setting, which extended backwards, a growing distance between old and new civilizations. The locals had migrated a long time ago to the new cities, and it was like traveling back in time, walking through the bush, eastwards. Gnarled trunks of trees, large waxy greens, shrubs and creeks and crickets, rich soil and poisonous vines, grew outwards from their respective places, and they seduced the team members into closer looks, the team accompanied by one addition, a local man, named Carlos, who was their guide to the ruins, over the next fourteen days. Through thick underbrush, they traversed eastwards towards the Javari River. Flowing throughout the northern part of Peru, the Javari River, which the team was to follow even further northwards, meandered, with thoughtfulness, into uncharted territory and into an overgrown village, which Carlos called Malorana.

"Malorana," Carlos said, "hasn't been visited in decades. We don't mention it to the children. We don't want them to search for it, getting killed out here." His shoes pressed the soil as he walked. "I am one of the few who know where the village is."

"And how," Dr. Phillips said, "did you learn of its whereabouts, if you were a child once yourself? I assume you were young at some point."

"You'd be surprised," the guide replied. "I know the location," he added, "because I am one of the last decedents of those who lived there. They knew something larger than the mountains, my ancestors, and you people want to find it in the village." He laughed. "Best of luck."

"We aim to please."

The team trudged, invigorated through the jungle. Rest between hikes involved water, cheese, and crackers. The team had been on foot for two days and they were now a half-day's walk from the village. Pre-camp meal was underway.

"How 'bout those pillars, huh?" said Lloyd Caston. "I can't believe they haven't eroded more."

Bridget Alcoy stirred her beef and broccoli with a metal spoon. "Lloyd, you would be into that. The mountains are far from here too, aren't they?"

"I mean, listen," said the geologist. "The stone must have taken a long time to get here, and it would have taken a lot of effort. It's not like they lived in clear terrain. They had to navigate through the trees." Lloyd thought of the mud and the rain. "They didn't even have shoes."

Five miles back, Carlos's hand pointed to the right, off their path. "Come, I want to show you something." Through a cascade of vines and fronds, dew catching onto the clothes of all the men and women, Carlos strode, not hacking, but maneuvering, with politeness, the foliage so that everybody else could follow him to his tangential destination. He had regressed into childhood, feeling the forest as he had when he was young, the trees tall and rough and the air crystal and

26

wet and refracting rainbows into his eyes. Carlos pushed aside one final curtain of frond, and he stepped into a small clearing, which was overgrown with vines and roots; the team shuffled into the ovular pocket in the forest. "Here is a piece of the village," Carlos said. The forest was quiet. The pocket was insulated. Carlos went to the apex of the oval and ran his hands up and down a tree covered dense with Fungi, and then he peeled the Fungi and vines away from the tree covered dense with Fungi to reveal not the bark of a plant, but rather the eye and nostril of a caricature hidden beneath the Fungi. Carlos said, "Malorana." Carlos brushed more dirt off the face. Two narrow slits comprised the nostrils, and two thick lips were beneath the slits. The guide further cleared the face. The team was enraptured. Two wide set eyes were elongated and were pulled back at their corners, by opal stones. The face of a frog stared back at the team, melancholic.

"My god!" said Lloyd Caston. "This stone is not indigenous. It's not indigenous to the area."

"It doesn't matter," said Carlos. "It doesn't matter what kind of stone it is. What does matter is what's carved into the stone."

Dr. Phillips stepped forward and felt the awe in the elongated eyes, and he drew in a breath and took his cap off of his head. He said, "The frog, Malorana."

"Yes. Malorana," said the guide, and he proceeded to remove the Fungi from the statue. He moved his hands over the totem, clearing it, and in entirety.

Alcoy approached the statue. "It's obvious. The frog was a god. Look at the skin on the animal. It's less rough than the rest of the statue." She went closer. "And look—wow, I can't believe this—look Doctor. There are lips on this frog, with lipstick. The statue was an idol."

"One can preserve dye on stone by rubbing types of sap into the figure," said Gus Reichen.

Another face, which Carlos was clearing, appeared below the face of the frog. Everybody watched as a human face was revealed, beneath the face of the frog, and through the nose of the human resided a long bow, which did pierce the nose. Carlos continued removing long strips of foliage and uncovered another face. This one was, too, human, and the face had paint and carvings panted and carved into its features, and sapphires pulled back at the corners of its eyes, showing deep rounded bulbs, which made the face of clemency. Carlos stepped back and then turned to the team, and said, "Here, on this totem is what you seek. The symbols, at least, and here you've seen the three points, Malorana, Man, and the Goquum. Now, underneath them lies—" He removed the final section of Fungi, and then he turned towards the team. The gasp, which was returned to the guide, was one of aghast and appalled breath. The team looked, all six of the individuals who incorporated the excavation team, at the face, which adorned the totem and claimed its base. Nobody moved. A shutter was heard; Becca Holmvik had snapped a photograph and then another. Carlos shifted and crouched and looked affrighted, and then there was another shutter from the camera of Becca Holmvik heard. Two long and bent horns curved downwards from the head of the fourth countenance, and two rabbit ears pointed skywards. A long snout pointed downwards, and the eyes on the creature closest the ground were batted and shot, and they were narrow and piercing; onyx had been set deep into the pupils of the creature. Carlos said, "This is the creature of choice, the Draikam."

"Hideous beast, isn't he?" said Dr. Phillips. "Shit, it is."

"—shit, it was," said Lloyd Caston, back at camp. The fire crackled and licked the spit, which held their cooking meat. "Shit, shit. Thing was ugly, but I'd be damned if I let that thing take up space in my mind. We should have left the thing covered in leaves."

Bridget Alcoy, the psychologist, nodded and swept her almond eyes over the geologist. "Yes, no need to think too long about it, but it is something to marvel, how people believed so much in evil."

"Evil?" Carlos growled. "Evil? Is for the weak. There is no evil. There is only choice. Do what you will with evil, but what lives underneath evil, what goes on underneath that face, is something entirely, entirely different."

"You know this, Carlos?"

"Of course, I know. I've met the thing. Now," Carlos smiled. "A choice to you, Dr. Phillips, corn," Carlos asked, "or hare?" The spit rotated over the flames.

***

Alcoy was not able to get to sleep. Lying in her bag, she turned in her matted hair, identifying small ticks and pains in her body as associated marks of the trip in towards the village of Malorana. Little sleep and too much pressure on the insides of the soles of her feet, which were well fitted with footwear, and caffeine did tire the mind and keep it awake. She slept, with soundness, in the first few days of the hike, through the Masanao and through the village of Anstape, where they slept in real beds. In her roll up bag, with tousled hair, she slept with a notion of reckoning, and it was a disparaged reckoning, upon the group, and the only item she was able to place in regards to the disparaged and maleficent locale, was the totem and the irrationality, which was a disguise, and which was faith, in time and ephemeral—the frog on top was the first to go and to sleep was to have the frog recede from the conscious mind and into the subconscious, where then the dreams did start, but she blocked them out and it was not hard when the schizoid conception of who was foreign and who was centric was a scintillated *we*, the totem Malorana relentless in the senses of the psychologist, with the washing and ebb and flow of crickets and winds; Caston was over the pit, and he was having trouble aspirating.

Swirls of purple and blue grew deeper behind Bridget Alcoy's eyelids. Out, from a blue inkblot, came the one who kept her tentative—the frog totem, Malorana. "You, you are good." The totem teetered on the rim of dream and nightmare. "Are you good or bad? Good or bad?" The frog watched her, and licked its lips, and spoke, laborious and slow, from behind the polygons, and it was morning.

***

Carlos, with his bag and canteen and medical kit on his hip, moved towards the unbeaten trail in the village of Malorana, and the team walked, for hours, in the muggy heat and bug clouded air and through waxy fronds and animals. They walked until the guide stopped to regain composure and refill canteens. Carlos said, "There is a stream there, beyond that brush. You may go there to refill."

Exasperated, the group sat, breathing and struck by the feigning mercy of the Peruvian rainforest. The team sat in two huddled groups. Alcoy, who had been expert in her silence and observant since the morning, and Gus Reichen and Lloyd Caston in one group; and off to the left, speaking in hushed words, were Becca Holmvik, who had been snapping many photographs this day, Dr.

Phillips, and Carlos in the other. Carlos was saying, "We have come far. The village is just past the next clearing."

"It is taken by water, correct? The village is flooded?" asked the professor.

"It is, and we must walk carefully, however well prepared we are. It is very spectacular," said Carlos, turned towards Becca, who had been searching for shots of large trees and limber cats.

"Very good," she said.

"Now," said the guide, "we must refill our waters. The following segment is not a tough one," he said. "But it is trying. Sit though, for a moment, sit."

Becca looked at the others, the other three sitting in a triangle, heaving and drinking the last droplets in their canteens. Becca could not see, though, why their eyes were so hollow, why they looked so sunken. She had slept and slept well. The soothing voices of the forest had lulled her into exceptional sleep, where minutes passed by as hours, and hours as days; and she woke rejuvenated. Even Caston's snoring had put her in a good place, purring. She snapped a photo of the group. They turned, looked exacerbated, and returned to themselves and their shared piece of earth.

Rising to the canopy above the six of them were light tufts of pollen. Becca felt uplifted. She wondered if she could get a shot of the canopy before she left, a bird's-eye view, so to speak. She wondered if she could climb a tree. The branches were far too high, nothing on which to grab a hold. She took a photo of the earth beneath her, the rich red and brown soil, the brown rocks and the dried leaves and the Insecta. An arch of dense brush and refracted light was beheld, and Becca took another shot and pushed through the arch of dense brush, towards the stream. Snaps and cracks of twigs carried on, underfoot, and then a small clearance was evident, with the Insecta and a specimen Dasypodidæ, with its reflexive and spherical armor. She followed the light gurgling of water, and there were aquatic fauna and Planta—Becca Holmvik scored the earth with her heel, leaving a brown swipe—and in Becca Holmvik broke, in through the viridian outlays of the large, waxy leaves, and in between two mahogany trunks, which stood, motionless, and in through to the stream, which glimmered white and topaz, and which had a few lily pads. Freshness, the scent of water in this atmosphere was wondrous. Incredible crispness and coolness, in certain places, were by far the inseparable life sources of this forest; all creatures came to the stream, at which Becca Holmvik stood. She dipped her soft, light hands into the stream and drank. The water flowed fast and was clean; and the small breaks in the surge created cusps around her hands and wrists and turned sapphire, a wider blue, and amethyst yet around her fingers when she removed them. Her tin was beside her, as was her camera, and she chose the latter, grasped the rough, black edges and felt the familiar impression of the shutter button, and clicked. Flash, flash. Life, the water was speaking to her; the forest was more alive than she, or perhaps, she and the forest together felt as so, not thinking of the village, Malorana, nor the people behind her, nor her home, which felt so superficial in comparison to a place like this, nor her own head which seemed far above the canopy now, and another—flash. The lily pads danced atop the currents like native tribes, celebrating their freedom. She capped the lens and traded the camera for her tin and dipped in the canteen under the rushing water.

The fluid rushed by, with the bubbles and the foam, and the stolid brown eyes of Becca Holmvik were entranced by the beauty of the place. Becca was still under the trance of pleasantness of the hallowed area, and seconds passed so ill-regarded that when, from down the stream, a small creature riding the waves came and shifted and penetrated the photographer's vision with its red and orange and purple skin, she had not the reflexes, nor the sharpness, to move her hand, before the creature slid, flowed, and grazed the backside of her hand with its soft, slimy skin. Becca jolted away, following this small, living, pressurized sensation down the stream with a glance, and she noticed a frog, a tree frog perhaps, had just grazed her hand, and she laughed, laughed at herself, laughed at her zoning out in this place, letting her guard down, laughed at her life, really, laughed at her incredible fortune of being in this place at this time, and she sat, smiling, and had good feelings, good feelings that they would find what they had come here to find, and with exactitude.

* * *

It had been five minutes of Becca's absence before the rest of the team stood and went to refill their canteens. They had been planning, conversing on when, who, and how they would go into the village of Malorana. It was decided, it being late, four in the evening, they would camp here by the stream, and by morning's light they would move to the next clearing and set up camp once more and excavate the village. Rubber johns, goggles, picking sticks, gloves, and ointments were all ready. They were going be the first to enter the pyramid of the old village, which was still hidden in the densest, most forsaken part of the world. The remaining four—Dr. Phillips, Reichen, Alcoy, and Caston—strode through the arch and light, through which Becca had strode, and they strode through the two mahogany guardians, towards the gurgling water, and into the brilliant reflections of the stream to refill their tins. Sitting and slouched on knees, before the water, her knees in all of actuality in the water, drenched though, rigged and supporting her, her tin still in hand, was Becca Holmvik. Caston approached Becca Holmvik.

Caston said, "Becca, nice to see you again," expecting her to turn, maybe flash a photo, take him off guard, or catch him dead in his tracks with her bright, creased smile she always had on, but when she did not move, did not respond, did not flinch nor breathe in response, he said again, "Becca, very nice to see you again," and again she did not respond, kneeling in the water, her back rigged and erect, her hands folded in her lap, facing away from them, across the waters towards the lush greenness across the way; and the team was all around, with Becca, kneeling before them, in the middle.

Her eyes, they saw, were open, glazed, transfixed in one direction, and her mouth was a perfect straight line—no dribbles nor imperfections anywhere on her face. She looked, as the Doctor said, kneeling down in front of her, waving his hand in her face, "Clement." He said, "Becca, Becca, what's wrong. What did you see?" The young girl sat and stared at nothingness, a blank inward glare at all that composed her—her past, her mistakes and rewards. Becca Holmvik sat in complete silence and solemnity as the grounds around her splashed water in her face and in her eyes, which did not blink in reflex. She had no reflexes. Lloyd Caston pinched her, and she did not move. He pinched her nose and her cheeks and the inside of the bicep where it was sensitive, and still, there was no reaction.

Dr. Phillips said, "Caston, maybe you should grab our guide. I fear something terrible has happened." He spoke, not taking his eyes off the glazed and petrified glare of the photographer, who returned his glare, and who had just five minutes ago, been alive and well and communicable.

*****

Sunburst images and colors took the mind's eye of the girl, Becca Holmvik. There were stars and phantasmagoric images of men and women and children, and frogs and trees and boats in the mind of the girl, and she watched in total relaxation the evolution of the indigenous peoples of this place. She saw them walk out from the caves in the Andes; she saw them with long, knotted hair; and she saw them conceive and give birth to children, who grew and killed and conceived; she saw the birds and the foliage as bursts and blooms and into a complete ouroboros with the life force of the Amazon rainforest, where she remembered she was located, on knees and in front of the stream. She saw the loud and intricate frequency of the forest; yet, the frequency of the forest was so simple and singular in its dynamics, one may well have heard the constancy—all senses were combining as one, and the frequency, to which she had been listening, was a constant, and she had been perceiving the chronicles of the present day, in its oblique situation, for many seconds. How long she perceived them, she dared not pay attention; the sunburst cycles, which were perceived in her head, were depictions of her own interpretation of the exchange, which was occurring, with rapidity.

She grew apprehensive, and the yellows and purples and oranges turned darker and blacker, and when she grew ambivalent, the colors grew virile; it was all inside her own imagination, and she thought to herself of hallucinogens and of the frog, which had encountered her, and that the Batrachian may have been coated with an hallucinogenic solution—she still was able to think—

her mind was still hers, and she thought, quite with precision, this place was the true meaning of their existence; it was the beginning of all items, notion, and ideas. The severity of pursuing ouroboros surfaced in that she was to wake deranged and demented by the poisons of the frog, and she was to return to the United States, to be institutionalized and to be victimized and beaten and cast down by society and publicized, capitalized upon, as the girl who had lost her mind in the Amazon rainforest with the group who went to excavate the pyramid of Malorana. The colors grew darker and she pushed the thoughts away. It was quite curious. She could take this where she wanted. The ancestors of the area were there, should she want to pursue them—the forefathers of our guide, Carlos, perhaps. She could pursue the vibrational frequency of this place—the birds and trees and people back there in the village of Anstape and Masanao. She could even pursue the intimacies of the origins of the frog itself, and come to think of it, the team was surrounding her now. She could feel their presence, though could not pull herself away from the sensation and perception. It was like nothing she had ever experienced before. Her mind was not high. There was no body sensation, as of now. She did not feel euphoria, to any extreme extent. She was only perceiving the forest for what it truly was, something of an entity, or deity, in itself, something that wished to teach and communicate.

"That damn frog," she laughed, and she heard it, her laugh, resonating. Then she realized, "That damn frog!"

The totem and the word itself, Malorana, all pointed back to the frog, and she had touched it, or the frog had touched her, in that sanctified place by the stream. The realization grew, "And behold," she thought, "the colors grow brighter."

The audio frequency was still present, she heard the high-pitched choir of the forest, and she pushed, pushed through the colors, pushed through the sounds, and pushed beyond her own expectation, for she now understood the reason of their being here—it was the frog, Malorana— the frog is what they were looking for. She only wished she could photograph this color. It was dancing now, dancing to depths of this noise, which had grown, and redoubled, since her push. She found it hard to let go, however. She could not give in to the forest. It was too heavy and too important, and she felt unworthy, and now, with this thought, she said, resonating, "I can't. I can't. I am not worthy," and booming, booming from the innards of the geometrical phenomena came a bellowing word, "Duaph," and she was expelled forwards, into the heart of the forest, where the birds sung brighter, and where the air was cleaner, and where the trees were greener, and the word, "Duaph," resonated equal in her head, and it had its own frequency, one higher than the forest and one higher than the multitude of the living here in the forest as she knew it; she was casted by her own spirit, and by the spirit of the word, "Duaph," upwards, and she lost the sensation of herself and all she ever knew.

***

Four hours later, after Carlos had come and carried the poor girl back to the camp, a candescent flare exited the crown of Becca's head, and Carlos smiled. Nobody else was around. It was only Carlos and Becca, together, as the rest of the campers were again, filling water. He had heard the stories, of course; he was one of the ancestors. He had never experienced it himself, however, the true essence of the village. He had only heard the stories.

There would be a moment, when all falls away, then one's light would come from the person, his uncle had told him, and the man would be with Malorana.

So, it was true. She had been touched, he thought. She had been touched. The four remaining team members came from the brush and towards Carlos and Becca.

"How is she?" asked Dr. Phillips. "She is now one with Malorana," said the guide.

"What? She's dead?" yelled Reichen.

"No," laughed the guide, "she is not dead. She is merely one with the forest."

"I don't follow," said the Doctor.

"There is nothing for you to follow," the guide said. "The following is up to her now."

"I noticed her respiration is very low," Lloyd Caston said. "I think she's in a complete

vegetative state, at the moment."

"Complete meditative," said Carlos, laughing again.

"I don't see what's so funny," said the geologist. "This woman could be dead."

"She is not dead, far from. Opposite actually, she is more alive than any of us here, you'll see, you'll see, the blessed frog Malorana be willing."

The four Americans stood appalled at the native's words. How could poor Becca, this girl who was, with completeness, besmirched by some essence, poison in forest, be alive, more alive than them? It was not so much his words, but his confidence that had them in half belief. All except Alcoy, who had been studying the lack of perspiration, the lack of heart spindles, and palpitations, all the usual symptoms of typical hallucinogenic experiences.

Alcoy said, "We need to get her e-vac'd immediately."

"I don't think that's the best idea," said Carlos. "She's fine where she is, and she'll be out of it soon, have trust."

Alcoy snapped, "I don't think you understand, Señor Carlos. This is an incident that needs to be addressed professionally, and by the looks of it, I am the one medically in charge here, in terms of psychological and even medical know-how, and she needs to be evacuated, I am not taking no for an answer. Dr. Phillips, we need to call the excavation off now."

"Now, wait a minute," said the guide. "You five came here in search of what? Gold, treasures? No, you came here in search of answers to a higher being, a higher cause. The girl here is in a trance, yes but she is not unhealthy. I don't know what is happening right now, but neither do you. Have faith in something greater than medicine and science. Dr. Phillips?"

The Doctor paused, breathed. It had been ages, ages since he had asked himself the question—what is more real? Faith or fact? What is more powerful? People kill over faith, but fact? Never. He remembered himself as a child, searching in the bush behind his home for Native American artifacts. He had never found one. He had never found a single treasure, physical nor psychological, proving his faith true, and he had been losing faith. He had come here to put a staple in his faith, to understand life as what it used to be, to understand the lives of past

generations, and maybe, just maybe prove their beliefs true. His eyes narrowed, he inhaled, and he looked at Becca, lying atop her bag inside the mosquito net, thinking, *Why has this happened?* He turned to the guide, then the children, whom he had brought on this broken trip, and then turned to Alcoy, and said, "We stay. We stay, Ms. Alcoy, because we are here to find something. I brought you all here to uncover the meaning of the Amazon, the meaning in ourselves. We can excavate the village, but we can also excavate the very foundations of ourselves." Ourselves, he thought, and who am I? Who is this man who brought these children down here? A crazy old man, with whitening hair? A derelict? A daffy professor? "I need to know," he said.

"Desire," Carlos said, "can sometimes be an ugly thing, professor." He turned back toward the others. "We stay, as the professor has said, and tomorrow we will excavate the village and—"

"No," Alcoy belted. "No. Tomorrow, we are dispatching recue for this girl, who, god help her, needs medical attention. Sunrise, I'm going, and at least one of you should come with me. We can follow the trail. Lloyd, you're good with rocks, whatever, can read a compass. You're coming with, right?"

"Bridget, I'll come, just so you don't kill yourself in the process. Becca does need

attention."

"It's settled," said the professor. "Tomorrow, Alcoy and Caston go back to Anstape and radio for a chopper, and Carlos and I will go to the village for reconnaissance. This excavation is not over."

"Settled, and we just may find something there that can help our friend Becca here" said the guide.

***

Enveloped in green, all was quiet. Small Becca, in a small clearing, was peaceful. She lay in the arms of the leaves. The forest was at her back and she was facing, with undeniable beauty, the stars, and far off, though not seen, were the planets, sensed soft and round. From the external gaze, into this atmosphere of leaves and vibrations, she lay, thinking not where or what this was, but who she was.

Through all her years of being alive, the constant feeling was there—Becca Holmvik— borne into this strange design, with regularity, through the eyes of her mother. Now, all was different. Her perspective seemed not her own up here, suspended by the moon and stars. It was the perspective of another being who had been with her since the beginning, old as the moon's craters and the burning stars and young and virile as the present moment. Becca Holmvik, lying there, was reborn, into the universe, and it said, "Welcome," to her as she approached the external band of radiation around the earth. She exited, lifted into the atmosphere, onto the platform above the clouds and into an eye there, and through it she looked—a ring around earth as she knew it, not like Saturn's, but a thin ring around the earth, on its slant, and it spoke again, "Welcome," and she returned to the leaf canopy, with little recollection of the occurrence, only the feeling of homeliness and past mothers she had had, and there, upon the canopy of leaves, her eyes opened and before her was a man, clothed in garments of the people of the area—leather loins and shoulders, red paint on his thick abdomen, where he crouched, and the man, with leather skin, dropped red leaves upon Becca's belly, and she realized she wore leather loins and shoulders as well, and the man said, "Welcome," and rubbed the dry red leaves into her skin and dashed on it cinnamon and water. "Welcome, Becca," he said.

Chimes were jostled. The wind blew through the open window. Drapes fluttered in the breeze. "The bath is nearly ready." It was comfortable, the acquiescent taste in the air, with the wit and clarity. Outside of this immediate area, she could not see much. It was rainforest, and the man introduced himself, "I am Goquum."

Becca was lying inside of her mosquito net, at camp, still unconscious. The day had fallen into night and the team was asleep, desperate and trying to gain energy for tomorrow's expedition into the village. Dr. Phillips had gone to sleep early, Lloyd and Bridget Alcoy stayed up, preparing themselves for the morrow's hike in the opposite direction, and Carlos and Gus grew enamored by the campfire, across each other, exchanging stories of their homes and what they had dreamt about as children—both dreaming, wishing they had been born animals, rather than human.

However, when Gus finally decided to turn in, Carlos stayed, watching the fire, thinking of his uncle and grandfather, what they had taught him as a child, how the animals were gods and how humans could learn from them.

The team, all the members of which asleep inside their tents, was silent. The jungle had ensued with its temperate buzz, and the guide, Carlos, looked transfixed into the flames. He remembered his uncle's words, a rhyme that some considered tradition and hokey mystical garbage, words that were spoken only by the deranged and wild. *A true loss of culture*, thought the guide.

He wondered if he dared say the words. He wondered if they would have any effect on the situation. He wondered if it was Malorana that quieted this girl. It must have been, the evidence was too clear. Her silence, her relaxed atmosphere, her respiration low, and her pupils dilated—all evidence pointed to the mystical, as Carlos was raised to see it.

His eyes darted and touched each of the team members. He cleared his throat to see if there was a reaction. There was none. Embalmed by the memories of his uncle, he went to Becca's net and kneeled.

The girl was silent, but very active. He could feel it in his gut, the very spot his uncle had touched with his words all those years ago. Carlos closed his eyes, the bird-track creases deepening in his face.

The trees swayed, the frogs—the frogs—spoke to one another, the wind tumbled through the fronds and made cool the beaded sweat on his brow. The words— what were they? Tradition? It was said the soul enamored would be lifted by the words.

He unzipped her tent and touched her hand and muttered the words: *Elo-uante, El-banante, el-loranta, Malorana.* His heart began beating hard, his breath took a new tempo, he cursed under his breath. Entre. The frogs hushed, and the wind stopped blowing. All that was heard was Becca's slow breathing. It was done. Becca's soul was lifted. Carlos wished he could be there to see, to see the transformation of Becca, into the forest, one with its spirit forever, should she be worthy, for it was not only them who would be affected but the entire world.

***

The next morning the team woke up pleasant and surprised to see Carlos cooking breakfast—nuts, tuna, and powdered milk. "Good morning, everyone!" he said. "Just in time for breakfast."

"What a night, huh? Slept like a baby, myself," said Gus. "How is she?" he asked, talking about Becca.

"Still no movement. I was watching over her last night," said the guide. "But she seems to be stable."

"Very well," said Alcoy. "We will head back to the village to get help, after breakfast."

"Eat, you will need the energy," said Carlos. "And professor, how did you fare last night?"

"A rocky sleep, but I am well for the day. Tell me, Carlos, are we heading to the village today?"

Carlos looked up for a moment, then dropped his eyes. "Yes, we will excavate the ruins today."

"Good," said the Doctor. "I will ready my things." And he left.

"Should anybody want seconds, just ask me," said the guide, talking to the remaining three. "You two especially," to the two returning to Anstape.

The Doctor rustled among his belongings, Bridget Alcoy and Lloyd Caston were readying themselves for their hike, the guide, Carlos, was eating breakfast, and Gus sat alone.

Gus had slept well. Not only had he slept as if on a cloud, but he had had dreams, images of the night sky, crowded with constellations and marvelous pictures of faces, cascaded by the descending starlight. He said, "So I stay here today?"

Carlos pretended not to notice.

"I'm staying here today?" asked Gus.

Carlos looked up and between his chewing said, "Yes, Gus, you'll stay here today."

Gus was quiet, appalled. He had come all this way for what? Manning the camp? He said,

"Really, this is not why I came here."

Carlos said, "Becca needs a monitor. Don't worry. You'll see the village soon enough."

Gus grumbled, but otherwise felt assured. Becca needed assistance.

"My things are ready," said Carlos to the professor.

"Mine are nearly packed," he replied. "You two," he asked. "Are you nearly ready?" Bridget nodded in assent.

The team would split up and go different directions in this wood, on their own quests. However, what they did not know was that this was the last time the six of them would be together; and just before eight o'clock, they separated.

***

The bath was exquisite. It was unlike anything she had ever prior experienced. The clipped orchids surrounding the bath, the bubbles, the soft scents of lavender and sugar, the women washing her so beautiful the Norse gods may have been jealous. It was like a dream, a daydream out of which one snapped, with instantaneity. She could not take her eyes off the bronze skin of one woman. It radiated health and fertility. An ambience that only an angel could have, lighthearted and pure, healthy in touch and voice, something to which Becca did relate.

Becca stayed silent for many moments, being scrubbed and washed, her feet and hands soaked and cleaned, her face, arms, and legs oiled, her hair perfumed, total perfection in terms of cleanliness and purity. She lay pampered by these women, the women introduced to her by Goquum.

The women talked amongst themselves in shallow voices. Becca did not speak, and they appeared not to be offended. They scrubbed as if she was their child.

After a long breath, Becca asked, "Where am I?"

The bronze woman said, "You are in Malorana."

"Malorana?" Becca said. "I thought Malorana was the name of the frog."

The bronze woman giggled. "It is," she said. "It is the name of the frog and the name of

this village. You are in the heart of the Amazon." She smiled and began again scrubbing.

Becca felt solid. She felt confident but confused. How did she get here? Where was the group? "How did I get here?" she asked.

"With Malorana's help," was the reply. "But perhaps our friend Goquum is the best one to answer that question." The woman beside the bronze one smiled. "You will talk with him shortly, after your bath."

The bath lasted many more moments and at one point the bronze woman and her two followers helped raise Becca from the tub, which was made of a thin, golden metal.

"What is your name?" Becca asked.

The bronze woman replied, "Jade. My name is Jade." And she showed Becca her earrings made of gold and the precious stone—jade. "Here, come with us. It is time."

Becca, Jade, and Jade's assistant exited the hut and were met by a floral and vibrant place, where colors stood iridescent—all colors mixed as one, but at a higher frequency. The huts were brown and white, the soil was red and white, the sky and clouds blue and yellow, negative depictions of themselves that sent the one observing high into atmosphere, entrancing one's eye and mind.

Jade said, "We will go see Goquum."

The triplet walked slow through the village, emblazoned with pictographs upon walls and children's chests, the children crowding the newcomer—Becca— and showering her with laughter and humility, it was almost unreal the incredible energy of the place.

It must be real, she thought. In fact, this is the most real and perfect place she had ever been. Everything struck direct into her core, the scents and smells of another generation.

She understood the intonations of the area, with ease. It was as if they were innate, the knowledge and curiousness of the place, there somewhere in her heart since the beginning, in her mind since she had touched the frog in that stream. "Where are my friends?"

"Your friends are on Earth."

"Earth?" Her stomach dropped like a stone.

"You will see them again. Here we are, Goquum's hut."

Earth, Jade had said. Then, where was she? This place had all the qualities of Earth—soil, wind, trees— but there was something extra, an extra element that added such composed nature to the place that it seemed surreal or divine. Not long will she see her friends again, she knew. It was an innate notion.

Jade pushed the beaded doorway back for Becca, allowing her inside the home. The fragrances of incense were heavy and present. Flower petals adorned the dirt ground. When inside, her eyes adjusted to the dim lit room, she could see the man who had welcomed her, Goquum, sitting with his eyes closed on a roughened linen-like material. He opened his eyes, knew who had entered.

"Welcome," he said. "Welcome, Becca."

She took a warm spot on the floor beside him and muttered, "Thank you." She looked behind her. Jade and her assistant waited by the doorway.

"Do you know why you are here?" the elder man asked.

Becca studied his boyish features, though could not understand how he looked so young and vital. He had creases in his face, bags under his eyes, but there, there it was—the eyes of the youth, the type of eyes that understood and acknowledged places and things most people ignored. "No," she said. "Where am I?"

Goquum said, "You are in the village of Malorana."

"The village of Malorana?"

"Yes," said the elder. "The village of Malorana." He could not contain a loud guffaw. "Finally, someone has found us." He smiled. "Do you know who I am?"

Becca shook her head.

"To the people in this village, I am Goquum, but you may call me Johan."

"Johan," she said. "You look like a Johan."

He raised his eyebrows. "You know," he said. "You and I are now siblings, under the great god Malorana."

"Siblings?"

"Yes," he said, leaning close. "Siblings. For I am the one who found him, Malorana. I am the one who found the creature that touched your hand. I was the first one to find this place."

"And what is this place?" Becca asked, inquisitive, enraptured.

Johan leaned back. "This is the village of Malorana, though not the same village your friends are approaching now. We are in a cloud, above the lost village of the Amazon, on the planet Earth. We are in the heart of the Malorana now. A truly higher plane to us, a plane created by the One." He paused. "Your friends will find trouble in the dwellings on Earth."

"Trouble?"

"Yes, and the priority right now is your warning them. They are stepping into something much too heavy for common souls. Those who enter Malorana without his touch will surely die, or worse."

Becca was anchored in Johan's eyes. He spoke such true words, not relenting in intensity at all, but seeming to chase the edge from Becca, leaving her with wit. "That pool there," Becca said. "That is where I can find them."

"Correct," said Johan, impressed. "Yes, you must approach the pool."

To Becca's left was a shallow bowl filled with water. She approached it and looked at her reflection. Her eyes were greener, her skin more lurid, her hair and teeth straight and perfect. She looked inside, and images and sounds began to appear, as if from a deep channel, a channel straight into the physicality and the subtle plane of the planet Earth, too far for one to reach.

Becca looked inside, peering as if through a looking glass into minds of the men. She noticed there Dr. Reid Phillips and their guide, Carlos, hack and trudge through flooded terrain, up to their waists in black water. They were entering the village limits.

As if from a cloud, inside her own head, behind her own ears, she heard the whispered words of the Doctor, as if from a far-off place. She had to concentrate to hear the voices. When she began thinking for herself, the voices and the images faded. She concentrated and heard, "Are we nearly there?" The professor, on his crusade to open the doors of mysticism.

"Nearly there, yes," said the guide. "Keep your eyes open for snakes."

From this great height, there was nothing left to opine. Everything heard and seen was pure, true. Nothing was left to subjection. Everything was pure and demonstrated, pure and heard and seen, nothing out of place, and perfect. The guide took point.

"It gets deep here," he said. "We will be up to our necks in water."

The cloud had taken Becca's mind. She could hear, with perfection, her mind clear. She must warn them of their fate.

"You must speak through the jungle," said Johan. "Speak, like you listen."

"We are going into the village now," Dr. Reid Phillips said to Carlos. His eyebrows were twitching with anticipation. He had already begun to sweat under his arms and on his brow.

Fervent, he snatched his canteen and took a sip. "We go to the village and find what is there, the hidden mysteries of Malorana."

Carlos took a deep breath. He also was anticipating the trip into the village as much as Dr. Reid Phillips was, but did not show it. He had never been there; and he had heard many tales as a child, how the village enriched people, how the village was sacred, how the village opened the eyes of youth, trading desperation with the place of deliverance. He had filled his canteen. He, too, took a sip of water, and said, "Are we ready?"

"Ready as we'll ever be," said Dr. Reid Phillips, pulling himself up from his sitting position and toward the guide. "How long is the trek?"

"It is not long," was the reply; and then they were headed through the bush, towards the village of Malorana.

A quick adieu to Reichen, who was staying at the camp, watching over the girl, Becca, was the moment Dr. Reid Phillips had his breakthrough: He was discovering the hidden, he was living his dream, and he was uncovering the masked treasures of the Amazon. With a hand, he had clapped Gus Reichen on the neck and told him to be well, until they returned.

***

Dr. Reid Phillips and Carlos hacked through the dense, dark green forest, growing closer to the village every second. Every second Dr. Reid Phillip's breath became more full, more wholesome. He felt it in the chest, in his heart, his growing closer to greatness. In one hour, they were at the edges of the flooded village.

"We wade through the water here," said Carlos. "Be conscious of the footing. Don't slip or I'll have to scoop you up."

Dr. Reid Phillips nodded his head, having fallen into reverie. The pyramid was in their sight. Layered and one hundred feet high, the impressive pyramid stood as a symbol to Dr. Reid

Phillips as liberation. He had found his escape from the modern world. The contemporary banter of civilization was far behind him. He felt grandeur, though not delusional. For he knew—and it was for sure—they were discovering something of greatness. Excavating the pyramid had been on his mind for years; and he had reached it, the pyramid of Malorana, the massive monolith structure, coarse beneath his hands as he rubbed the stone structure with his palm, exasperated and thrumming with disbelief as to how large it was, how grand, how with such solidness it represented his thoughts, which were large, solid and unbelieving, and yet, he did believe. He believed this was an unmistakable and treacherous terrain; and he and everybody else in the team, Carlos, the guide, included, had braved it, all having become one with the forest, having become one with the pyramid, and having become one with Malorana.

His thoughts dashed back to the girl who was incapacitated at the camp. He wished the best for her, but his thoughts and his legs carried him forwards in a garrulous way, which tended on the border of hysteria.

He broke into laughter, ghastly laughter, deep and reverberating within the hollows of the pyramid. They had entered the portico and pushed through the anteroom, which gave way through to the rest of the pyramid. The Doctor screamed into the pyramid a deafening word, the word, "destiny," in three drawn out syllables, which had the guide, Carlos, shoot a look over his shoulder.

The guide said, "Silence! This land is sacred."

After that, the two remained silent and meandered slow into the pyramid and were brought upon a large doorway, which was closed and had on it hieroglyphic writing. The guide said, quiet, "I can read this. I might be able to decipher the hieroglyphs."

"Very good. Very good," said the Doctor; and he sat back against the wall, taken aback by its brilliance. For the sunlight refracted into the anteroom with gusto, alive and teeming with energy, a high sort of feeling entering the Doctor as he breathed the air of the pyramid of Malorana.

The guide took his time, brushed some dust off the archaic writing and said, "There are levers somewhere. We are to pull them simultaneously. Then, the door will open."

"Very good. Let's find the levers."

"They're right here, by our feet." The two moved to grasp the levers with their hands, pushed the levers, simultaneous; but the levers did not budge. They had been frozen in time, unable to be moved with the force of a man's arms.

"Our feet," said the Doctor. "Let's step on them, like giant buttons."

The guide, Carlos, nodded in agreement; and they pushed, with all their strength, on the levers, simultaneously; and the levers, with a sickening creak, gave way.

"By some pulley machines, I think, they open," said the Doctor; for they had pushed, and with ease did the door lift open. They were granted their first view of the sacred ceremonial room. The doors opened, and darkness came spilling out, as well as a few frogs.

Carlos and Dr. Reid Phillips shined their flashlights into the room and saw thousands upon thousands of frogs.

***

Bridget Alcoy and Lloyd Caston were, meanwhile, on their way to the village of Anstape. The e-vac was necessary, thought Bridget Alcoy, *That girl is incapacitated; and I fear the worst.* Though the paranoia had drifted away from her thoughts, the omnipresent idea all of the team was in danger was pulling at her, pulling her forwards, closer to the village of Anstape, with fervor.

Candid, Lloyd Caston made a comment on the girl's hair and the girl's looks. She did look dazzling in the rainforest, her golden blonde hair playing perfect off the lush green forest, giving the impression of extreme balance in the woman, as she stepped careful over obstructions in her path.

It was time to end this, she thought. The excavation had gotten out of control. As if by some means of inner communication, Lloyd Caston snorted, in disagreement. He was having the time of his life; and because a girl got injured (not even injured, but incapacitated) was not going to dampen his view of one of the most historic times in human history. For he was the geologist of the group. He knew the absolute and extraordinary occurrences that must have happened here in order for the pyramid and the village of Malorana to take prescience; and he cracked his knuckles, which sounded like stone pebbles under a foot of stones in a shifting of a tide. Sifting through thoughts, the two, who were silent, meandered through the forest tracking back from whence they came, back toward the village of Anstape. It was a two-day trip. So, they would have to set up camp this night and sleep in the forest, without a guide.

However, they knew where they were going; they knew the dangers of the rainforest; they knew they had each other to watch the other's back; and, most important, they had much water, having filled their canteens at the camp, with Gus Reichen. Really, it was simple. The entire way back followed the stream, which filled their canteens hours prior. If and when they needed a refill, they were simply to approach the stream and refill their canteens. If and when they got hungry, all they needed to do was pull up a stump, or if there was not a stump or a log, take a knee and fill their bellies. The thought of air conditioning drove Bridget Alcoy on, with candor, toward the village of Anstape. Converse, the evening drove Lloyd Caston further toward sleep and his reverie. Because he was so infatuated with the rainforest, distance meant nothing to him. He was more enticed by time—the time at which they would set up camp and the time at which they would enter the village of Anstape. He was riveted by the high canopy of trees, the shining and glistening petals and fronds of foliage. He felt in his element, the element of Earth, the stones they treaded upon, the soil, and the fragrance of the rainforest, humid yet comforting to Lloyd Caston. The soft leafy fronds graced his arm as he walked by them. For hours, they treaded through the forest sharing few words, but finally, something came out of Lloyd Caston's mouth, "You look beautiful."

Bridget Alcoy snapped around. She was not expecting the compliment. Instead, she was expecting something closer to the lines of, "Let's set up camp." Nevertheless, she turned and smiled over her shoulder a smile that spoke to Lloyd Caston and gave into a prelude of their night together. For they would make love this night. They would make the Choice to share a sleeping bag; and in the hot, toiling recesses of the sleeping bag their Choice was going to be made, to have a long time together, to take into account nothing but the foliage, the thick aroma of the South American romance, listening to the crickets, the swaying of the trees, the wind blowing through the canopy and into their hair, cooling them in the moments it saw fit; cooling them, because it was hot in that sleeping bag, a warm, incubated lair, where love and feelings reigned supreme, but, it was very spontaneous—a lustful coming together. There were very few attachments here in this place. One felt more attached to the rainforest, its means of humidity congealing into the spirit of a person. That was what pushed them together, the humidity, the virile atmosphere. That and something unknown. For there was obscurity between the two—Bridget Alcoy and Lloyd Caston. There was that unknown factor, which played a part of their coming together. The space in between light, the difference between light and darkness, day and night, brought them together, because what was more powerful? The light or the darkness, which resided in between light?

It was said that nothing could travel faster than light. Light was everywhere, traveling

thousands of light years from the stars above, changing one's perception of time so much so that viewing the stars was divine. It was divine in the manner that one experiencing a light had been touched by light shed thousands of years ago. Everybody knew the stars existed; but not everybody knew why or how.

As to why, the two, light and darkness, exchanged places, they gave perspective to one another. There could not be darkness without the stars; and there could not be stars without darkness. The two played off one another, perfect, giving toward the ebb and flow of the heavenly precession, turning, twisting in its ever-rotating axis—the stars and the darkness changing place, forever, until in twelve thousand years the precession started all over again. How many lifetimes came between the start and the end of that rotation? Many. It would depend on the times it started. Perhaps with modern medicinal advancements people could live until two-hundred years old. How did the stars make that twinkling intrigue? How did the precession change with such ease, when in their static point of view the difference was able to be seen only by a trained eye?

Over thousands of years did the light of stars travel and find Earth. Over thousands of years the light of stars traveled and found the eyes of the human, and they gape and wonder—how? How could this be? The time was so fragile. It took a delicate eye to see any difference; but that depended on where the eyes came from. Where the eyes under a dense canopy, filled with animals—crickets, monkeys, and panthers? Was it the eye of the city, where light pollution gave certain obstruction to viewing those celestial entities?

No, it must be simpler than that. In must be the second, at a glance, when one has awe in sight that matters most—that must be why the darkness came to light and light came to darkness. No Choices had been made. It was natural, as if some divine understanding took place every twelve thousand years, every night, when the stars and darkness and light exchanged places and

people made choices. People made Choices to observe the stars. People made Choices to entertain thoughts and ideas. People made Choices, and that was what was the most mysterious aspect of all of Malorana. The village had made Choices and had disappeared in time. They licked the backs of many a frog, many a god, and were delivered into the hands of that exchanged liking, that exchanged part or point in the sky, or in the Earth, or in their minds, where Choices gave, with absoluteness, to individuality. It was for that reason the people of Malorana were gods. It was for that reason the two eloped under the shaded canopy of the rainforest, and it was for that reason Choice had more power than the person; because Choices happened when people lent to themselves. People made Choices. Choices did not make people. Or did they? Lloyd Caston supposed he was lucky. The salty taste of the girl had him thrumming in the loins.

But, did Choices make people? Choices made people different. Choices defined people; but did Choices create? If they did, it must be on the microscopic level, where small electrical synapses and chemical exchanges gave way to adrenaline or long-lasting ideas—a short thrill or longevity of sorts.

In that small and hot sleeping bag did Choice reign supreme. Choice had dictated that evening and that night more so than any other aspect of the forest. Choice dictated that evening more so than either of the two— Bridget Alcoy or Lloyd Caston. For they were incapacitated. They made the original Choice to come together in that hot night; and everything following was natural. Everything took place, from the cracking of a toe to the pulling of hair to the nighttime singing of crickets, which seemed uncoordinated, but must have been, because all was too perfect and all was reverie, and descending upon the two—Lloyd Caston and Bridget Alcoy—was the following day, a hot day no doubt, and their eventual arriving at the village of Anstape, not knowing they had changed the future, not knowing they had changed destiny, because a Choice was important. A Choice brought one into life, and a Choice took the life out of another. It was only a matter of who and when, and the answer they were looking for was in the form of a chopper, a chopper high above the ground, a chopper, which would give them another look at the canopy, not from the bottom up, but from the top down, and then, they would be more like the stars, viewing the Amazon rainforest from a bird's-eye perspective, much like with what the stars were enamored.

They rose late in the morning, collapsed camp, and treaded towards the village of Anstape, the village, they thought, would render Becca Holmvik saved, the poor girl, from her sure death, bringing her out of her trance and back into reality.

***

Becca Holmvik took a sip of tea somewhere in between fantasy and reality. There was a lingering effect of touching that frog; and people watched over her. There was something about the girl, said Johan to Jade, that changed the future forever. The village will be changed. We will be changed because of the girl—she is the first outsider to touch the frog of Malorana.

The tea went down her throat warm. She shuffled into an upright position, sitting cross- legged on a pillow and still taken aback, at awe of the whole scenario. The frog was hallucinogenic? It must have been, but these people did not call the frog hallucinogenic. They called it divine.

It was time to take Becca Holmvik to the next level, thought Johan, the Goquum. It is time for her to hear the forest.

He came into the room, in which Becca Holmvik was relaxing. He said the word again— Duaph—and a crack sounded in her ear and gave through to a hissing sound, which expanded and overtook all thoughts of the forest, the village, Malorana, and everything within arm's reach and all else in her head. The hissing dropped its tone to a primordial throbbing. "Listen," said Johan. Becca Holmvik could hear the heart beats of all the animals. Becca Holmvik could feel the wind through the trees. There was complete body/mind separation; and the tone dropped further into an unmistakable and present intellect.

"I'm here with you," said Johan, in her head. "This is how my hearing is always. I saw you when you entered the village. Very beautiful, and now, look at you. You are with me, as I knew you would be—and we are taking steps into the mystical. You will change, Becca, our time. You are not going back to your body."

At that, she jostled and twitched; and a sharp pain shot up her arm.

"Don't move. We are in treacherous territory. Your body has not had time to grow used to the frequency, but, we are taking big steps toward your destiny. I had much experience with Malorana before I reached this stage in meditation, but, you—you are being taken on an extreme journey. You are being taken straight into the belly of Malorana and our village. Take my hand..."

"I can't move," thought Becca. Johan took Becca's hand, and they burst into the belly of Malorana.

Back at camp, Gus Reichen was feeling well. The girl, Becca, was still lying on her back, arms at her side; and Gus Reichen knew something was not right, although he was assured and peaceful. The twigs snapped, the ever-present creaking of the forest went on, and it was at this

time when Gus Reichen decided to go down to the stream to refill his canteen. He would leave Becca alone for a few minutes. What could go wrong? She had been in this catatonic state for over a day now; and nothing could lend further to its strangeness, not even the night, not even the forest night, which was so strange, thought Gus Reichen. He heard so many bugs chattering. He thought this was the place to find new species. He, as of yet, had not taken any samples. Perhaps he would on his trip to the stream. He would gather some vials, with holes punched on lids for samples of bugs. He could study them at the camp; he did not need to bring them home. He would take notes at camp, there beside Becca, on the husks of beetles, the legs and movements of Insecta, the smallest of animals and the most reassuring animals, reassuring Gus Reichen of the fact he had power in this camp, and he was not going to let anything happen to Becca Holmvik.

He descended the shallow ridge toward the stream and dipped his canteen in the stream, filling it to the brim. He felt chaste. He collected an ant, a rather large specimen, into a jar and went back to camp. However, he stopped at a rotten log and looked beneath it: large beetles. Hakuna matata, he thought, as he collected a large, juicy beetle into a jar. He took a step closer to camp.

***

"I know of these frogs," said Carlos. "They are the frogs of Malorana. One touch and you're done." They took only one step into the ceremonial room, not daring to go closer to the frogs, which numbered in the thousands. The frogs were hopping hither and yon, paying no mind to the two people.

"I don't dare." Dr. Reid Phillips was captivated. Before the two of them was a statue.

"Look at this statue," Dr. Reid Phillips said. "It looks like a shrine."

Carlos said, "She looks Caucasian."

"Indeed," said the Doctor. The statue was of a woman, tall and striking, and was adorned in an airy robe.

"In fact, she looks strikingly Caucasian."

"Oh, yes? How so?"

"Well, look at the forehead. Caucasian, definitely, and the jade in the corners of the eyes

make the eyes green."

"Indeed they do, but what are you implying?" said the Doctor

"Nothing. Nothing at all." The two paused silent for a moment. "I suggest we go back from where we came," said the guide. "Lest we have an encounter with one of these frogs."

The two trudged back to camp, through the anteroom and the portico, which Dr. Reid Phillips had, with such admiration, touched. The notion held fast in his mind, however, that the girl, the statue, looked much like their Becca, back at camp. It was peculiar at best. How could a girl having just entered the sanctuary of Malorana be in the pyramid as a statue? It made no sense; and it defied logic. Nevertheless, it seemed to take in the mind of the Doctor that it was a Caucasian girl who was portrayed in the statue. A god among the South Americans. It would not be the first time a Caucasian was deemed a god among them, and the idea was facsimile compared to the schema of Malorana. A single god, amongst thousands and thousands of frogs, which were, in turn, gods, as well. Dr. Reid Phillips took a long sip from his canteen and slung it over his shoulder. The trip back to camp would take an hour; but the thought of the pyramid would last in his thoughts forever.

***

In Anstape, the two, Lloyd Caston and Bridget Alcoy, with success, had rallied a party for the e-vac. They had told of the emergency to the officials at the department of securities; and the helicopter was dispatched fast, with both Lloyd Caston and Bridget Alcoy aboard. Now, they did have a view of the rainforest—the view was spectacular, unlike any sight either had before seen, a deep and lush rainforest, green and teeming with life. They could see the stream, which they had followed back into the village of Anstape. Nevertheless, they knew it was there, just like they knew of their coming together, just like they knew of Becca and the danger she was in. It would not take long—a mere three or four hour chopper ride back into camp would prove them successful in their e-vac; however, what they did not know was that Becca was not going to be aboard, when they returned. For Becca was going the opposite direction, deep into the Earth, while the chopper was approaching the camp with speed.

***

A freefall into the depths of the Earth and Becca, screaming in terror, all the while sitting placid on the pillow, was the hallucination Goquum had divined. Becca was fast approaching the source of the power of Malorana, the frogs and the people, who had disappeared years and years prior to the arrival of the team at the outskirts of the village of Malorana. The throbbing was louder than ever; a screaming tone rang in her ears. Then, breaking through the sound, with the screams and the terrible visions of frogs and corpses and death, was a drum, hollow and ritualized.

"Duaph." The feelings of Becca Holmvik were reaching into the belly of the frog; and she knew then her life on Earth was no more. She was to spend her time, eternity even, in the depths of the Earth, as an anchor and as sturdiness for those in tribulation. Like the rainforest breathed oxygen, Becca breathed hope. Into the lungs of billions of people, she felt her exhalation reach. She lost track of Johan's hand. She was released, and she saw the totem, which Carlos had uncovered a day prior. At the top was Malorana, the frog. Next was Goquum, or Johan as she knew him. Next was Man, as the entirety of the species, and then there was the Draikam, looking horrible and lively, looking deep within her eyes with his onyx glare. She blinked, and the totem turned to a stone illustration of herself. She felt her body harden, like stone. Her breath was released from her lungs, violent. Into her ears and her hindquarters was the air of the rainforest; and she shot up, like a rocket, into the pyramid of Malorana, ascending, yet descending, like a shaft of light through the top of the pyramid, paradoxical. She was granted the image of thousands of frogs. Her eyes wanted to shed a tear, but they were hard as stone. Then, by means of a gravitational pull, she was brought into the statue, the girlish statue, which only minutes prior had been discovered by Carlos and Dr. Reid Phillips. Only Becca, back at camp, was not at camp anymore; for she had disintegrated and had disappeared into the forest; and upon knowing this and feeling it, she felt the weight of the world ascend off her shoulders; and she closed her eyes and became mist.

***

Gus Reichen returned to camp with his samples to find Becca missing. Where had she gone? He was devastated. Had she walked off? Woken up and went searching for the others? But no, she did not get up. She was gone; and Gus Reichen kneeled before the sleeping bag, on which Becca had been lying and sweated into his eyes, crying tears not of sadness, but of perplexity. For she was gone; and he knew she was not coming back.

***

The chopper arrived two hours after Carlos and Dr. Reid Phillips had returned to camp. They had found Gus Reichen sitting on a log, shaking his head. "She's gone," he said. "She's gone, and I don't know where she went."

The two—Carlos and Dr. Reid Phillips—looked at each other. The ominous image came back to the Doctor, the statue of the Caucasian girl. "Where has she gone?" asked the Doctor.

"I don't know. I went to the stream and came back minutes later and she was gone, disappeared is all, and I don't where she is."

They sat and mourned and drank water.

Hours later, overhead, was the helicopter, which dropped a ladder and an airlift, for Becca. Down came an officer, to set Becca into the bed; but she was no more. The team decided to e-vac, in totality, and send out a search party. They ascended into the hovering helicopter. They found Lloyd Caston and Bridget Alcoy sitting, strapped into their seats, so that they did not fall out of the chopper, which would shift with the new acquired weight.

"Where's Becca?" asked Alcoy.

"Gone," said the Doctor.

"She's gone. She's disappeared."

"Disappeared. What do you mean?"

"We're sending out a search party. She's gone. Reichen went to the stream and came to

find the camp completely empty. Officials are staying here to search, but I fear the worst."

As the helicopter cascaded toward the village of Anstape, Gus Reichen had a peculiar thought and voiced his opinion on the matter: "We just don't know. We just don't know what the world has to offer. In terms of peculiarity, I'd say this gets a ten out of ten. Where Becca's gone,

I don't know, but it's strange, Doctor, strange.

"Indeed it is, and as for what the world has to offer, it's been my thoughts for years that we will never know. We will never know of the undiscovered, unexpected circumstances in which we find ourselves. That's why I set up this excavation; but it's only lent itself to further distraught questions."

"What discoveries have been made over the past twenty years," said Gus Reichen, "have only given way to more questions... Thusly, we find ourselves here in the Amazon, wondering about questions. Questions on questions. Where has Becca gone? How was the pyramid created?"

"What are the frogs, really?" said the Doctor. "The village believes they are gods; but my guess is that they are demons, demons, which walk the face of the Earth without our knowing. That's why I fear, Gus. I fear the demons. I fear the frogs. I fear Malorana. When I was in that pyramid, it was like somebody was watching me; but really it was the thousands of frogs, the thousands of generations that have disappeared, and the hundreds of people who have disappeared, which have me fearful—and now, now we can only wait to see if Becca is one of them, one of those lost, in mystery."

"We truly will never find or discover all things, Doctor. You have to know that. It has me guessing as to my origins."

"Yes," said the Doctor. "And mine, as well."

Origins and final resting places and the journey in between the darkness and the light—all were closed, and all were opened and all had a middle ground. It was only a question of what was Malorana. What was the village? An origin of man? A final battle ground? Or a peaceful impasse? The team would never know; but Becca did. She knew it was the end. It was the end place, Malorana. The people, who were leaving the village of Malorana, were, as she saw it, lucky. For they had short lives. Now, she had a long existence; and as long as the rainforest kept breathing, she would live. The team pulled out. The excavation was over. One had been lost, thought the team, at disparaged instances in the travels home, and little had been learned, but what *had* been learned was the primordial and imposing character of the naturalistic world and the wrath, which played a part separate from civilization, keeping Man ignorant.

The team might have been a small bit enlightened, thought Becca, from her high point of view and staging ground. Her body was preserved as the statue and her spirit was preserved as the forest; but she was desperate, and she wanted to come home. At that thought, all vanished, and all was the forest. All was breathing as one and all thoughts lent themselves to Malorana and the Amazon and the rushing forest, which was mobile, beneath the team and the chopper, with the billowing trees and with the noisy shadows, which had been draped by the helicopter, atop the tree canopy. The team ate well in Anstape. Becca drinked tea, on her omniscient pillow. Meanwhile, thousands upon thousands of frogs leapt, precocious, within the pyramid of Malorana.

A Philosopher's Lexis

Nothing can ring more true than my following words as I, upon my writing these words, have found that many have succumbed to the wrath of the Curse. That I have written words, which many have read, and live, however doleful, is pertaining to the fact these words are portentous in that those who read these words are, too, sure damned. For that reason, do I implore the reader to continue with due wariness, so that they do not end with the same Fate as those others who have read my words, in past times.

It seems I am borne with a gift no other on the face of the planet has been given. That is, my words, scribbled on a page or typed, are assured and Cursed. Many times have I written in transcendental prose and poetics to balance or counter the sure Fate, which descends on the victims of my art; and do say that now, as my words are being written, that I feel an unprecedented sense of longing to speak to those who have passed on, fallen prey to delusions, or have been instated in hospitals for the mental ill—those who have, whilst bravery having brazened their thoughts, become subject to that darkness, which I house in my right hand. For it was said, when the Saints of old raised their hand and then lowered it, many a tiding of emotion and waters went into the lungs of the disheartened, and sure died as a result; and thus do I write in sure undertones of the savage ritual, which has made the reader, too, Cursed.

Read on and sure will he find the truth; for it was when I was a child the Curse found me, and now it shall be passed on to the reader, who reads with confidence, but will sure wind up forgotten and forsaken by the very gods, who rained upon us the duality of all things. Where there is light, there is darkness; and where there is darkness, there is light. Only now, do I think in acute and profound notions that there is a threshold betwixt the two and which is regulated not by Earthy entities, but those who are of the dæmonic. This is why I write in warning. It is for this reason I have become aware of my placement in macrocosmic nature—that I write with sure script and regulate the tidings of madness with penmanship. Over time, I have conjectured the unthinkable and have written down words, which have rendered my enemies overcome. I have been the culprit of tragedies, taking the willpower of men, women, and children from the very hands of god, and placing them in my own. I have been the inventor of many an obscurity; and I have taken away power from the sirens and philistines with my ecstatic literature. Broken the bounds of the timeline have I; and have learned that all men, women, and children are confined to a singular and dimensional timeline, which their lives follow. Learned have I how to break the confines of this prison-like dynamic, setting all those who read to run a course unknown to them and unknown to their angelic protectors, for danger is always a theme in the comprehending of my words; and, as I have said, have destroyed many an enemy, ally, and impartial person, by my words, set them off course, as in a gale of winds whilst traveling the seas, so that they never again saw land, always in the midst thereto of insanity and even of death. This is my warning; and reading on, I assure you, will lead to a certain Fate, over which I have henceforth lost control.

It began as a child. Many times, in my sketches, I drew of demented faces, eyes which spun in twirls and mælstroms, mouths which drooped, and ears which pointed upwards to the unrefined skies of a background, which in many cases involved mountain ranges or river settings. Yes, I, in youth, was an artist not of literature but of feigning sketches, which made the viewer wince and take breaths in order to exact a confidence in that I was not unusual. However, that could not be farther from the truth; and as I grew into adolescence fell into the camaraderie of young men and women who had interests in the occult, exacting séances and dark rituals in the attic of a home I remember only too well, as so much time has gone by, and which I would not for the sake of nostalgia, want to forget; for it was in that attic the Accursed hands were given me. Candles had been lighted; five young men and women sat in a circle around a drop cloth, on which was painted a red pentagram, and, slow, I was eased into reverie. The night was black, and from the inside of the attic, which gave through to a small window, I could see the sticks of a dead tree faltering. Overcome was I with a sense of dread not ten minutes into the ritual, and I was seeing with my eyes a man with black skin and red paint on his face, standing in the center of the pentagram, which reigned upon me sure horror, as the black man was looking at me, with a look in his eye like some animal found only in the jungles of the African continent. No, it was not a living animal, for no animal could have those eyes. It was a cross between the living and the deceased—an extinct form of a feline's eye, split down the middle with a sharp pupil, black as the night, which was blowing outside of that small attic. My eyes were closed, and yet I was seeing this man with sure accuracy, seeing not with my two physical eyes, but with the third, which was until then obscured with skepticism and foreboding thoughts of fear—my sketches, drawings, and scribblings of blurbs on the back of those demented faces rushed into my head as a wave of paranoia, and then he was gone. I felt numbness in my right hand and a dutiful feeling in my gut; and when I opened my eyes, I felt as though I had been struck in the mouth by an angry fist. Dark sparks came from my hand and from my eyes and chest, sounding like flares and darker than the attic in which we were sitting. This was August of 1991; and still to this day, I feel that strike upon my mouth and still hear the flares of those manifestations when I write and when I sleep. Upon standing, I felt uneasiness about me. I went straight home and drew a sketch of a black man having been hanged from a tree. This sketch was the action, which got me instated into the hospital for the mental ill, two weeks following the séance.

I was brought into the psychiatrist's office with resentfulness. He sat, arrogant, with one

leg crossed over the other and asked my name. I said my name was John Forstead, though names can be deceiving. He asked me why I had been instated; and I was quiet for a moment, resistant to talk to this man, in all honesty, and decided to say I would write down the events, which preceded my institutionalization. He agreed, and offered me a pen and paper, the tools which proved my dominance in the setting, and which would grant me freedom that very day. I wrote down the occurrences of the séance and gave the paper to the psychiatrist. He read, and as sure as evident illness were the thoughts and beliefs of this man, about halfway through reading the long paragraph, shuttered and screamed. The air about him flickered and shuttered, and he, estranged from then on, looked at me and told me to get out of his office. He saw no other patients that day; and from that day forth decided never to practice medicine. I was discharged, as per the psychiatrist's orders later in the day, and was brought home where I wrote down the events which had happened in his office.

It was peculiar, having power over a man who was thought omnipotent in a hospital setting. My freedom was given to me without a second guess. He wanted with dearness, never to see me again I assure you, and as I mounted the steps to my home that evening smiled at my dominion. Never had I went into the hospital for the mental ill after that incident; and I was sure to cover my queer pursuits with wariness and even lies as time wore on. I drew still. I wrote but showed nothing to anybody. This power was my secret, that is until I went to the University to study English; and there did this power take a more significant turn.

I wrote essays upon essays, which many a professors read and critiqued. Many a time, those professors called in sick or were absent following days on which essays were due. I wrote on Miltonian poetics, Shakespearian theatre, studied the practices of Buddhists and Cabbalists in religion studies classes, and wrote essays on all and everything on which I could write an essay, and time after time, teachers came back from critiquing those essays estranged and seemed absent-minded after reading my writing. Once even a teacher failed to show for a meeting and it was told to us she had died of a stroke the preceding night. I gathered this was an effect of my writing; and do not think me mad, for peer critiques from students whilst in these classes, gave way to shrieks, and I was lambasted for my writing and evident personality. A girl once slapped me after reading what I had written, a rather eloquent writing on the coming of age from feudalism to common day economics. People feared me, and I was forced, as no people read my writing after the Curse was evident, to leave the University without achieving my degree. It was then I started writing as an escape, showing nobody my writing, but keeping this secret a perfunctory weapon against whatever might be lying on the other side. I had heard of dæmonic battles, when writers and their respective dæmons duel in the poetic craft. This, I fear is my Fate; and as I write I think what will I, in the moment of ethereal judgment, write? That I think the dæmon will read and be Cursed does not resound a great deal of courage in me; and yet I, thoughtful, am pulled to the notion that all who in fact, read my writing are just that—Cursed. For, as I have stated, many have become mad, many have died, and many have reacted violent to my being present and writing. I know not what has come of many of these readers; and yet I am forced to the knowledge that I, someday will know what has become of them. As the timeline is further skewed by peculiar writings I am enlightened to the fact that when I perish, there will be the culmination of the three faceted personalities—the first person, the third person omniscient, and the second person. This is my Fate, as I see it; and will be subject to the literature, which I write and have written, Cursed, no less by the peculiar savage

I had seen in August of 1991; and now, my fellow reader, you have read my tale and my peculiar story. I know not what will become of you, nor will I know until the effervescent time of death penetrates my being, and

I am taken from this realm and brought into one of high craft or simple devastation. All I know is that those who read my writings are god damned. You may think me mad, but when the time arrives and delusion slips, slow, into your subconscious, waiting for you to go to sleep, and when you wake, feel the paranoid ghost pulling at your arm, telling you to wake, when you are paralyzed with fear, then you will know that you, too, are subject to Fate.

The Split

1

In a rather spontaneous attempt to preserve my memories, I, Carl Redham, have decided to put on record a set of events—the exploits of Friday, June 4th, year 1971—which has tinted the looking glass through which I view the world, for I am an aging man.

I will begin by saying I find myself observing the night's expanse with more and more frequency and with deepening veins of reverence, sitting, perched under the silken canopy of starlight, which has become my only home, marveling not at the stars themselves, but more so at the darkness in between them.

It is my knowledge, children today discuss the intellect of modern man—it is on the television, I've seen it. I also know these children grasp its concepts with much more wholesomeness than I, myself, do, these theories atop of theories of possibilities, branches of science human beings may one day harness and develop into god conceptions, the stars, but the tragic notion occurs, what of the darkness in between? What of the things no human has or will ever touch upon? The things, which make people people, and gods gods.

In that blackness are where my thoughts dwell and my hopes extinguished—hopes my experiences may, one day, be conceptualized in full and understood, and are the outcome of the stars, rather than of darkness.

I am viewed as a derelict by the people—their eyes show me in how they catch on to mine and release, scared of turning to stone, it seems, as if I were a demon, and I add with humility it is not so. While they look, I wonder, who are these people and what is waiting for them? And then do I wade through the swelling and receding tides of possibilities—the origin of the Split.

A great many years have passed since I began calling the incident by that name, and I do think the reader would find it notable to recognize my experiences as so from here on forth.

The Split—it is a divide between science and religion, logic and mysticism, common knowledge and the occult, delicate and separated yet brilliant and entwined into the fabric of human emotion. It is through great time and consideration that two viewpoints hold fast in my mind. One: that of a logical skeptic, awaiting scientific and testable evidence to verify my assumptions. And two: a faithful mystic. It is natural I find myself on a rotating axis, in and out of these viewpoints, continuous.

I must say, yes, in my lower, more trodden moments, there have been regretful times when I've pushed the recollection of such memories off the bounds of reality and into the dark abyss of delusion. Though, perhaps, trodden and contradictory are a better description of such down times, contradictory in the sense that I know the events of June 4th, 1971 had, in fact, taken place, and had not been fabricated in the corners of my imagination.

Now, after half a lifetime, a single night consisting of too much red wine and the better half of a cigar, births thoughtfulness for a radiant memory, which is just now finding its way onto paper.

1971, dinner in Miami with my darling daughter, Claudia. A soft breeze giving off the ocean pecked kisses at my forehead, cooling me a slight bit and rippling my shirt and tossing Claude's hair. She was young then, eighteen, and I dare say she had become a sort of symbol of the evening, for her hair was the first thing I had noticed upon my return. Such small details are such potent triggers in recalling memories. In my case, it is her hair, extravagant set tables, palm trees, and a cigar. It is hard to separate the two, the night in Miami and the Split; though, they still can be recalled with great ease and fondness. Sitting across from me, with her eyes set cool on mine, was Claudia. We had been in Miami for two days at that point and the weather was agreeable, not quite the blasted heat the place is chalked up to have had, and not rainy in the least. There was a breeze, which Claudia voiced her thankfulness for and I replied, looking east out on the ocean, "Yes, doesn't exactly work wonders against this humidity though," saying this purely for humor; I was in fact quite comfortable, this being my first time south of the Carolinas.

"Feels nice," Claude said, and a pleasant silence had hung among us for a moment until she spoke up again. "Thanks, Dad, for taking me down here. It's been good getting away."

I had agreed; Claudia's hair, her eyes and eyebrows, bore striking resemblances to my late wife's, auburn and wavy and thick, and it felt almost as though she was there with us. I had learnt not to dwell—it was stifling—letting Gayle settle in mind. Like crude oil in water, it stuck to everything.

Claude said, "Ah, here he comes," smiling. "Thanks, Alex." She had a ripe genuineness, along with a dash of conservation, which made our waiter raise his eyebrows in curiosity. Claudia was and still is a blessing.

Unknown by myself at that point in time was how her role and her undeniable residence in my heart would brandish the courage and wisdom needed to escape the Split; it was not noted until very much later.

I had ordered another beer, said to Claude, "So, are you trying to get that same lifeguarding job when we get back home?"

Her skin glowed bronze in the lighting, statuesque. "I thought I would," she said. "They reserve positions for previous employees, and it's good money. Not hard work."

As so had our conversation continued, and before too long, I realized three quarters of my steak was gone as well as three beers; I looked up at Claudia, capturing her odd and frozen image—her head cocked slight to the left, looking past and behind me down Ocean Drive, the wind blowing her hair back from her forehead, supple, her right arm up at her side, limp at the wrist, on its way up to replace her burgundy sundress's fallen spaghetti strap to its position on her shoulder, panoramic and precious; the café's conversation again picked up into a steady vibration. "How're the scallops?" I asked.

"Delicious. Melt in your mouth."

"Same with the steak," I laughed. "I think they used cinnamon sugar as a marinade."

"We should try that."

"We should."

"Dad," she said, prompt. "You're going to have to excuse me. I have to use the ladies'."

I replied, "Don't take too long, hon. You wouldn't want to bore me, would you?"

"Not a chance. Don't go anywhere," and she walked away, inside the café and out of sight. Now, I do realize it would add to the suspense of the story to say this was the last time

I'd ever see her, but the fact is the statement couldn't be farther from the truth. Begging consideration at this point is a pivotal question, which reads as follows: if she had taken a few minutes longer in the bathroom, if she had not come back to our table the moment she had, to give me the breath of life, would I still be alive today to write these words which you now read.

This is the essential focus of this story. Did she save me—or did I save myself? I decided not to order another beer. 1971 was a time when one could in fact have a smoke in a café and not get persecuted—I started smoking heavier after Gayle had passed, a cigar most days out of the week—so I patted my breast pocket in search of the smoke and cutter.

An expression in my left-side pocket all night, the tool was reaching out to me, and I stretched, just far enough to grab it, into my left pocket for the metallic piece; the cigar from my breast pocket was on the table now; and in reaching, I had bumped against the table, setting the cigar to a roll. It fell to the ground and taunted me.

Nowhere could I have imagined that in only a few short moments my coronary artery would be backed up and choked and I would fall victim to a heart attack.

The cigar had hit the ground and rolled still. Lazy and with my white chinos tightening around my legs, I managed an attempt to snatch the brown tube off the ground; a detached, warm burst of unrefined pain surfaced in my chest and began soaking through my shirt. Short time had passed before I had even the slightest notice of its presence. It was like lukewarm coffee had been spilled on my chest; I looked down at a dry shirt, with no such wetness found. The only wetness— sweat—clung to my forehead; the hot flashes had begun; my shirt collar was in the unrelenting process of making of itself a noose.

Claudia was distant; everything was distant. It was a very uncomfortable feeling I wish no one to ever experience. Air came in wisps. Panic had grabbed ahold with conviction. Time slowed; thoughts ran like wild horses. Pressure began pressing on the inside of my left arm, and I had no choice but to drop to one knee for support.

Abstract in the way one feels when connected with two seeming and opposing things, in simultaneity, life and death, I was lying on my back humbled, all my strength and

willpower draining from my body and with nature's fury acting as an anchor and keeping me immobile and incapacitated on the café floor. Further taking my breath, the realization hit me; my life and my death were moments away from merging as one.

Faces hovering over me went all but unnoticed, and I thought of Claudia again, trying hard to find her in my mind, trying to catch her, or maybe hold on to her, so I wouldn't fall into this end. I was dying while she was in the bathroom; she would come out and see my corpse lying on the ground and she'd be alone.

Those were my thoughts as I exited, exited a place considered home, a place considered comforting, gratifying and pleasant, a place considered livable, a place considered real.

I exited, and as though life were nothing but a child's daydream, the Split had taken me.

2

Science or religion? Stars or darkness? All ends double back to these dualities.

One taking a scientific standpoint might say the light which had consumed me had been nothing but a fantastic array of bounding and rebounding chemicals in my brain, an explosion of neurological essences, the peak of all there is to know about the finality of death. Crisp and to the point are the beliefs of these scientists, as were mine prior that night.

I was undergoing a radical transition. Nothing before seen or sensed could be described as anything close to the rush of energy I was feeling. The rapidity at which I traveled was immense, hurling through a boundless expanse of light. There was no friction; not even the familiarized weight of my body was existent. The physicality of the gliding and the light was so beyond description, to say the least, it cannot be put into clear context; the English language does not have sufficient words for such things—the way the light had intensified in spots and dulled in others, into shades of grays and pearly whites and everything in between, all flashing in unison with one another as if a four-dimensional kaleidoscope, the shifts in hue and color related as an unparalleled, discernable means of communication.

Still traveling forwards in this velocity, new connotations and nuances of this language being spoken, or rather showed to me, optical, were just starting to unfold in precognition as if they had always been there, dormant.

It was like a celestial collision of sign language and metaphor.

Dancing on the edges of empathy were the overtones of these flashes, and I had a very vague sense of self awareness, in the context my previous self was not myself at all; I felt a very different person, fresh. There was no Claudia and there was no Gayle in my thoughts; the absolute gravitation towards this light had my complete focus, and, slow, I began to realize the selfishness of this act, this separation; it was at that point I did begin to slow, the language starting to be understandable, and in full.

My god! Where to begin? Perhaps it is obvious. Through all the light shown to me and through all the subtleties this light had lain upon me, only four words could be articulated atop of all the emotion—look, illumine, and see—and I lingered in bliss for many moments. A pop resonated outwards from my head moments later, as well as from my chest, and my extremities began to have feeling in them again, warming, and I felt something like water flowing around my skin, very cool and complimenting, and quite revitalizing, and I opened my mouth and the water trickled in my mouth and onto my tongue, and I swallowed.

The light turned into patches then, other colors seeping through—greens, blues, and

whites—I couldn't identify what they were, these colors, only that they seemed very tangible and real, as my arms and legs and head were beginning to come back to me.

Then, yes, there was a branch, with leaves, and a cloud and blue air. My ears were pulsing, and then the sounds of birds and gurgling water were present; the patches congealed into a place in which I would dwell for a time, how long I will never know. Only in that moment, when the patches had congealed in full and I had complete control over my thoughts once more, I realized I was lying in a stream in this new place, and without any clothing.

3

I was in a daze, I tell you, but I did feel aware. The trees smelled fresher than any tree I'd ever smelled, pine or oak or any flower. It was as if a middle man of sorts had been cut out, like there was no need to think or to actualize. Everything just was; the trees were my very senses, so vibrant and thick I needn't even process my surroundings—I was accepted by this place—the air crystal. I'd never felt more alive than in that moment, and I do not know if the beaming sensation will ever be felt again.

As it may be, my mind, however new, was mine again, and I was in a daze. It seemed apparent: I had passed on and was dead somewhere, lying on the ground in a place, which now seemed, in retrospect—and this thought was entertained in full—quite despairing, and my lying here in this quiet stream was another part of me, somehow, a much more important and meaningful part.

I stayed in the stream for a bit, just feeling the area around me for many moments, the water flowing over my skin, supple, the clouds wakeful and bright, the residue of wonder in my veins. Then, I was reminded of Claudia, and I let out a diluted sigh of warm air. She was alone, without family, young, and it seemed as if she was dwindling in some way, being evaporated off my shoulders; I stood from the water and walked ashore.

It was quite strange, this caricature of life. I strode, quiet, taking in the waxy leaves, touching them and feeling their ripeness, and I became uncomfortable; I realized I was naked and wet and cold.

I couldn't help but think—Adam and Eve, how they were born nude and stayed nude until the original sin had been committed—knowledge—and they had been clothed ever since, and I did feel uncomfortable, standing there with a leaf in my hand.

So, this wasn't a playpen of the gods. There wasn't just blissfulness here, there was real emotion, yearning, embarrassment my current one.

However, even through the embarrassment, I was surprised in my clear-headedness. I remembered the words—look—beauty, color, the soil, rich and full; illumine—the high power, the lights and sparks, the awakening moment; and see—the downcast appeal of all I've left behind, somewhere behind me, the breathing of the Miami shoreline, this stream beside which I sat, the air and my own breath, which was of constancy.

It began with sympathy, for the loved ones, Claudia and Gayle, our separation from each other too early; intense nostalgia like something had been churned just then; and something too powerful to endure if it wasn't for the stroke of hope brushing across my brow at that moment. The wind carried me far closer to old age and death then, than I ever care to be. An essence, which seemed trivial at first, was erupting inside me. The dirt begging to be crushed, I dropped to my knees and expelled the cries of a man weary and confused—it was becoming evident and truly inevitable I would never see my home again—and this place was radiant with light, yes, but more so radiant with energy of which I had never been aware, the true loss of power. I lay and slept in the soil. Dreams accosted me, fragmentary wisps of the past and present; terrible cracks of the future, gore and violence of places I didn't recognize. I slept, tumultuous, until a moist caressing woke me; it was nighttime, and the crickets and frogs were chirping amongst themselves. I felt peace again, and a breeze carried mist into my eyes. Follow the water, maybe. Maybe there were people somewhere. Maybe they could help me. I followed my tracks back to the stream and dabbed my face with water and drank some. I started down the way, south, east, west? I had no idea, I just walked and walked and tried to find a meaning in all this—I felt as though there was something incomplete, something outstanding in this place and needed doing. I walked in what seemed like a limbo, a wild sense of roundness complementing this mystery, and through the moonlight and the starlight and their reflections from the trees and water, the blackness of the sky lay on me a somber grip, saying, yes, this may just be all that is left.

4

I was amongst trees and tree stumps, as if the trees had been cut down for lumber, for houses, or civilization. There was something here, people, curious. A clearing, full of tree stumps, was casted before my eyes and I had the peculiar sense I was being watched, from the tree line. I stayed in the clearing for the majority of what was hours, until the orb in the sky I called the sun descended; and eyes looked outwards from the trees, or rather they looked like eyes—giant purple orbs, emanating from the woods. I gathered my courage quick and ventured into the woods, still unclothed.

Snaps and cracking of twigs came from underfoot. There were no thorns; it was a peaceful wood, and I navigated with confidence further in to find a glimmering light, a fire, in the distance. The smell of smoke found my nose. Chattering birds, the first and far from the last example of life, entered my ears. I heard a shout, as if somebody was playing with children, then giggling children. It was as if I had descended into a ghost place, the laughter far distant, and yet, I found myself unaffected by my nudeness and approached the sounds, my body surrounded by cool air and confidence, walking through this strange land, unbeknownst of the trials I was to undergo.

I reached, in the distance, a small house, in what seemed like a short walk, but in this would-be reality, my feet ached, and my body had grown cold and I was, much like the feeling I had felt before leaving Miami, Florida, hungered. I felt hunger in this place, which meant physicality was evident. I needed material nourishment, like I needed in the Earthy setting I had departed. I needed food. I needed shelter. I needed clothing. This land seemed fertile, almost like a feudalistic place. I pictured farms, animals, and families working in fields, and a city nearby.

A yellow wall breached my eyesight just as I entered a clearing, which housed a small cottage, with thatch roof, a cottage made of wood, and a woman hanging clothing out to dry. She wore a traditional gown. I approached, and she greeted me, unsurprised, as if it were indifferent to her.

"Another one," she said. This woman was to be my wife for the next three years.

5

I pranced through the woods, carefree, disregarding to the growing wind, the speed picking up to a steady, gusty evening-time rainstorm. I had learned miles east was the ocean, a large expansive ocean, which was called the Big Sea, and which separated the rural-esque place in which I was living and the kingdom that was the greater area, where many people lived.

The woman had clothed me, and we had had a conversation, which brought us together in friendship; she said this was common amongst farmers, or peasants in this area, the smaller and more rural of the two areas in this grand place beyond the place Earthy, from whence I had come and where I was going to make a return in ten years. Her name was Phillyna. She told me of people who came to this place after their separation from their former world—she told me not many returned to their former world—and, in fact, she said those who returned to their former worlds were known as legends in this place and she wanted, with dearness, to help me return, for she saw I was distressed, and I did talk much about my daughter, Claudia.

Phillyna told me there were ways to bring my body back together. There were multiple forms of the body, she said; the part which had left and came here is the wondering body, the part of the body, which yearns for understanding and knowledge. The other part, which stayed on the former world is the concrete body, the body where desirable things are manifested and acquired, the part of the body which seemed to know all, until the former of the two bodies I have mentioned leaves and is ascended to this place; after days of deliberation I decided I was going to listen to her word, depart from this new constructed place and find what I was looking for, so I could return to my concrete body, my Earthy body.

"I will be trying."

"I gathered as much." Those were the simple words Phillyna and I had spoken to one another, upon my bringing about the conversation—I wanted to go to the city; I wanted to go home. She was excited. In a way, she was passive and excited. She wanted the best for me, but

sometimes she seemed as though on, for the lack of a better term, auto-pilot, as if she had lain down in the cut, stayed balanced, and went with the flow, very rare in doing things, which were to change the surroundings, with greatness.

She only mentioned the city, the maze which was the streets, and the haphazard people, who walked through them. I was well taken care of, however, clothed, bathed, and fed. We slept together. We ate together. We spoke together; but she was quiet, almost downtrodden in her words and actions, as were the forests and the forest floors, in which we lived and lived well, and she departed in the morning to fetch water from the stream and she harvested fruits and vegetables from the garden behind and beside our cottage and she spoke little of her endeavors, for it was a slow place, trodden in its nature, and she looked tried by the elements and one reason I decided to leave was that she seemed one-dimensional and singular. She spoke only when spoken to, for the most part. She clothed herself quick and mechanistic, avoiding my eyes sometimes, and playing with her hair, interacting as if there were a preoccupation or something on her mind.

Days had passed, and it was rather on a fluke we had come together. Phillyna, at first, was full of life and had gumption to the degree which made her irresistible to me. It seemed inevitable, at the time, and as time went on, she seemed to lose the luster, lackluster instead, and in was then the wandering pursuits of my mind took residence and were internalized, my wanting to go home, my wanting to see Claudia, and my wanting to tell her that everything was okay.

My living at the cottage brought a degree of knowledge, as to my existing in that place. Home, in my former world, and raising a child had with it many distractions, psychological obstacles, which made raising a child difficult, or like a chore, or rather, something close to a risk, for the distractions were offsetting of a child's psyche and changed them to degrees, which may not have been retainable, unbeknownst to them, or to the absent-minded parents. Here, in this cottage, there was pure reciprocation.

6

My wife, back home, where my Earthy body was still lying on the ground in the restaurant, in Miami, Florida, had died years prior to our visiting the sub-tropical climate of Florida. It had been a rather boisterous and uncomfortable realization and death. She had been healthy her whole life. I had taken care of her. She didn't smoke cigarettes. She ate well. She exercised sometimes. She, it seemed to me, was going to live to see one hundred, she, an example of health and fortune, leading by example the ways of a good life.

Claudia and I outlived her. Her years ended abrupt, and it was not an easy surfacing of her sickness, cancer, which killed her.

We had eaten dinner, a delicious meal of roast beef and fried potatoes. The table was cleared by Claudia. We had taught her to do her chores and she did them well, without question, and my late wife, Gayle, and I were pleased with the way she had turned out, the way she had developed from adolescence into teenage years and we were thinking about buying her a car as a high school graduation gift. That ended up not being the case. Our money went to Gayle's therapy, short as it was, and expensive therapy, in which Gayle did not want to participate, and she ended up dying, leaving before the brunt of chemotherapy and radiation set in. She died with a full head of hair, with meat on her bones, albeit sick was her demeanor and it seemed quick, almost too quick, her leaving.

We had cleared the table, washed the dishes, and the three of us went to bed. I fell asleep, quick. My head hit the pillow and I was out just before I said, "Good night." I think I said good night. I was already so deep in my regular food coma the vague recollection of my saying goodnight may have been a hallucination.

Nevertheless, I have the memory of her saying good night to me and she sounded well saying it. Hours later, I was in mid-dream state. I remember the ascending of birds through a tree canopy. The birds were a vibrant red. The trees were a deep green and I just saw the blue sky through a porous section in the tree canopy. I was silent. It was all visual. I was observing the birds and they were silent, as was I. I did not hear their wings fluttering. I did not hear the innate sounds of wildlife, found in a jungle setting. There were so many birds. A dozen red birds ascended through the tree canopy and as the last bird penetrated the leaves, a bloodcurdling scream woke me, violent from my dream.

I shot up. My wife, Gayle, was sitting upright and turned her head towards me, mechanical, in a way which can only be described as horrible.

She had awoken, she said, with the most exquisite pain in the center of her skull. It was so exquisite that it woke her from her sleep, woke me from my dream, and I saw the shadow of Claudia casted on the wall as she approached our bedroom, also awoken.

Gayle was silent, her eyes bloodshot and her hair tangled. She looked skinny, her eyes sunken deep into her skull, dark circles surrounding the eyes, and she said nothing for many minutes.

Claudia and I only watched her as she collected herself. After collecting herself, she said, "I need to go to the hospital." The words came out in a cracked meter. She was, in all honesty, shattered. Her psyche had been broken by what the doctor, days following the MRI, had said was a brain tumor the size of an avocado in the center of her brain. "There is nothing we can do."

That was when I knew our lives were going to be changed forever. Claudia was going to college in two years. I was working steady at my job at the paper, editing. The house was going to feel empty, and it did, following Gayle's death.

Our visiting the state of Florida was a coping mechanism for me and Claudia. To my own horror I died on the floor of the restaurant and, to my fear, was leaving Claudia alone, to fend for herself, in the big world, in which she knew so little; she was only nineteen and beginning college. Without guidance, how was she supposed to be successful? A woman? It was going to be trial and error, her maturing, if I did not make it out of the Split.

I do not know what Gayle had experienced upon dying. I do not know whether or not she was in a dream the night of the wretched scream. All I know is I have the hope it was similar to my experiences upon leaving the Earthy body, for the longevity granted in the place I found myself, in this alternate existence, was remarkable, and there was the changeability of the very fabrics which composed the solid earth, from whence I had come.

Now, I had, in this place, a new wife, albeit lessened in dynamics, emotional or otherwise, but she had told me, upon our first meeting that the city, the city far beyond the waters of the Big Sea, held something for me, for the people like me, who came to this land, and who came to this land, temporary.

7

It turned out I did not leave as quick as I wanted. I did not leave as quick as I wanted because something came over me. It was an unbound source of inspiration to listen. That is correct. While in the Split I was given a never-ending source of inspiration to listen to the communicable force, which came back to me in sleep and in mid-day, and I listened to the poetic communication. In reality, it was much more in depth. In reality, it was much more mysterious, for my hearing it had a power, the power of manifestation. It was not as if I, with immediacy, got put into the Split. In reality, it was the poetic speak which came first; and the poetry manifested the coming path of fatherhood, in this place; the poetic speak manifested the undeniable and challenging voyage, which led me out of the Split.

I sit here now, writing this for the reader so they may be enlightened as to the higher realities of the world in which we live. I sit here now, remembering the words I heard and saw, by means of flashes and sparkles. I do not remember them verbatim, for they were lost upon my leaving. I can see it now, a bundle of papers, my words, on my desk, just before lightning cracks and I am brought back at incalculable speeds to Miami, Florida.

One thousand times, the fluttering of birds reached my ears.

(This was a message sent to me in a flash, when the air, the sounds, the birds, the winds
gave me that limitless source of inspiration.)

One thousand times, the fluttering of birds reached my ears. It was written in a song, a
sound untold, pledging away trifles of the daytime wounds. One thousand times those birds, the wind blowing sure of those lost still amounted to nothing.
When the wind blew it read something deep and different, as if none of those listening were to be similar at all. Those lost were lost, yes, out and through the quiet; but the wind blew sure at night to those who listened and spoke to one another in hushed whispers, birds and winds:
They must have gone from whence they come.
For one bird heard himself anew and mid-nest by the sounds of them!

It is a poem I had heard in rudimentary flashes. It is a poem, inspired by the Split. I always thought of myself as the bird mid-nest who has heard something and is anew. I am the bird. Now, as I write this for the curious reader I am forced to remind you the above poem is not a verbatim account of the words heard in the Split, but it is close to the original.

The days following the viewing of the poem, I did much walking. Exploring the surroundings was an interest of mine and I did so, with wholesomeness, much influenced by the freshness of the place and the birds and the winds. I was quiet. I spoke only simple words to the woman who was going to mother my son. My mind was occupied by observation, for the most part, and I did observe much throughout my journey. It was an even-keel place, an even state of mind, where I found stability and confidence. I experienced a total of fourteen writings in the Split; and by the time the fourteenth poem had manifested its contents in this quasi-reality, I was released. I went on a trek into the woods one day, excitable in the thick forest and expectant of the fantastic happenings that occurred in the forest. There was some magical quality in the forest, the trees thick and brown, the tree canopy thick and bountiful, green and pleasant, contrasting the reddened soils of the ground. I was going to the stream to swim.

Many minutes had passed without words being thought. I was transfixed by the forest. I ran my hands over the rough bark of the trees, wonderment escaping my mouth in the form of Oohs and Ahhs. There was a peculiar energy in the forest and I felt vibrant, walking through it.

"Do you feel that?" I asked myself. I was playing games. "It feels like a good morning."

I nodded my head. I was always agreeable and now at fifty-five I was just starting to take on aspects, which made me an individual—tying my shoes, so to speak, in a metaphorical way. I was a grown man, I thought, and I entertained the notion. I helped with the food in the evening.

It seemed people here were capable of much more at my age. I felt young, as if I had aged with wonder.

I was navigating through the forest, following the sound of the stream, walking, for the lack of a better term, east, for what I called the sun rose in that direction. I was knocking the tree trunks, listening to the sounds they made, putting my ear up to the tree trunks and hearing the internal workings of those organisms. I was infatuated by them and I walked, and I knocked on a tree and listened, laughing, entertaining my boyish side.

The most peculiar thing happened upon my knocking the tree. I knocked on a tree and just before I knocked on the tree, stepped on and snapped a twig beneath my foot. When I put my ear up to tree, the wind in my left ear heard, while my right ear listened to the tree, the wind, in a peculiar, livable way, directing me to the west; or what I called the west, for what I called the sun set in that direction. It was more so a vague sense, or realization, that something awaited me to the west, over the mountains, the dawning thought and original thought I was to escape the Split.

I had given up hope short after my arriving there, short after the experience, which set me in this place, curious. I was granted, in my right eye, which was pressed against the tree, a vision that I was to cross the mountain range, which was opposite the direction Phillyna said I pursue, which was east and across the Big Sea, to visit the city and attain something, speak to somebody, to do something to escape the Split.

I knew I was going to go west, towards the mountain ranges. I knew I was going to cross the mountain range. I knew I was going to escape the Split, but I didn't know what was going to happen between then and now. I arrived home, to the cottage, after a swim in the stream and I must admit I was a little off-ended and spaced out, after the realization that what was over the mountains held the key to getting back to my real home, and I told Phillyna about the occurrence.

"The forests hold much mystery," she said. That was all she said. She said so with little conviction, as if she knew already where I was going to go, what time, how I was leaving, that is, short and brisk and without much notice.

"I am going to leave soon," I said. She nodded her head in assent. "I want to get back to my real home, my real family." She had a little scrunched up face of annoyance when I had said it, as if this was my real home.

She said, "Do what you must." I think she forgot to add, I'll be here for you.

I thought what I would need—a heavy jacket, a flask of water, bedrolls, blankets, a cap, good shoes, extra socks. I was going to wear two pairs of everything, two pairs of socks, two jackets, I had decided, and I added on another jacket to my thoughtful pile of belongings, two shirts, two pants, and an extra flask. I was going to bring along with me a knife, flint for fire, food, that is bread, a brass ring, which I was to use for bartering, when I found civilization on the other side of the mountain range, if there was any civilization on the other side of the mountain range.

I would pack with me dried fruit and nuts, too.

I knew I was going to escape the Split, but I didn't know how. I didn't know what obstacles, outside of the massive and white gray one before my eyes, I was going to have to cross and overcome. How was I—by some ritual?—going to leave this place—backtrack?—through the communicable light and back into my life, back into Miami, Florida? It sounded absurd, but I knew it was possible, for there was a glinting light of inspiration and not exactly of hope but of knowledge that this place had a never-ending sense of yearning which did deliver one's desires to the individual. This was what I went out to achieve.

Desires come in many different types. People desire the flesh; people desire the material objects of life; people desire power. I desired my returning home. Perhaps the third desire I have listed, in all of effectuality, was my desire—a desire for power, for I was powerless in this place, as of yet. I was brought here unbeknownst as to why and was powerless in my transition to this place. I was brought here, unexpected. I was brought here, with force and with violence, for my dying on the floor in the restaurant was not painless. I was brought here with the notion there was some test which must be completed or passed, in order to return home, safe.

Look, illumine, and see.

That was what was shown to me upon my entering this fantastic place.

Look, illumine, and see.

However, nowhere in the declaration was there the notion or hinting I was to return home. I suppose those lights weren't as telling as I wanted them to be, but that was the best part of the Split—the growing form of individuality and freedom granted in the place. There was peripheral willpower, when, at home, there was only what was before you, behind you, to the left and to the right fof you. There seemed to be in this place a degree of in and out, the acknowledgement thereof and an ability to form and create destiny.

8

Easy did the rain fall in the days following the original poem. I lay in bed with the woman who was going to be my wife, for there was only one bed in the small cottage, and the rain came down in sheets. I did not know what was more soothing, however, those bed sheets or the rain pat-patting on the rooftop. They were both very soothing and I lay awake for a time, thinking of the days to come, what was I to do in those days, thinking of Claudia, thinking of Gayle, thinking of how and in what way I was supposed to escape this place, thinking Claudia was alone, thinking I was alone, thinking and thinking some more.

I rose from the bed in one incredible storm and stood in the doorway, watching the rain. It was quite revitalizing, and it lent me some sort of power, some sort of understanding I was in a predicament and I was to conquer and succeed. I saw another flash by the candlelight, and it reads as follows, though, I remind you, it is not a verbatim account of what I saw, for the words and meter and the way in which the original poem was telegraphed is beyond comprehension, and the words were lost upon my returning and the inspiration I now feel is not like the inspiration I felt while in the Split. It is dulled down, as is my psyche, ever since my return. Perhaps there was some kind of release of passion upon my returning. Perhaps my being introduced into the Split was just that, a culmination of passion. Nevertheless, I remember the gist of the poetic verse and I remember what had occurred following my seeing the poetic verse, and the poem goes like this:

Easy, I lay on a hard night, softened by sheets of linen and sheets of rain.

The answer to problems: The rising of the early arrivals and the gray wisps to slay. Walking slow one morning, I heard a whisper from afar,

where the mourning men whimper like barking strays.

When the gray haze speaks of morning and willpower, arriving large and unforgivable, and stays for cheap, there is, by and by, my bed and breakfast.

***

Upon seeing and hearing the poem the rain grew stronger. It drove down in thick pails. It was spectacular, watching the impregnated mass, which was the storm, and I ran. I ran out into the rain and cut the sheets with my arms, as swords, and became soaking wet in the rain, and stripped myself naked, out of passion, and returned to the stream, where I had awoken. It was a long run—I ran back to the stream—but I felt nothing, no pain and no heat. It was a cold night, and I felt impenetrable by the cold and rain; and I ran to the stream and jumped in, naked, as I had been when I had awoken, and cried. I cried for the days to come. What was I to do in those days? I cried for Claudia, cried for Gayle, and cried more. How and in what way was I supposed to escape this place? I cried because Claudia was alone and cried because I was alone, cried and cried.

I did not go to sleep in the night. I whispered to myself, as a man in mourning. I thought myself selfish, mourning my own death. How could a man mourn his own death? By the circumstances alone, I mused; and I listened to the gray rain pounding, slapping on my head, my forehead, and ears. I listened to the raindrops. I listened to raindrops, trying to find an answer, trying to hear an answer. I lay in the stream until the morning came, hoping I would die again, die for the second time, but that was impossible. The morning came, and the rain stopped, and my willpower was all for nothing in the night, for I rose from the stream and walked home, flustered. Every time I lost my willpower it came back. It went, and it came. It went, and it came. It was drained from me with reason, and this place reinstated my willpower by its wonder.

I said goodbye to the stream and I walked home to find my bed and my breakfast made and ready for me, for Phillyna was worthy.

9

Winter had come. Snow was falling. I wore my coat, jovial in the daytime sun. I was pestered by memories—memories of my wife, Gayle. Her death did bring heaviness upon my shoulders in this place. I felt her, very vivid. It had been years since her death and yet I felt more connected to her here, now so more than ever. It was not a connection having to do with the immediate place. I knew she was not floating around somewhere, in a town or the city or in the forest. How could she? That was a far-off imagination, taking place where my hope did flourish, and I felt connected to her on a very deep level, deep within my bones, as if my bones were the very trees lifting up into the sky my skins and leaves, myself covered and wearing the trees as brown and stylish attire, admired by the birds and winds and the frogs and flora and even the weeds, which grew up my flanks, like worry, and which apprehended my emotions to a standstill—a static place, which kept me in a state of memory, of longing for Gayle, and for the past. For the future was very present here and I did not fear the future, nor did I fear the past, but I wanted what was in memory to be here with me then, and now, as it may have been; for I am sitting late in the evening with my cigar finished and my wine finished and with my lips chewed into a wrinkled fatness and with my hair descending down onto my forehead and into my eyes, because I am writing of this taxing experience and I do feel fatigued just recalling it. Writing it down and remembering these poems is taxing to another degree. Perhaps another glass of wine will do me well. Perhaps another glass of wine would sharpen me up, if I drank it slow and let the taste descend and trickle down into my throat by its own means and speed, mine being far too expedited, far too excitable for a relaxed evening of writing and smoking and drinking; and yet I relax, I smoke, I drink, I write. I relax and recall the feelings, the wholesome, thick and smoky feelings in the Split. I smoke cheap cigars, made of tobacco and leaf, cheap cigars which hit the stomach like an uppercut and flatted the heart until the exhalation. I drink this wine, tasting thick and red, and I write. I write about my experiences and my feelings, and that is why I am so confounded in thought right now, because Gayle, my Gayle was not resolved. That problem, those feelings, those heavy, hard feelings were not resolved as a result of my escaping the Split, as were other problems—loneliness and self-actualization. They were not resolved, the mixed feelings of Gayle; but that was why I escaped and that was why I had a window, through which to jump, at the end of my experience in that strange world—because there was inconsistency and because there were things that didn't make sense, and there were things which shouldn't have happened, and things which left me to wonder, things which may have left the epileptic mass of light wonder, Why did I get placed in that world? Why did I escape? Just as the question, why did Gayle die so young, is prevalent, nobody knows. Perhaps it is just an anomaly of psyche and of existing. Or maybe it was an anomaly of the human heart.

I saw one aubade, simple, in the cottage, in that time, and it was a rotating two-sided dish, on which was written the poem. I was thinking there was not a proper goodbye, in regards to Gayle and I, and Gayle and Claudia. She left with such suddenness I was overcome with bewilderment.

10

I came out of my depression. It was temporary. Phillyna and I went for a walk down to the valley, which was just north of our cottage, for she had proposed the walk to further distance myself from my state of mind, the state of mind, which held me captive to far off thoughts, the state of mind, which could not help, the time being where it was. Now, I was to relax and get accustomed to my new surroundings; and we walked down to the valley, where we grew much closer, so close, in fact, the trip down to the valley solidified the possibility that I was to marry her, marry Phillyna, as my wife. It was spectacular, jagged tree lines separating the would-be Earth and sky, red dirt caking our shoes, light air propelling us forwards in the valley, in the trip, in a way which could only make one happy and expectant of good things to come. It was remarkable truly, for in the trip down to the valley I had the time to appreciate, in full, the surroundings in which I found myself—the nature, the atmosphere, and Phillyna.

Without doubt, I saw a few more poetics, upon our returning home, but only after the incredulous journey had been completed.

We saw many things, animals, outlandish and comfortable in our presence, outlandish plants and trees and flora, which I could not identify.

Wan, she lets go of my sleeve. She says, "No way I am going down there,"

speaking of the valley below, and I say, "It's nothing—"

I grip the hand, which has just been holding my sleeve.

She proposed going to the valley and over-looking the valley from a vantage point. I proposed, upon our arrival, to go down into the valley. She was hesitant, a cute head, as I have written, wan in comparison to the mighty natural comings of the Split; and yet she had nodded her head in assent and we had descended into the valley below, with high expectations and high eyebrows for the night to come.

A flash while in the valley:

Turning, I have forgotten my place, the looming trees supporting only my head, my time. Faint pressure grips my throat; and somebody else my arm.

I supported her weight as we navigated over the tan rocks of the valley. The walk was insurmountable, as far as experiences were concerned. The Grand Canyon had nothing on this place, outside of the sheer mystery of manifestation. How did something so grand become so real and so alive? It was as if it had been placed there, with intention. How could something so vast be unnoticed by so many people, and in this place, this valley by us two? It was impossible, for people did notice. We did notice the sheer beauty, the sheer cliff face, the chipped rocks by our feet, which crackled the rocks below like hard candies. The soft, thin sand snug in between our toes, found itself in many places. Sand always tended to find itself in the most unpredictable and small places. The leaves of a tree were so grand, long and thin and waxy. I felt one with my hands. I felt energized by the wax-like feeling and I felt this place taking me, in full, to no ill satisfaction and with pure expectation. I was excited to be here, and I knew I was getting home. I knew I was getting home, with such sureness, that the walk down to the valley filled me with pure hope and joy.

I forgot about all my troubles.

Again, a flash upon our returning home:

We drift, shady, toward sleep, sleeping together after another uneventful day.

We feel cold, agitated, and restless in each other's arms. Warmth cometh.

11

I woke in the night, worried, and saw a brilliant display of poetics. I do think some intelligence was talking to me:

We break, midnight—an explosion of relief and expectation.

We wish, while asleep to be together. While awake, I think of stars.

The woman thinks of trees, and then color and texture,
the cumulative recollection of us both—
the trees and night's sleep, which would soon come, taken by aeronaut.
I cinder, lacking in sleep, and she shifts. She has heard something.
Otherwise, why did she move? She has heard a thought, or my tempest
that is the morning and my gift to her,
morning coming in a short time and not foreboding.
My gift to myself: her face towards mine, in proper direction.
So I see. I, too, shift and have captured a glimpse of her inspiration,
a never-ending sense of imagining: the day growing nearer.
I, underneath the sheets, think of nothing but the countless stars,
pulling me back into her world.
I wish for nothing and am granted my wish.

These were our nights together. My curious fascination with the poetry took on the role of perpetuation, making happen their contents; and Phillyna and I looked at the stars at night, I was taken into her world by them, I lay awake and thought. I, complete, at ease and listless, turned in my sleep, far too often; for I had had concerns pertaining to my getting home and concerns pertaining to my daughter.

Nevertheless, I had seen the poetic flashes and things did happen. After I had seen the above poem, we, Phillyna and I, had started sleeping together, taking full concern for one another, and it was fantastic. In not long at all I would depart, however, as those poetic verses would state, and I would escape the Split, this curious, fascinating escapade on which I found myself, and henceforth would be the carrier of knowledge that a place so full and alive and separate from our world existed. It was truly remarkable and fantastical.

People, however, with rarity ask me of my experiences, for I am an old and dirty man now, valuing only wine and cigars and the lofty and occasional memory of such places. Thinking of my daughter has become a bypassed notion. She now works as a nurse in a hospital, taking care of the geriatric, the ill, the young, and everybody one can imagine. She takes care of everybody and I am so proud. I am so proud of her.

Perhaps it was that reason, pride, which had me so down weeks later. Again, a flash of poetics a few days after the first time Phillyna and I had slept together made itself prevalent; and days following the writing of the poem I had begun feeling down, one can say, and it was not the fact I was here, a part of the Split and it was not the fact I was separated from my daughter or separated from myself even. It was the fact and the omnipresent notion, uncertainty was all too the case. There was uncertainty and there was also worry. The worry and uncertainty were most present during the morning, in the tub.

Turning on the thespian light, as so did that calling say, turning and lighting the light

did I, exasperated after two long, grueling years, lighting the same light,

the electrified circuits of the brain, just as powerful as that of the illuminated vessel, which carries me to slip-shod wakefulness, mind and eyes shut in the tentative morning of my long, last life, a picturesque turning from darkness to day, for I have been awake for long, long hours and can see no difference.

The light through the window is wholesome. I feel gray and natural,

forgiveness and forgotten, foresightedness.

I see my reason: a toast, a cup, a butter knife, and the ability to know the difference, the bed, the wooden chair, the old house, my hair, the house, the bird feeder, myself,

stuck in time. I do rise to take a bath and piss instead. Bathe when I, later, will think.

That was the turning point of the entirety of the Split. I had been there for two years, two years having flashed by in a moment. I believe when in water there is some circuitry, which is in better usage. Perhaps it is the fluidic, filmy texture of the water, which permeates thought and feelings. The water did in the two days which followed procure much thought. I lay awake for a while after writing the poem and days later lay for hours after the bath, which I have above illustrated. The poem manifested my reality, and, also, I was lying in bed for hours, because the poem I had seen a week prior the one above had manifested something different and in entirety. The manifestation: Phillyna was pregnant.

12

My memory has become shoddy. Sitting here and thinking of the events which occurred on Friday, June 4th, 1971, I can feel only mystified. Even now, as the stars sparkle outside, high into the reaches of the atmosphere, I think of Gayle and I think of my wife in that maybe she is up there listening to me, watching me write, and watching over me as some high and portentous protector watches over their children, because really, even though I have aged and even though I am an old man, with gray hairs and wrinkles, I feel as a child does, alive while writing this account. Perhaps she watches over me; and if she does I could not feel more thankful, thankful I made it out alive and thankful she was there to guide me in life and in the Split, because she was there. She was there for me while I was alive, and she was there for me when I was in the Split.

I do think now that when we separate, when our bodies detach, and the concrete body separates from the other, which drifts, there is the old and late family which protects us and guides us. I do feel now that the light, the communicable light was her. Perhaps it is me only being hopeful, rationalizing what is not understood, so I can digest the extraordinary occurrences of that day. Perhaps she had had a moment with me, when I was ascending into the curious place. Perhaps she had had a moment with me, and one which she was expecting, with greatness. She always was an excitable woman. It was her. It was always her. Now, Phillyna and I were having a child; and I don't think it would have upset Gayle too much. It is a natural part of, for the lack of a better term, life. Phillyna and I were having a child and the pregnancy, along with the wanting and the needing to escape, was suffocating. If I were to have a child here, and then leave, I would be abandoning a child, but I already had abandoned a child, my daughter, Claudia, who was now, unbeknownst to me hunched over me, getting ready the breath of life, to revive me from the Split. However, the omnipresent question lingers: Was it her who saved me, or did I save myself? Did I escape from the Split, or was it only an extraordinary hallucination, Claudia truly being the one who saved me?

That brings up another question, the question of truth. Was I truly alive? Sure, I was breathing and sure I was feeling with my hands the trees and rain; but was I alive? Was I alive on a quasi-level, a place where life and death meet and dictate where one goes? Was it a middle ground or a mere hallucination? I do not know. I fear I will never know. However, the poems I had written are real. I have recorded them here. The memories are real, and what can be more real than memory? Instances have been recorded in my memory, my mind recalling them in as much a reality as the chair in which I sit. Who is to differentiate? My mind recorded, lived, and navigated through the Split as it was real, just as I had recorded, lived, and navigated the occurrences in Miami, Florida, on the 4th of June, 1971. If such a notion is any basis to go about, believing and deciding what is real, then everything is real. A dream is real, for one remembers it. It truly happened. It is not a hallucination, but an alternate state, which surfaces, and which is rooted in the mind of the dreamer—same as with the Split. My mind and quasi-body surfaced in a place with which I was not familiar and yet I remember, with explicitness, what had happened; thus, my recording of the occurrences only solidifies my belief that what had happened in that place, in the curious place, was real and not a hallucination.

I hesitate to speak of my experiences with people— they might call me crazy, not crazy, perhaps, but they would dismiss my occurrences and the experiences with such ease, not having the proper viewpoint to ascertain in full the words spoken from my mouth, from the mouth which ate food in the Split—because I believe there is little difference between the two, the Split and Miami, Florida.

They were like two sides of any single thing. There was the left side and there was the right side. Sometimes, when much is happening around a control, the left side does not know what the right side is doing. This was the case regarding the Split. Oneself did not know what the other was doing, until much later.

Months after Phillyna had gotten pregnant, I started getting serious about my returning home. Until that time, I had been patient, waiting for the right time, waiting for another occurrence to get into the place or state where I was able to make a conscious move back to my concrete body.

I had seen the escape-state to full prescience. A poetic verse had been viewed. Following the viewing of the below poetic verse, I left Phillyna and followed my goals and dreams to escape the Split.

The poetic verse reads as follows:

A tender darkness folds along the lines of a perforated skylight
and descends dew upon grasses and leaves—
the light of the previous day, the gone day.
Passed has the drained light of yester-dawn and, with a yawn,
and greeted by the humble sounds of my forgotten life, passed themselves,
are the ones who divided the darkness. I smoke and throw a butt passionate upon a leaf, which folds under weightlessness and shameless—these momentary lapses.
Be, my day; be bright as the morning passes.
Be light and shine upon hair the unfolding, never-closing sources, limitless inspiration, circles and craning

heads, forever knowing lonesome roses, thorns and throes,

teeming life and the unclosing verses close.

As far as the many times I have turned my face are concerned, it seems life keeps spreading its wings wider, so I can see more differences. They seem the same, however, and the divide furthers two bodies, and the night keeps passing like the one preceding it had passed and there are few times when I circumspect the feeling, which tends the reader and the writer; it is up to the individual to determine which, or it is up to the beds, which house us in the night, and which cradle our sleeping and ignorant bodies, if only for a time. What with which we most identify: identity, on a very deep and receded level, and it seems points and boundaries and hearts reach into the furthest reaches of identity to retain the very little they know. In between the poetic verses, with which the body does most identify, is silence. Silent and humble and from the author of lives, and with totality, words come and relay broken ideas and thoughts, which our minds accept, most appreciable.

13

My boy escaped. I imagined our child was a son and he escaped my mind into my reality. I envisioned a boy, walking the streets of Miami, Florida, walking the beaches and kicking sand. He was a beautiful boy, with long brown hair just past his eyebrows and dark eyes and light skin, walking through the sand at night, thinking of his father and where had he gone.

It was rather disheartening, but at the same time I knew he would want the best for me. He would want me to get back to his sister, in the land from whence he came, his father a legend, a story to tell all his friends and all who asked, who are you and who was your father? He left and went back to his world. He is a legend. He did what only a few have. He escaped. My son, I mused, saw this world as separate. We were so similar as I walked the reaches of the Split and approached the high mountain. We were so similar even he wanted to escape. That was why I envisioned him in Miami, in the hot Florida night, where he could live like I had lived, to see the concrete world from whence I came, and to live, perhaps, to tell about it, when he came back to his world. Funny, he would be born here, in the Split. He went to Miami and passed in that place, and was re-delivered here again, to the Split.

I liked the thought and strode harder past the trees, which whispered good fortune, and I decided to stop and catch my breath and rest my burning feet. For I knew I was reaching something. I knew I was reaching my destination.

I saw a poetic flash in the instant, brought on by fatigue and the burning sensation in my feet, and, by the poetic flash, I knew the Split was going to enlighten my boy when he strode through the forest, thinking of me. It is rather grotesque, but really what wasn't grotesque in a place of such uncertainty and such worry. I knew this poetic verse was going to craft an interesting young boy, who was observant, and who took time aside to grasp in full his surroundings. Perhaps the poetic flash was even going to teach him the art of mercy.

Forever glaring under the light, the boy finds two birds, dying and cradled—

they cradle one another—and these birds and the boy die a little bit.

Why? These birds do not fight. These birds, under the dying light not only fade, not only come together, but rather the two birds fall together, and he, the boy, lets them die, and finds his eyes wet. What? What is he to do, but be trite under the shadow,
which lies atop the birds an unrefined existence?
The two birds are soon lifeless and dead, a nuisance and a bother and how he thinks these thoughts when he lets fretted, whetted, setting birds, look comfortable!
He gives once again to his casual saunter.

My boy left Miami. He left the place and was delivered to the Split, as a gift, from perhaps even Gayle to me. That was why I left, because I knew she was watching.

14

That was when I felt the first breath of life in my lungs. Thoughts of Claudia came rushing back and I saw in my clouded vision the ceiling of the outdoor foyer in which we were eating before my coming into the Split, years ago.
I saw sparkles and flashes, my body lifting off of the ground out of itself, and she gave me the first breath of life and rescinded.
Again, I felt a breath of life and saw in a flash the following idea, spoken in silent words, but spectacular and foreboding in my clouded vision, as what I know was Gayle, communicating with me:

Still awoken by the crying birds, most pleasant and chirping, your eye grows stern to a crying one, who sounds rather raspy. No, it is not some pheasant.

For the cry sounds like booming horns, broken, and shatters your early arrival into sleep. The night has grown old and long. The bird does not shut up. The others flee

from the wretch, and, long after, you, awoken and shot by light, dilate the blood vessels

inside of your eyes, the middles, and find it was you who was the wretch,

crying into your own ear. You give your leg enough room to breathe coolness.

Some fog, you think, as the crying continues. You are reminded of your lost son

and you give a stark breath and find yourself in the reflection of a window.

You are searching for the loon.

Claudia was crying. I could hear her. This is exactly what would happen. I would look into a window, following my escape from the Split, not yet home, but closer. I would look into the window, seeing my reflection and many different Carl Redhams, simultaneous and escaping the Split. It turned out the situation was vast and larger than I had perceived. It was incredible. I was incredulous, and upon seeing the verse and upon hearing Claudia cry and upon feeling the first breaths of life and upon seeing my reflection I was transcended to a state of an in-between understanding. I knew there was life beyond what was seen by the concrete body. I knew there was life outside of what trickled into the eyes, through the pupils; and I knew I was just that, a student, learning how to escape, learning how to navigate through the trials of life and the afterlife, because it was I who was chosen to be here. It was Gayle who had brought me here, and it was Claudia who was going to bring me back. I was only an in-between liability of the present. I mattered little. Really, I mattered, as far as matter is concerned, one-hundred and eighty-five pounds, in Miami, Florida, but here, who knows how much I weighed? Who knows what my body temperature was, in Miami or here in the Split. Here in the Split I must have been a wisp, a thought, composed of nothing and in entirety, but more than nothing. It must have been here in the Split I was composed of memories, the lingering perception of who I was and who people thought I was. For here in the Split I had only my memories and the memories of people. For years I had been wandering around the larger area, confined within the airy mass which was the Split and amounting to nothing but wonderment, taken aback by the circumstances and not knowing where or who or why I was; but I had the lofty memories and the notion of Gayle, and she was with me, guiding me through this experience by means of flashes, inspiration, and sparks which still sparked even after her leaving the concrete Earth. We still had the magic, and it was magical, this place. The bottomless well of inspiration and wonder was incomparable to any other place I had ever been.

There was so little we knew. The classification of the animals and the plants was so deep and wise, one was able learn of the self and the human psychology through them. That was why it was so mysterious. That was why it was so magical, because when you came home from the botanical gardens in the evening and the smell still clung to your clothes like a child you went to sleep, and green and purple colored your dreams. The pastel flowers and their colors you had felt with your fingers are still there and you can feel them, as well as your bed sheet, while lying in bed; and they feel soft,

soft as can be, and you might even be able so smell them, granted your olfactory senses are just right and tenuous, recalling the mystery of the day, and the air from the ceiling fan or the open window in the night was just like the air from the skies, which blew the light breeze onto your shoulder and cooled you and you feel just like a silk robe, having ascended and then descended back into bed, the middle ground the lush forestry and livelihood of the larger world. The lush forestry and livelihood of the larger world extended their hands to you and you felt their hardness. For they have hardened over time, as my heart has since the time of my returning; but they were so wholehearted there for you there is no deceiving the keen eye and the expectant hands, which ran their course over the bumpy ridges and soft petals and waxy leaves of the state, which is so real, and which was so substantial it was impossible not to know they were thinking of you and they saw you and talked to one another, not gossiping but lending light comments to one another on your shirt or daughter, how well they looked and how fortunate they were to be a part of the botanical gardens for such a short time and they wished you back, because it had been pleasant to both sides of the exchange and they extended and even waved an arm in the wind because they liked you. They liked you came to visit. They liked you tried and fumbled with their long and cumbersome names. They found pride in that their names were unlike any other name for any other tree, flower, or bush, and they sent you on your way, past the souvenir shop and past the snack booth, because you took something, something you should not have taken. a flower, and it was in your daughter's hair, then, and the flower holds back her hair in the most sophisticated way when on the drive home the windows are down on the long, empty road and the flower got blown out of her hair and got placed in the highway, onto the roadside foliage—you extended your arm out the window and cupped a fresh handful of the breeze, letting the wind course through your fingers like water and into your shirt sleeve where it stayed until bedtime, and there it stayed as you recalled everything, the life, the thoughts, the inspiration found in the garden and you felt crazed by the thought it can always get better.

From the clear skies, by some miracle you heard a thunder crack in the distance—a boom, heard from whence it came: high above the Earth, in the invisible cumulus-nimbus, which was so far above and behind you you care not whether you get struck by its preceding lightning bolt. It would feel good, to get zapped, taken up into the cloud, with literalness, your electric brain and your brain chemistry and your thoughts and psyche elevated into the cumulus-nimbus, where it stayed for a while, before it descended again into the thoughts of many, collecting like a pool or high wind in the memories of all those who followed you, and the inspiration went on and on and the flash again, the final flash before the reflection, which told all:

Staring at yourself, you throw your shoulders to show yourself a side angle of your body. You are disappointed; it has shown you the losing story of your child, haughty,

for he is the tormented one, the tingle on the shin.

Your muscles are not the same, sticking sharp in between two blades, which tickle.

Two more crack, two more knuckles, your face with two more than it has had,

right across the forehead, making a total of five, you, a total failure.

The knuckles: you wish you could have more because you like the sounds they make,
  and futile, you are not anymore standing on your head, but feel the weight,
    pushing upward from the bottoms of your feet,
    the weight of your shoulders and your knuckles,
  and you shatter your face in a grin. It is the new day, the day the loon has escaped,
  and you are a prisoner, a man behind glass, living inside of an aphorism,
  a moderate aphorism, and you back away from the window
  and out of the corner of your wood-be eye you find a problem—
  a long crack in the molding.

The lightning cracked and split a tree in two before my eyes, straight out of the clear sky, and I was taken to seeing the crystallized trees, for, these trees were different and not made of earthen material. The crack of lightning crystallized the tree and I looked into the reflection: many Carl Redhams, performing the ultimatums, many Carl Redhams in their own place of receded psyche, my thoughts, desires, ideas coming to full fruition in many different places, Carl Redham cuddling, Carl Redham cuddling with forty Carl Redhams, Carl Redham gambling in the hand of his life, Carl Redham defeating another person in a sword fight, Carl Redham fighting in a war, Carl Redham, Carl Redham, Carl Redham.

15

"Carl Redham! Carl Redham! Carl Redham, can you hear me? Carl! Carl!"

I coughed and gasped. People were hunched over me, looking on in the curious restaurant, where I had had the heart attack so many years ago and only five minutes ago.

How the time can fly! How time can be so deceiving! How the time! How the time! "He's back," she said, my Claudia. I was lying on the ground in the small café, the burnt cigar by my head. "Are you okay?" she asked. "What happened?"

I coughed and gasped again. I was not able to speak. I was in a shock, of sorts, but knew, with completeness, what had happened was extraordinary and rare. I coughed, "I'm okay."

That was Friday, June 4th, 1971, Miami, Florida. The occurrences pushed me along the boundaries of enigma, and still I think of them. Still I think I see a flash and I think I have a thought, but am I really? Am I really here? Or is this just another hallucination, no, not hallucination, but a middle ground? Is this a middle ground? Are we only here for a time to be taken from everything we know and ascended (or descended) to another place, to another place in time, where ideas reign supreme and not as a figment of imagination?

I hope so. I hope I go once again into the Split, when I die a second time. That time, I suspect, I won't come back. That's why I am so excited to leave this place, because what you don't know is what helps you. It is the darkness in between the light lets one take a proper perspective, because we are ignorant and the root word of the word ignorant is ignore. People seem to have a wrong impression of what ignorant means. People think ignorant means dumb or unable to see the world, as is proper, but in "reality" it is because to ignore the truth, or apparent. People who are ignorant ignore what is apparent, and what is apparent is apparent and what happens happens and what is is, and there is only one thing able to separate the skeptic from the mystic and the logical from the faithful, in such a scenario, a kiss from the daughter, which was just what I had received from Claude, upon my returning from the Split. Claudia kissed my cheek, and I felt whole again.

The Phrenologist
(Part One)

The office was small. Purple carpeting with yellow stitches that had become old and discolored clothed the first level of the entire building. The office, on the first level with its purple and yellow carpeting, though small, was large enough for the small business which occupied it, and which extended psychographic tests to the public. The office was as all science professionals' or psychological professionals' offices are, that is sharp and striking; and the oaken shelves and leather-bound books and the brass, all-seeing-eye paperweight made it as such; it was quite satisfying to work there. But, perhaps the most striking or stunning piece in the office was the psychograph with its archaic support column and holding the helmet within which the patients' craniums were deposited. It held an eerie quality in the way the wires descended the arm, which too descended down to the purple and yellow carpeting, and it was even eerier when somebody, a subject, was sitting with their cranium within the psychograph which measured their skull to ascertain characters in the personality representative to the dimensions of the cranium.

My fascination with the science, however, disappeared as per the events of this past winter. The events which occurred following my most recent patient are the focus of this writing I write now months following the incidental death of he, Herbert Podrey, who had given me a call one September evening, saying he wanted to be a subject in a psychographic test.

The work day was coming to a close and as was custom the bottle of scotch was removed from beneath the mahogany desk and a glass was poured for immediate consumption. It was peculiar, the anxiety felt throughout the day, and my blood pressure had elevated to the point of discomfort. Exiting the building to get a breath of cool, Maryland air, the vertigo ceased, and I began feeling well. Inside, the scotch was waiting and there was no time for procrastination; it was in through the swinging glass doors and over the purple and yellow carpeting, into the small office within which was the drink that would settle nerves.

The scotch was downed in one drink and then the phone rang. Picking it up, the voice of what seemed to be a well-manicured man, who introduced himself as Herbert Podrey, was heard; to which I responded with my own name, Allen Earnhardt. This man, Herbert Podrey, with his quiet manner and precise diction, seemed the sort who would seek psychographic testing; he seemed to an extent eccentric over the phone and even a touch of loneliness may have been in his voice.

After the shot of scotch, ambivalence at having a patient was prevalent and the date for the test, which was to be September 25th, was jotted down in a notebook. He bid me adieu and hung up. The bottle of scotch was returned and, rising, I felt the lightheadedness of the drink and the expectation of the appointment coalescing as one. Briefcase in hand, I turned off the light and went out into the hallway. Outside, the day was becoming evening. The door, locked, would not be opened until Monday. It was a Friday evening the evening Herbert Podrey had called; and I do think that phone call was the mark that had sent him unto the last days of his existence.

I would not return straight home on this night. Johnny Hovan's was hosting the usual threesome, that was Raleigh Durman, Lenny Amaranth, and I; and over drinks we would discuss what married men should not discuss, the nothings of middle-aged men and the ins and outs of nineteenth century medicine. We were a good lot and had been together since the very early times. The small Chevrolet in which many commutes were spent cradled me and took me to Johnny Hovan's, where the parking lot was already full and where people were smoking, drinking, and crowding around motorcycles. Johnny Hovan's was not a rough place but from the outside one can see why a passerby would think it were a rough place. In fact, Cathy, one of the barkeeps, was the sweetest lady one could meet inside a place selling hard liquor, and she made Johnny Hovan's overall pleasant. The Chevy parked, I traversed the gravel lot and went into the bar where many people were speaking over one another and smoking and drinking and on the jukebox there was an Allman Brothers' Band tune. The three of us—Raleigh, Lenny, and I—never sat at the bar. Around the walls of Johnny Hovan's, there were booths with overstuffed cushions and olive-green upholstery, many of which were ruptured and poking out stuffing like faux snow. Raleigh and Lenny were not in sight and, so, I took a booth out of the way and over came Ms. Cathy and I ordered a scotch neat, please.

Herbert Podrey was on my mind. It was a wonder somebody in this day and age had scheduled a phrenology appointment. Herbert Podrey had called, and we had scheduled an appointment and I would perform a psychographic test on him. I was impressed somebody still knew about phrenology let alone had an interest in it. The tune changed from "Ain't Wastin' Time No More" to "La Grange."

Cathy came over with the scotch and I ordered another. The scotch glistened on my tongue. It would not last long. Yasmin did not have a big problem with my drinking but going home to a woman and smelling of alcohol was not appropriate behavior and somewhere I dreaded going home smelling like scotch. She was the woman I married and for good reason. She had mothered my child and was a damn good mother at that. The scotch was finished and already Cathy had brought the second glass of scotch of which I took a drink after a silence. My watch read eight-thirty, which was the customary time agreed upon. Raleigh and Lenny were never late and showed up together. They carpooled on Friday evenings to Johnny Hovan's and traded turns driving. It lessened one's chances of getting pulled over and arrested for a DUI which nobody wanted, and which could happen any given Friday evening taking into account the amount of alcohol consumed. Halfway through my second scotch, Raleigh clapped me on the back.

"Good to see you, you old dog!" He took a seat across me and flagged down Cathy, bless her soul. "I can see we have some catching up to do. How many've you had? Five, six?"

"This is number two not counting the one I had at the office."

"Good, good," said Raleigh, and waved down Cathy. She came over and took his and Lenny's drink orders. "How are things at the office?" Raleigh asked.

"I got a call today from a patient. We've got a date set for Monday."

"How 'bout them bananas? Somebody wants to talk to you, you old-timer?"

I was quite surprised somebody had called and, before Herbert Podrey's call, was convinced I was the lone and final phrenologist on the face of the planet. Now, there was hope phrenology might survive the day of neuroscience and biological hysteria. I, however, said nothing to Raleigh. He always got a little rowdy at Johnny Hovan's and railed on whoever was nearest him. Nobody ever seemed to mind.

Lenny Amaranth, who had gotten engaged two months prior, spoke up. "We've set a date, too," he said. "Gretch and I. Speaking of dates being set. We're getting married this December."

"That's wonderful."

Raleigh said, "We're invited, Amaranth? Open bar?"

Lenny said, "You're invited, the both of you. And yes, there is an open bar."

"She's three months pregnant right now, isn't she?"

"Yes," said Lenny.

Raleigh said, "She'll be a beach ball by the time the wedding comes."

"Yes," said Lenny. "She will be rotund."

Raleigh guffawed, Cathy came over with a pitcher of beer for Lenny and Raleigh, and the three of us drank. "Bad" on the jukebox turned to "Cisco Kid." A rerun of a past Baltimore Orioles-New York Yankees game was on the television. Lenny was talking about Mariano Rivera and the way he hit the sweet spot on the inside of the bat and left sluggers with shattered wood in their hands and Orlando Hernández's sidearm. Three glasses of scotch later, bed was sounding pretty good. The tab was paid and Raleigh Durman and Lenny Amaranth each got a handshake and once more I traversed the gravel lot, and the Chevy took me in the direction of home, sleep, and Yasmin. If driving drunk was a problem I could not tell. Since the beginning, one learned to stay between the lines and this was no different; and, like every Friday evening preceding this Friday evening, the Chevy pulled into the driveway. Walking into the house, one was met with a long narrow Persian rug and family photographs. On the wall to the right of the entrance way, carved wooden pieces were perched atop a narrow table against the wall. On the table was where the car keys went. Late, I traversed through the hallway and into the kitchen where I had a glass of cold tap water, and back through the hallway, into the master bedroom where Yasmin was asleep. I escaped my work clothes, brushed my teeth, and then washed off the scent of smoke and scotch in the shower. Lathering shampoo onto my cranium, a startling recollection overtook me—the dawn of my phrenological career, the day on which the realization that the cranium, not the brain within it, and the face, housed the device of human identity, personality, and intellect, that when people looked at one's skull their first impression was not made by brainwaves but of raw facial and cranial characters. At the time, early in my phrenological pursuits, it seemed foolish to believe the human, or humanity was housed within the cranium as gray matter. The eyes, the eyebrows and their arch, and the height of the forehead gave insight into the individual; and to the professional one could go so far as to regard placement of the ears, hairlines, and outstanding cranial characters. The whole field took the young and perturbed scientist, that was I, by force. And today the call from Herbert Podrey had awoken a lingering hope that phrenology was not quackish; the call had instigated a sub-strata of possibilities, past, present, and to come. The notion was exact and cerebral.

The towel, after I dried off, was returned to its rack. The bed received me, and Yasmin did not stir. She was out, and so was I, within thirty seconds.

***

The rain started at about one o'clock in the afternoon. The house in its little pocket of forest had a tendency to gray out and become quiet in such storms. The rhythmic swells of rain hit the window and the wind blew raindrops with hard force onto the windowpanes. The morning had been pleasant, a family breakfast with scrambled eggs, spinach, bacon, coffee, and orange juice. Our daughter, Lena, was a charm to have around the breakfast table. She was much like her mother in that regard, polite and for the most part kept to herself. The morning passed through noon and then the rain came, the morning blindsided. In the dark living room, the heaviness of the storm and the rainwater, the wind and Lena who was coloring at the table by the fireplace, had become overbearing and were bringing about the nostalgic feelings those sensations tended to bring about when present and together. On the end table to the right of the couch was a photograph that did not get much attention anymore. It was a photograph of my first wife at the Niagara Falls. I picked it up and looked at it. Tyra is standing before a rail opposite which are the Niagara Falls flowing into each other. Her arms are stretched out and she is wearing sun glasses and looks young and healthy. It was quite clear in mind, the trip to the New York-Canada border. That photograph of Tyra was the most recent of her; two weeks later she was dead. She had choked on a scallop and was found two days later by her colleagues. They had noticed she was missing from work and checked her apartment. She was found purple and lifeless.

Lena pulled at my shirt. "Who's that?" asked Lena.

"This is the woman I was married to before your mommy."

"Oh," Lena said. "Where is she now?"

"She died, Lena. She died too early." I put the photograph back on the end table.

"Oh," Lena said. The girl was young, but she understood. Perhaps she had not yet realized death was a thing and that it was all too real. Perhaps she was too young for that. Lena left my side and went back to her crayons and coloring. The rain on the windowpanes was a tirade. I went outside to watch it fall. The backyard had a deck which was covered by an awning. Beneath the awning were metal chairs which had not been affected by the rain and I took a seat. It was quite spectacular, the rain dousing trees and foliage, the wind swirling the rain at times into miniature tempests. The grayness overhead was domineering and absorbing; it was endless and deep and far too low. The trees doubled in height could have penetrated the nimbus cloud overhead and break them like a dam, leaving the house to deal with a liquid deluge. The air moistened the skin on my arms and the follicles stood upright; on them clung beads of moisture. My shirt and khakis fluttered, and my hair changed its direction. I recalled the Niagara Falls, the heavy commixing of roaring water, far down below the spectators. There, too, at the Niagara Falls, mist lifted from the centralized water, as it did now from the sodden grass and waxy leaves of oaks trees. The rain descended and descended. To the right, the gutter was spewing much rainwater. The rainwater collected in the foliage and was beginning to flood the deck. The gutter churned rainwater; the wind spun the water droplets. It defied gravity. All this coursed through my head, washing out post it notes of old rhyming couplets and shopping lists, paperclips and corks from drained wine bottles, spools of string and flaking lead. The rainwater from the gutter disgorged and the wind churned the storm. Within minutes the storm got more violent and I went back inside the house and into the kitchen where the clock read 4:46. For a second, it was as though Tyra, the Niagara Falls, Lena, Yasmin, and even Herbert Podrey were an unreality. But that was far from the truth. Within twenty-four hours, all was going to become much more real.

***

The phone rang the following morning at nine A.M. and woke me from a heavy slumber. It was Gretchen, Lenny Amaranth's fiancé. "Quick," she said. "You must hurry. Something has happened to Lenny. I don't know what it is, but hurry over here. We're still at the house. I don't know why I didn't call the paramedics first."

I told her I would be right over. I brushed my teeth and changed into a tee and khakis. Yasmin asked me where I was going and I told her Lenny Amaranth's, Gretchen called and something may have happened and I would be back within the hour, which, in fact, was far from the truth.

The Chevrolet ignited, I turned on the heater, pulled out of the house, and made a right to go to Amaranth's. My mind was clear, but Gretchen sounded pretty riled up and in truth, I feared for Lenny. Within ten minutes, I was pulling up to Lenny Amaranth's house. There was a car in the driveway and I doubted she called the ambulance. They were home. The doorbell chimed, and Gretchen opened the door.

"Come in, Allen. He's in the kitchen." Gretchen led me into the kitchen where Lenny Amaranth was sitting on a chair drinking coffee. He seemed fine to me.

"Amaranth," I said. "Good morning." Lenny Amaranth did not respond. He looked at me expressionless.

Gretchen said, "He woke this morning and he was fine. Then, ten minutes later in the kitchen he was asking me who I was and where am I. He doesn't even know his own name."

"Lenny," I said.

Lenny Amaranth said, "Who are you?" He sipped his coffee.

"I'm Allen Earnhardt, your friend. We went to high school together. We drink at Johnny Hovan's every Friday night."

"Where am I?"

Gretchen said, "You're home, Lenny. You're home and your name is Lenny Amaranth. I'm your fiancé. Don't you remember?"

Lenny took a sip of his coffee. He did not respond.

"I think we should take him to the hospital."

Gretchen said, "I agree."

"We're taking you to the hospital, Lenny. Something's wrong."

Lenny Amaranth did not respond. He sipped his coffee, remained seated at the kitchen table, and seemed carefree.

"Come on, Amaranth." I took the coffee cup from his hands and put it on the kitchen table, and then I took him under his armpits and lifted him as Gretchen took his other elbow. We led him to the Chevy, put him in the front seat, and took him to Ebberfield Hospital South.

Gretchen was silent as was Lenny. The hosts of a radio talk show prattled on about some baby in Indonesia who was born with three arms. I was not listening. Amaranth was throwing me off. It was as if he had regressed to childhood. His words were unexplainable and so was this predicament. We parked the Chevy and got out. Lenny still sat in his seat. When we opened the passenger side door and took him out, he asked, "Where are we going?"

"Something's wrong, Lenny. We're taking you to the E.R."

We signed in at the window and were told by the secretary it would be an hour, hour and a half wait. That was fine. That Lenny was without intellect and social graces was a problem. He needed attention. By minute thirty, the lights seemed more florescent than they should have been, ailed individuals seemed more crippled and sick than they were, and my morale was taking a dive. It was not so much the wait or the hospital atmosphere. It was Lenny's absolute inability to carry on a conversation and to act mature. He asked childish questions; daftness had taken place of Amaranth's otherwise privy personality. I drank a paper cup full of water and brought Lenny a paper cup of water, which he drank. He thanked me. I said no problem. Gretchen was scared to her wit's end. She had not spoken in the sixty minutes we were in the waiting room. A nurse called out Lenny Amaranth's name and the three of us were taken back into an infirmary where many people lay strewn hither and yon with broken bones and undefined sicknesses. Lenny lay down on a hospital bed and said, "Where are we?"

"The hospital. We're in a hospital room."

"I have to pee," he said.

"One second." I asked the nurse where the bathroom was, and she gave me directions. Then, Lenny Amaranth and I went to the bathroom to pee. It was odd having a man acting childish urinate for forty-five seconds, zip up, wash his hands and thank you. Back in the hospital room, he lay back down and within twenty minutes a doctor, who introduced himself as Dr. Oliver, entered.

"What seems to be the problem?" he asked.

Gretchen said, "Lenny, all morning has been asking 'Where am I?' and 'Who are you?' and 'Who am I?' It's as if he doesn't know a single thing but how to drink coffee and pee."

Dr. Oliver said, "I see." He turned to Lenny. "You're Lenny Amaranth?" he said.

"Who are you?" said Lenny.

"I'm Dr. Oliver. I'm here to help you. Are you Lenny Amaranth?"

"Where am I?"

"You're at Ebberfield Hospital South, because something seems to be the matter. Can you tell me your name?" said Dr. Oliver.

"I'm thirsty," said Lenny.

"We will get you water presently. Who is the president of the United States?"

Lenny looked thoughtful and shook his head.

"Peculiar," said Dr. Oliver. "This has been the case for the past three, four hours?"

"Yes," said Gretchen. "Since this morning."

"Did he fall, hit his head? Has he had anything alcoholic to drink this morning?"

Gretchen said, "I don't think so."

Dr. Oliver looked unnerved. "I will come back in fifteen or twenty minutes," he said. "We'll get this sorted out."

Gretchen thanked him, and Dr. Oliver exited the room. I fetched Amaranth a cup of water and he downed it. Gretchen said, "I'm nervous. I don't know what's wrong with him. I've never seen this before."

"Everything will be just fine," I said, but in secret I, too, was nervous.

Dr. Oliver came back into the room and said he may or may not have an explanation. "If this memory lapse lasts for more than forty-eight hours what may have occurred to Mr. Amaranth is a miniature aneurysm. However, if the memory returns within forty-eight hours, this lapse of memory is what we call retrograde amnesia. It is very rare. When the memory escapes the individual, it is usually only for five hours at most. When it comes back, all is as before. You get regular old Lenny Amaranth. In the meantime, we will keep Mr. Amaranth here until his memory returns. If it does not return within twenty-four hours, we will take an MRI of the brain to see if any blood clots have become manifest or if an aneurysm has taken place."

Gretchen thanked Dr. Oliver. Dr. Oliver left the room. I turned to Lenny Amaranth and said to him, "You may have had an aneurysm. Or maybe you're experiencing what people call retrograde amnesia. Just wait, Lenny. Just hold on." He looked at me and I felt helpless.

Hours passed, and I made a call to Yasmin and told her about Amaranth. Then, I went to the cafeteria and brought back sandwiches and juice for Gretchen, Lenny, and I. We ate in silence. It was all very eerie, the way Lenny Amaranth unwrapped his sandwich and put it in his mouth and chewed like a child when he was a 220 pound man with a full time job at the tax collector and had a fiancé whom he was to marry in a few months. When Lenny was finished with his sandwich, he wadded up the plastic wrap, handed it to me, opened his juice, and finished it. Nurses stopped in every so often and asked Lenny who was the President of the United States and in which state he lived. Lenny after each question scrunched up his face and shook his head, frustrated. It was nearing now three P.M. I called Yasmin and told her if things did not change here I would come home around four or five o'clock. When things did take a change, it was about four-thirty. Gretchen was sitting on a chair flipping through a magazine. I was sitting on a chair and, too, reading an article in a *National Geographic* issue. Lenny on the hospital bed was lying supine. He had not spoken in two hours. Reading the *National Geographic* issue, in my periphery, I saw Lenny Amaranth sit up, swing his legs out, and place them on the linoleum. He shrieked and looked at me and shrieked again. He rose to his feet and started crying. "He's going to jump out the window." I stood up and his face contorted. "He's going to jump out the window. He's going to jump out the window." He just cried and cried, saying over and over, "He's going to jump out the window. He's going to jump out the window." He put his face in his hands and cried and I took his shoulders and shook him.

"Lenny! Lenny! Lenny Amaranth!"

Amaranth shivered and I took him into my arms.

"It's okay." As I stroked his hair, he cried into my shoulder. Gretchen had gone to get the nurse. The nurse came in and Lenny, sitting on the bedside, was sniffling and shivering. She took his blood pressure and lay him down, and then she asked, "Who is the President of the United States of America?"

Lenny gave the correct answer.

"What state do you live in?"

Lenny again gave the right answer.

"I'll get Dr. Oliver," she said, and she left the room with haste.

Dr. Oliver came in and Lenny Amaranth was lying on the bed rather disconcerted. Dr. Oliver said, "Lenny? That's your name isn't it?"

Lenny said, "I'm Lenny Amaranth. I work at the tax collector. That is my fiancé Gretchen Pinter. We live in Maryland and the government is a farce."

"He's back," said Dr. Oliver. Amaranth groaned. "It seems to me," Dr. Oliver said, "his memory has returned within forty-eight hours and, today, he has suffered from retrograde amnesia. These events aren't recurring. You have nothing to worry about, Mr. Amaranth. We can rule out an aneurysm, but I would still like to run a MRI scan."

"To hell with your MRI scan," said Lenny Amaranth. "I want out, now. I want to get home and eat dinner and lie down."

"We'll get you out of here. Okay," Dr. Oliver said. "Okay."

Lenny was discharged within the hour, which was quite fast. Gretchen, Lenny, and I got into the Chevy and I drove them back to their house. Lenny invited me in for coffee, but I told him I needed to get home to Yasmin and Lena, the day had been really trying, and to try and get some rest, Amaranth. It's been a long day.

***

The appointment with Herbert Podrey was Monday morning, the Monday following Amaranth's amnesiac episode. Throughout Sunday night, the temperature dropped. Herbert Podrey was in mind as was Lenny Amaranth and what Lenny Amaranth had said upon regaining his memory. It was striking but it did not occur to me what he had said could have been correlated with the Podrey appointment and the psychographic test I was to administer on him. The parallel did not occur to me until much later. The appointment was set for ten A.M. and, showering, the cold reality of the following three days could not have been more elusive. Driving west towards A.E. Phrenology, the streets seemed rather empty for a Monday and likewise cold; the cars drove atop gray streets, the sky, too, was gray, crows in number dipped from phone lines, timeless. The building in which A.E. Phrenology was located was about fifteen minutes from home and the drive to the building, windows cracked and letting in the coldness, was, too, timeless in the respect that within an hour I was to perform my second to last psychographic test. This sent me through intersection after intersection. There was finality in that commute, a finality too elusive and so it seemed conscious and intrusive. Pulling into a parking spot, I shut the windows. Then, I got out, locked the doors, and walked up to the office building. The doors slid aside and welcomed me with their all too familiar purple and yellow carpet, faux ficus, and painted harbor scenes. It was nine o'clock and Herbert Podrey, within the hour would knock on the office door and the psychographic test would commence. I unlocked the door to my office, went into the office, and took a seat behind the desk. The psychograph was to my right. Accustomed to the medieval machine, its twisted wire and feelers interweaving and set upon a metal frame, I was not affected by its otherworldliness. I never had been, but that would change. As surely as Herbert Podrey had been a subject of a psychographic test that day and within twenty-four hours of the psychographic test, proceeded to jump out his window, that would change. The machine's otherworldliness, its archaicness, its medieval nature and even malevolence would be internalized and capitulated. However, now, the confidence of a professional phrenologist was in my demeanor. Exacting this psychographic test would be no more self-absorbing than setting a clock. It would be done with simplicity and with professionalism. The results would be given to Herbert Podrey who would be sent on his way, no strings attached. That was what I had thought, sitting behind my desk the morning of September 25th, ten minutes before Herbert Podrey's arrival. There was a knock at my door and I answered the door, a collected Herbert Podrey standing in the hallway. The man was well-built, with long brown hair across his brow. With confidence, his back straightened, he shook my hand and I could tell the psychographic test would go off without a hitch. He had a smooth voice and an angular nose and already I could tell, from the high frontal arch of his cranium, he had a high aptitude for reason and spirituality.

"Welcome."

"Thank you," said the smooth, gentile Podrey. "I've been waiting for this, with high expectations."

"Good. Good. Firstly, I want to thank you for coming to see me. Phrenology is a dying science. I'm surprised anyone is still interested in it."

Podrey smiled and said, "Mr. Earnhardt, I feel death is not in the aged sciences but in contemporary studies of science. Children eat this age up, microchips and gray matter alike. Immortality, Mr. Earnhardt is in the aged sciences. Immortality."

I, too, smiled and noted the insight in this young and sophisticated man. He was unlike anybody to whom I had ever before spoken. It was in his voice, the resolute acceptance and thoughtful consideration. His was a dying breed. As, too, was mine, I reflected. Two men sitting across another, one a phrenologist and one a phrenological subject. That he and I were living a scenario frequented throughout the nineteenth century was substantial and yet jarring in that this science, phrenology, was lambasted by modernists as being pseudo-scientific. It was as though Herbert Podrey and I were an underground phenomenon, one which surpassed contemporary logic. It was as though the psychographic test which would occur within ten minutes of our introductions was, together, terminal and eternal in that Herbert Podrey, the young, confident, and handsome man opposite me would, following the inevitable psychographic test, descend three stories from his bedroom window and upon hitting the cement patio expire, though he nor I knew it at the time. "This is a psychograph. Have you ever seen one before?"

"I have not," said Herbert Podrey.

"You, the subject, sits on this stool and your cranium goes beneath the helmet. The psychograph adjusts to the undulations of the cranium, by its thirty-two feelers, and breaks electronic circuitry built within the helmet and sends signals to the printout mechanism. It tells us which of your aptitudes are strongest and which are weakest. The test is not long. I would like to begin. Do you have any questions?"

Herbert Podrey shook his head.

"Sit, if you will, beneath the psychograph."

He got up from the seat close by the desk, moved to the stool attached to the psychograph, and sat on the stool. The psychograph adjusted to the subject's cranium and within a minute the printout mechanism would spit out the results which read of Herbert Podrey's mental aptitudes. The results gauged aptitudes like reason, memory, and spirituality in the forefront of the head and destructiveness, mirthfulness, and servility in the posterior of the cranium. I asked Herbert if he had any expectations in regards to the results. Did he feel he would, in one aptitude or another score high or low?

"I haven't put much thought to it," he said. "I'm pretty calm and down to earth. I can't see myself scoring highly in negative aptitudes. But who knows? I'm particularly interested in the aptitudes of time and sublimity."

"You've done your research, I see."

"Oh, yes," Herbert Podrey said. "Yes, I've done research. I know phrenology was considered by some a religion."

It had not occurred to me phrenology was religious. In fact, quite the opposite was my own viewpoint— phrenology not as a fulcrum between the mystical and the corporeal but as a divergent study no less of biology than of psychology. That the brain fit into the skull like a hand fit into a glove was the premise of phrenology. By assessing the skull one gained insight on the brain and the personality and traits of the subject. Which was more powerful, however, the brain and skull or the equitable hand? That was not my dilemma with which to contend, however, at the time the psychographic test was in progress, Herbert Podrey, pleasant and sitting on the stool. But, now, as I write this account, the parallel between the brain and the hand, their differences and the question—which possesses more power?—now is a problem with which I contend. For what writes these words, which the reader now discerns? The hand or the brain? Which is the device used to communicate? It seems not the brain, for it is enclosed in the cranium and the hand as I write trembles and aches, fatigue finding residence not in the head but in the hand: a sure reason to believe the hand is more powerful over the brain, the hand of Fate, the hand that giveth and taketh away. These parables live not in the head nor in the brain but in ethereal forms which take shape as abstract as thoughts and are extrapolated into symbolism and typography.

The printout mechanism to my right spit out the results and I tore them from the printout mechanism. I switched off the psychograph and it slept. Herbert Podrey got up from the stool and once again took his seat before my desk. It was as expected. The aptitude for spirituality was quite high, as was the ability for time, the perception of which and how malleable it was to the subject. Destructiveness and mirthfulness were low in activity.

"Great," said Herbert Podrey. "But how are the results for sublimity?"

I scoured the results for the sublimity reading. "They are not high, Herbert. Well below average." I set down the results. "This by no means indicates a lack of appreciation, however. Sublimity is of the most abstract, under-actualized aptitudes. And it is rather token in regards to the grander aptitudes, of which you have scored highly."

Herbert Podrey, from the seat across me, looked demoralized. His face darkened and his brow furrowed into wrinkles. "Damn."

"It's no reason to become distraught."

"Damn it all to hell." Herbert Podrey muttered to himself. He was reddening, and I felt nervous. It was as if Herbert Podrey had changed, irrevocable.

"Can I get you a cup of water?"

"How about a shot of whiskey?"

It turned out I had the bottle and two glasses beneath my desk. "It's early. But I have here a bottle and a couple of glasses if you really want a drink." I removed the bottle, which was half gone, and the two glasses from the bottom most drawer.

"Pour the drink," he said, and I did. I poured two glasses of scotch for Herbert Podrey and I, and we saluted each other and downed the contents. "Better," he said. "That's better. You know, Mr. Earnhardt, sublimity is the most important aptitude in the whole of phrenology."

That was his opinion and I did not question him. I could not trust him after the outburst and I was rather taken aback by the swing in mood from well-to-do young man to one angry and fuming. "Would you like a copy of the results to show a significant other how highly you scored?"

Herbert nodded yes, and I made a copy of the psychographic results and handed them across the desk.

"You have scored highly, Mr. Podrey. Don't fool yourself."

"I thank you," said Herbert Podrey. "And I apologize for my lack of composure."

I told him he was not to worry. Phrenology was a worthy pursuit but losing control of one's passion can lead to failure. I did not want to end our encounter on such a lectured tone, but it came out that way. He did not seem to mind. His face had brightened and the Herbert Podrey who left A.E. Phrenology was the same Herbert Podrey who had entered—jovial, high-minded, and earnest—only now he had in his hand the results of the psychographic test, which, I believe, was the mark delineating long-lasting life and a quite immediate death to this jubilant individual. For, that night as I lay down to sleep beside Yasmin, having tucked Lena into bed, kissing her goodnight and turning out the light, Herbert Podrey was throwing his leg over a windowsill. It did not occur to me until the following week, when I read Herbert Podrey's obituary in the newspaper, that perhaps it was I who was responsible for the death.

In hand was my morning coffee and my eye caught hold of a familiar name in the obituary section. Herbert Podrey, 31 years old, fell to his death from his bedroom window. Date of death: September 25th, 2017. I was in shock. I could not believe what I was seeing.

Herbert Podrey, that was my Herbert Podrey, had killed himself?

Dumbfounded, I sat back in the kitchen chair and recalled an incident all too similar; and, also, much more personal. The incident in question had involved my first wife, Tyra Earnhardt. Tyra's funeral struck my eyes, a closed casket, the crying parents and uncles and aunts, the memoranda, a large photograph of her face framed and surrounded by red carnations. At the time, it seemed unrelated, Tyra's death and her being subject in a psychographic test two days prior her death. It was all very unrelenting and unnerving, the way the events, one following the other, recurred. This time it was Herbert Podrey who had died, the night of his psychographic test. Herbert, however, requested and even paid for his psychograph test. Tyra on the other hand had not. It had been my desire to test her with the psychograph and at first, she declined. Perhaps she was embarrassed. Perhaps she was only uninterested. I wanted insights on her aptitudes, character traits, and personality if not for my own curiosity but to show her how she scored in the phrenological aptitudes and faculties. And when I pressed, it came out she was scared of the machine. She was scared, she said, of the psychograph. It sent a cold twinge up her spine, she had said, and by the mere sight of the thing she said she felt doomed. But, I would not be defeated. Perhaps this was my flaw. Perhaps forcing a psychographic test on Tyra was the chain link which had broken, and which had led to her undoing. For two days, I implored Tyra and beckoned her with gifts so she would allow me to perform the test on her. She conceded, and the test went off uninterrupted. Tyra scored high in reason and time and even sublimity. Her entire reading was quite uniform and balanced. She was healthy in her mental faculties, as per phrenological aptitudes. The night of her psychographic test, we ate dinner at a restaurant and drank well, went home and made love. The following day, I was in Pittsburgh to attend a convention on phrenological antiquities and the retaining of phrenology as a culture. I was to stay in Pittsburgh for two nights, both of which had events scheduled, the former night the portion of the convention regarding phrenological antiquities and the latter night's portion involving the survival of phrenology and its future, followed by drinks at a local watering hole.

On the former night, my wife, Tyra Earnhardt, choked on a scallop and perished alone in the kitchen. I arrived home to an empty apartment and a note on the kitchen table reading: *Allen, its Ruby, Tyra's colleague from work. Something's happened. Call me as soon as you can. 555-4978.* The phone call to Ruby was very short, sixty seconds at most. She had told me Tyra had not arrived at work in two days and she, Ruby, had come over to our apartment and found Tyra, and it was *ohh, so horrible.* The colleague told me to contact the hospital where Tyra was being kept. I did so and the morgue told me over the phone the autopsy results— *"Her trachea had been blocked and she asphyxiated to death"*—and they gave me their condolences, which were rather automatic and commonplace. We hung up and I went to the refrigerator and looked inside of it. There was seafood linguine still leftover.

Herbert Podrey's obituary filled me with anxiety, to an extent that raised my heart rate and had begun

142

making my hands tremble. The two incidents could not be related. No, it was impossible. That Herbert Podrey died, as did Tyra, following a psychographic test was coincidental. There was no foundation to support the sequence of thought—Herbert Podrey and Tyra were subjects of psychographic tests, within hours each passed away, I was the phrenologist who exacted the psychographic tests and I was responsible. It was all very muddled and dense. That the possibility the two incidents were related existed was leaving me irresolute and rendered itself cacophonous. The idea bounced around and jostled my head. It was not possible. That the events correlated was anomalous. Believing they were related, as per the common denominator that was a psychographic test, would be delusional. And yet, something in my head jarred me into believing, however slight the belief may have been, the deaths of Herbert Podrey and Tyra Earnhardt were related, and I was responsible. The obituary had the date of the funeral. Herbert Podrey was to be buried at White Egret Funeral Home on October 3rd. I was going to attend. And not only because I felt responsible for Herbert Podrey's death, but because I felt in regards to Herbert Podrey's death guilty, too. Not to Yasmin nor to Raleigh Durman nor to Lenny Amaranth would I tell of this seeming consistent and symbiotic trend. The deaths and their preliminary commonality were not to surface. For one, because it was incriminating. And two, because anybody who believed the two deaths were because of the psychographic tests appeared a lunatic, a word far from desirable when it was meant to describe a person. The newspaper lay on the kitchen table and for minutes I sat at the kitchen table recalling Herbert Podrey and his contorted face when he was relayed his test results. It was minutes before I took a sip of cold coffee.

I folded the newspaper and threw it in the trashcan. Then, I dumped the remaining coffee down the drain and went upstairs into the bathroom. I looked into the mirror and saw a man sturdy in frame. I saw a phrenologist. And then, what I was going to do following Herbert Podrey's funeral was quite clear. It was all too clear. This conundrum would be solved but I hoped it would not be solved with another, more dire fatality.

***

Stained glass depicting the Virgin Mary, St. Paul, and other patron saints, an organ with its pipes fifteen feet in altitude, and a marble alter on which strewn the Good Book and a silver crucifix were the components of an otherwise timeless and heartfelt service. The day prior the funeral, the visitation of the now deceased Herbert Podrey was held, an event I had missed, but the morning of the funeral I rose, dressed in my tuxedo, which I had not worn since my second wedding, and traversed eastward towards the Church of Heavenly Saints and the services being held for Herbert Podrey. Upon my entrance into the small building made of stucco walls and brown roof, a fragrance between a rose and Frankincense wafted into my nose. The service was already underway, and many people had filed into the wooden pews the priest faced, his nose directed toward the assembly, addressing the distance between life and death and the significance of the afterlife. The casket, which was made of mahogany and brass, was sidelong, and the casket was centered upon the marble before the altar. It was closed and the image of Herbert Podrey following his death, his wife standing over him in shock, churned my heart. It could not be that I was the sole proprietor of death. If it were true, this woman to whom Herbert Podrey was married had the right to my head. It

144

should be given to her on a platter. But, the notion of manslaughter—it was not murder; death had not been my intention exacting the test—released its grip on me as the service continued and as the priest's words entered my ears.

"Death is not the end. Death is the beginning. Death is of god and not the devil. Praise he who takes us from this place. He who is taken shall not be forsaken."

The priest, dressed in black, went on with his monologue describing the few times he had had interactions with Herbert Podrey. From his words, it seemed Herbert Podrey was lackadaisical. It seemed he was carefree and pleasant. This did show in his test results, so I was not surprised. Nobody was. Everybody present knew Herbert Podrey to a certain degree but nobody expected his time would come so very soon.

In the foremost pew, a woman veiled and, too, wearing black stood with her chin down and on her right side was a child who must have been five or six years old. This was, I was to learn, Mrs. Podrey's and Herbert's son. Introductions would be made. But not during the service. Not here. The atmosphere was too great, the high ceilings and stoic eyes from the windows staring down the assembly like spirits. What to say to Mrs. Podrey had not yet been conceived. The standard condolences—*he was a great man*—were overdone and improper. I knew Herbert Podrey for only thirty minutes. A conversation between Mrs. Podrey and I would take place. But, not here. Not in the Church of Heavenly Saints. I felt as though mine were the dominion of the devil and as though my presence here was imposing and secretive. Mrs. Podrey did not know of Tyra's death, which had preceded Herbert Podrey's, and the peculiar synchronicity linking the incidents. To her, I was Allen Earnhardt, phrenologist and acquaintance of the late Herbert Podrey and I was here to pay my respects.

The assembly shed tears for Herbert Podrey in unison, but my eyes were dry. They stayed dry throughout the service and through to the end of the day when the sun dove into the Earth and the waning moon took its place. For the time being, the rear most pew was my own and it felt quite like a shelter or means of protection against the people before me and the priest and the casket within which was held the corpse of Herbert Podrey. The priest muttered a final prayer nobody heard over the casket and then gesticulated to the pallbearers that they might take the casket outside to begin the procession towards White Egret Funeral Home. The people's heads—there was forty or fifty people present; family and friends from out of state or even abroad, acquaintances and colleagues—all followed the mahogany and brass casket down the aisle. The rows of people, beginning with Mrs. Podrey's row, followed the casket and pallbearers. Row by row, the assembly adjourned and I, being in the rearmost row of pews, brought up the rear. The doors behind me closed and eternity was heard in the form of a hollow thud. It was then that people surrounded the hearse into which the casket and the corpse of Herbert Podrey was deposited. One car and then another exited the lot of the Church of Heavenly Saints, following the hearse towards the cemetery. I once more brought up the rear. A police escort blocked off intersections. The hearse sped westward. Countless cars and family members and friends, too, sped westward. The iron arch, which was the entrance to White Egret Funeral Home, stood unfaltering yet shoddy as a gateway into eternal darkness. For within this place lay the people from before, never again to see the sun, to never again

146

embrace their loved ones. Here, they were sent into the Earth for an eternal sleep. It was something never before pondered, a theory unexplored by myself, the concept of death and everlasting life. It seemed to me one perished and gravitated not outward but inward to whichever primordial center was most powerful or intriguing. The aptitudes of spirituality, time, sublimity, and even destruction and sex were centers in which the deceased could reside for eternity. This, as I have donned it, was the only and most practical means by which one could ascertain the concept of eternal life. As a phrenologist, it seemed almost coy, the device used by Providence to convey this impervious schema. Using deductive logic, during the service in the Church of Heavenly Saints, it seemed obvious that the mind of Herbert Podrey had been set helter-skelter by the results, perhaps because they were not as he had desired, and his demeanor toward phrenology had unraveled him in a psychic way or the psychograph had deviated, pulling and pushing and oscillating the electro-magnetic waves within Herbert Podrey's cranium. The causality of this death, and even more so the two deaths, which were synchronistic, was very uncertain. The green and rolling grave sites, the gray tombstones and their chiseled typography were all too symbolic of the immediacy of the circumstances. Cars upon cars lined the narrow road off of which Herbert Podrey was to be buried. There was not space enough for every car on the narrow road to park—it was almost a path—and I parked the Chevy around the lot, and then strode upon the grass towards the grave site. Once more, I stood in the rear of the assembly and tried to listen to the wistful words of the priest. They went unheard and only the high swooning of a breeze and a screaming baby were audible. The casket, which was to be lowered into Earth, was not visible as per the amount of people assembled and obstructing the view. When the time arrived only the mechanical clicks of a pulley system descending the corpse of Herbert Podrey into its grave site was heard. A timelessness in the chirping sparrows, the shifting of weight from one leg to the other, fabric against fabric rubbing and creating static electricity, the assembly's immense blackness absorbing the sunlight and reflecting an absence, a void—all these representative images of finality were weightless shadows in my eyes. Upon the end of this segment in the services, the priest blessed the assembly and the remnants of Herbert Podrey with a wave of a white hand and dismissed the assembly's patrons from the cemetery. We were to move to the home of Herbert Podrey, where the introduction between Mrs. Podrey and I would occur. Retracing my steps across the green, my thoughts reached for a phrase or word, anything to convey my feelings, guilt and regret, to Mrs. Podrey without sounding too derisive or self-incriminating. Doubtless, she would be accosted by family and friends all speaking in similitude. I wished to say something different, poignant and unexpected; for I was different than these people with whom I was in close proximity. They were the good men and women of Herbert Podrey's life. I was—it started taking hold in mind—a culprit, his murderer. But, the notion as I got into the driver's seat of the Chevrolet—*(You are a murderer)*—was pushed from mind. It shook me, abrasive. It was not a murder. It was not. What happened could not even be called manslaughter. There was no corporeal relation linking the meeting, which took place between Herbert Podrey and I, and his death. There was only the notion of the past recurring. There was only an observation, an uncoordinated parallel which had become manifest. Herbert Podrey's death was not my

148

responsibly. Yet, it was. I knew it but dismissed it. It was heavy and domineering, tantalizing and suspended overhead. The Podrey household was northward twenty minutes, located in a part of town that was quite rural.

Homes, developments, and shops turned to forest and pastures. It seemed the existent town rearwards was feigning into nonexistence. A.E. Phrenology, Yasmin and Lena, Raleigh Durman and Lenny Amaranth, the backyard deck, the master bedroom and bathroom, the psychograph were all figments of unreality. Wafting upward, these ideas, people, and objects seemed phantasmagoria. The procession headed towards the Podrey household hit the brakes. Red lights on cars ignited, starting from the foremost car and traveling backward, systematic. The procession had arrived. It had arrived at the street on which Herbert Podrey had lived. Presently, I was making a left turn onto W Beverly Road and once more carried on as a part of the procession. The home, a three-story rural townhouse, was set upon an elevated landing through which curved a winding gravel driveway. On either side of the gravel driveway were bushes of hydrangeas. Long, thirty yards at most, the gravel driveway lurched towards the townhouse. I parked my Chevy toward the mouth of the driveway. There was just enough space. I twisted the key backward, got out of the Chevy, and walked towards the townhouse. Dozens of people were exiting their vehicles and entering the Podrey residence.

The front doors were tall and rounded at the top. They, like Herbert Podrey's casket, were made of mahogany; and I entered through the doorway into a home, which smelled of lavender and chamomile. Many individuals were already at the dining room table, picking at chicken tenders and pigs in a blanket. Some already had alcoholic beverages in their hands. Children ran and screamed, toyed with each other; and all seemed very cordial.

It was unknown to them the per chance instigator of Herbert Podrey's death, that was I, had stepped into the home. (*You are a murderer.*) It was not so. It could not be so. I told myself I was innocent of doing any harm. I told myself I was the lamb. It could not be that within me, within my studies, within phrenology or the psychograph, the grand and cosmological power of death was housed. I told myself I was guiltless, but that was far from true; somewhere in the depth of my being, I knew the psychographic test and the phrenologist who had exacted the psychographic test were at fault. (*You are a murderer.*) I walked into the kitchen. On the hardwood, the soles of my shoes tapped and, once in the kitchen, I spotted who must have been Mrs. Podrey. Talking to two women, her face was turned in my direction. She had removed the veil and a small, sharp nose and narrow eyes were exposed. Pouted, her lips added to the curve of the natural handsomeness of her face and I thought her very attractive. For a woman who had lost her husband not a week ago, the resilience in the arched eyebrows was omnipresent, though her eyes were dismal and fatigued, beneath them dark circles. She had been losing sleep, one could tell. I lingered by the refrigerator, looking at crayon drawings of the household and geometric tracings one atop the other in a sort of mystical contrivance by who must have been Herbert Podrey's son. The drawings had on them no name but the date of the drawings were written on the lower right hand side: September 10th and September 11th, for the townhouse scene and the geometry, respectively. Mrs. Podrey was exchanging kisses with the two women and I approached the trio before anybody else could seize Mrs. Podrey. The two women bid adieu to Mrs. Podrey and Mrs. Podrey turned toward me. Reaching out my hand, which she took and squeezed, I told her my name; and she introduced herself as Tina Podrey, the late Herbert Podrey's wife. "You are? A colleague? An acquaintance? Herbert was very well liked in many circles."

"I am a phrenologist. I run A.E. Phrenology in town. Your husband came to see me the day of his death. He scored very highly."

Tina Podrey's face darkened. "Yes, he told me about his phrenology meeting. Really, it had taken to him quite strongly, phrenology. He wouldn't stop talking about it. He talked about phrenology as a religion and related it to this and to that. It was, I must say, Mr. Earnhardt, overwhelming."

"Phrenology has fascinated me since youth. I'm not surprised it took to Herbert strongly. He did score highly in aptitude for reason, which is said to contain the fundaments of critical thinking and even creation."

Tina Podrey's eyes faltered. Her eyes darkened, and she whimpered. "Do you know what it's like to find a loved one lifeless?"

"No, I don't."

"I found him thirty minutes after he fell from that window. Thirty minutes. I was lying in bed and I didn't know where he had gone. We had dinner and he disappeared. I went outside to look for him—" Again, Tina Podrey whimpered. "I went outside to look for him and found him on the side deck, lifeless. It was not pretty, Mr. Earnhardt. It was not pretty at all."

"I can't imagine it was."

"What he was doing out that window, I couldn't tell you. It was an accident, Herbert's fall. It was an accident. He was not the type of person to do something like that to himself." Tina Podrey buried her face in her hands. She whimpered. What was I to do? Embrace her? The man who had indirectly murdered her husband? It was insulting, attending Herbert's funeral, let alone facing his wife. All at once, my attendance of both the funeral and the luncheon seemed foolish. It was not hard to believe Tina Podrey thought the fall was accidental, that Herbert Podrey took a nasty spill from the third story window without suicidal intentions. But, I remembered his contorted face, his anger at his sub-par aptitude for sublimity, the drink of whiskey we had shared. Most of all, I remembered Lenny Amaranth's words inside a hospital room during our visit to Ebberfield Hospital South.

"He's going to jump out the window. He's going to jump out the window."

And I knew Herbert Podrey's fall was not accidental. I knew it had been intentional. But, Tina Podrey would not find out about that. She would go through the remainder of her life thinking her late husband, Herbert Podrey, had a bout of bad luck or Fate and had tumbled onto the concrete side deck by accident.

"He was a good man and the love of my life," said Tina Podrey.

I squeezed her shoulder. "I know." Staying in the Podrey household seemed an atrocity. The woman before me was broken and my presence was to her, though she may not have known it, humiliating. Releasing her shoulder, I looked into her eyes and saw a woman who did not know what had happened to her husband. I saw uncertainty and perplexity. "I'm going to step outside if you don't mind," I said.

Tina Podrey nodded her head and walked past me. I walked outside through the sliding glass door and went across the wide back deck, stepped down six or seven steps and onto the manicured lawn in search of the side

152

deck. I hung a right, not knowing on which side the side deck was, and found myself approaching the side deck, which was, as opposed to the back deck, sunken. I stepped down the staircase of three or four steps and found myself standing at the site of Herbert Podrey's death. The side deck, small as it was, fit a glass table, in the center of which was a fabric umbrella. On my right, there was an area of twenty-five square feet. This was the concrete section of deck on which Herbert Podrey had landed following a three-story fall, ending his life. It was immaculate. There was no evidence of death. I looked up and saw a window above the twenty-five square feet of concrete, three stories skyward. I returned my gaze to the concrete side deck, not wanting to conjure a perturbed and maniacal Herbert Podrey in my vision. This was enough. My presence—I could sense it—was not welcome here. The guilt I felt, I was sure, was sensed by a mourning Tina Podrey, though the correlation between the psychographic test and her husband's death was not evident to her. Nor was it deductible. It feigned and eluded commonplace bystanders and victims. To myself, however, it was much more prevalent, even a certainty. That the psychographic test diverted Herbert Podrey's course and also my first wife, Tyra's, course was quite the case. To me, the phantasm was quite present and almost foolish. Magnifying it to an immediate degree was my course of action. Its congruity would not go unearthed. The psychograph would be used once more. But, this time, it would be used on somebody all but cognizant.

The staircase of three or four steps leading into the side deck was mounted once more and instead of heading back into the backyard towards the mourning family members and friends, I walked towards the front of the townhouse, meandering through azaleas and a cluster of ferns, not looking back. Tina Podrey would never again see me. Neither would I come back to the Podrey household. The Podrey household was gathering around my knees in essence, desultory and indistinct, as a reminder that a once healthy man had taken his own life as per my actions as a phrenologist. The grinding of pebbles was omnipresent as I passed twenty cars lining the gravel driveway of the townhouse. The grinding, the greenery, and the rationality I inhabited in most cases mixed and hardened. Yasmin was expecting me. Upon my return home, a drink would be poured and drank. All this, the Podrey household and Tina Podrey's demurred eyes, enshrouded me. On the drive southward towards my own home, the town that was Newbury, Maryland began once more to exist. Before me, it lay like a coiled serpent, black and licking the air with its pronged tongue. I could not foresee the milieu which was to occur. The coiled snake would strike, but, driving home from the Podrey household, it was unknown just how immediate and malevolent it would be. I drove southward towards Yasmin and home for the time being, thinking of the stark flavor of whiskey and the following day.

Pastures and forest turned once again to homes and establishments. The geometric patterns and the painting of the townhouse drawn by Herbert Podrey's son, the marble alter and stained-glass windows of the Church of Heavenly Saints were recalled in my eye. Somewhere between the saints, the geometry, and the stone lingered death. It may have been holy to some. But, knowing what I did—Lenny Amaranth's outburst in Ebberfield Hospital South, Herbert Podrey's psychographic test, and his suicide seemed to me very unholy. Through the fabric of reason, the hands of death had been activated and seemed to cease and rewind the ephemeral hands of time.

I, Allen Earnhardt, phrenologist and husband, father and friend, was a bystander, an observer of macrocosmic anomaly; and I had become in the case of Tyra and of Herbert Podrey, a murderer. How far the manipulative hands of death and the deceptive hands of time dared flounder the present would not be known. The truth would not be beheld, not until my plans regarding the matter were executed and I apprehended proof these deaths and the psychographic tests which had preceded them were, in fact, related. It was only a question of whether I would come to realize the connection in life, that was in Newbury, Maryland, or if it would be realized after the grave.

I turned off the Chevy once home, exited the vehicle, and went up to the front door. Yasmin was probably inside the house preparing dinner. I needed a drink. Opening the door, stepping in, and putting the car keys on the glass table, I could smell cooked vegetables. I walked into the kitchen and saw Yasmin hovering over a pot and stirring what must have been her vinegar sauce she had invented. I did not speak and went to the liquor cabinet. I took down the bottle from the cabinet and poured a glass of whiskey. I drank it in silence just as Yasmin turned around.

"Drinking whiskey," she said, matter-of-fact.

"It's been a long day."

"Don't get drunk before dinner," she said.

"I won't."

She turned back to the pot and resumed stirring. "How was the funeral?" she said.

"Disorderly." It seemed to me, however, that disorderly was how I felt, that it was not the funeral which was disorderly. The disorderliness was in me.

"Dinner is almost ready," she said.

"I'll go get changed." I poured another glass and took it down. Yasmin did not notice. Going up the stairs, Lena passed me, and I patted her head. Her hair had thickened over the past two years. It was much like Yasmin's, dark brown and voluminous. "Good evening, sweetheart. How are you?"

"Hungry," she said, and I believed her.

Escaping the tuxedo, which had become grainy and suffocating, the following morning's routine went through my head. After rising, brushing my teeth, taking a shower, and eating breakfast, I would go to A.E. Phrenology and do something, I mused as I put on a pair of khakis and a tee-shirt, which may or may not be suicidal. Downstairs once more, around the kitchen table the three of us sat and enjoyed the meal, after which the three of us cleaned the dishes. The night was becoming cool, cooler than average for an October evening in Maryland, but I decided to sit outside at the table anyway. The night had arisen from the forest and reached out from the lofty recesses of the stratosphere. The black sky was dotted with stars, which, when collected, made up constellations—all of which throughout the galaxy and around Earth proceeded into eternity. Order was present in the constellations, unlike that which was occurring presently in me. That order, however, the constellations—Sagittarius, Libra, Leo, Ursa Major and Minor, all the constellations—were constructions of man. Prior the conception of astrology, the stars were giant balls of gas, light, and heat, lightyears distant, manifestations of macrocosmic anomaly which had not been actualized until religion was formed. Then, order to the stars was given and they were ordained as deities, deities who, through belief and itemized idealism, reigned in man. These ethereal deities throughout the epochs of history, from Paleolithic times to the 21st Century washed in and out of him, exacting for themselves a quasi-real, quasi-actual existence which could only flourish within and confound man; it was an existence which was to forever seize man and within him grow a peripheral mind, a peripheral man who became manifest. Some called this entity religion. Some called it Fate. Some called it knowledge or pride. Unfurling before me was not the woolen possibilities of what was to come, but what had occurred, what was occurring, and what was to occur, all collecting as a predominant entity. It was not kind. Nor was it alive. The tripartite vacuum that was religion, Fate, and knowledge was becoming manifest in full. It was attriting its subjects. It had attrited Tyra to her death. It had attrited Herbert Podrey to his. And, within the next week, month, or year, it may well attrit me, too. My guilt and my responsibility for the deaths implored me to take this cohesive and linear phenomenon to a more immediate level. The stars which had evolved into constellations which had evolved into religion and Fate and knowledge may have been itemized and recapitulated into the very mechanism and field of science I studied, that was the psychograph and phrenology; and the application of these mechanisms and sciences were the dominion of the devil was to me all too evident. A.E. Phrenology had been infiltrated; and that which had been imposed upon Tyra, Herbert Podrey, and I, was soon to be uncovered. It was to be unveiled.

The sliding glass door behind me opened and out stepped Lena, who tapped my shoulder. In her hand was the photograph of Tyra at the Niagara Falls. She clutched it in two small hands and she asked me the following question: "Do you know where she is now?"

This little girl, six years old, was thinking of mortality for the first time. The circumstances being what they were, her thinking of mortality, her taking and bringing me the photograph and asking me the question, *"Do you know where she is now?"* was very pertinent. I looked at her and knowing of my intentions for the following day, I realized this may well be my last night together with Lena. She clutched the photograph in her small hands and I wanted to say *She's dead, she's gone*, feeling responsible, feeling guilty. But, I could not say that to the girl, my Lena. As morbid as it sounded, it was all too true. I knew it. Tyra Earnhardt had died asphyxiating on a scallop while I was in Pittsburgh attending a phrenology convention. Tyra Earnhardt died as a result of psychographic testing. I was the culprit. I knew it. And it had happened again in the case of Herbert Podrey. I sat transfixed, watching Lena clutch the photograph, hoping the end would not be the same in my own case.

I took the photograph from her and we were silent for many seconds. Then, I said, "I don't know where she is now."

Lena outstretched her arm, tiny and white, and placed her hand on my chest. The night had grown cold and something was making it colder. Perhaps it was Lena's touch. Perhaps it was what it represented. Perhaps it was that, within the next twenty-four hours, I was performing that which had twice proved fatal on myself. Lena did not know the psychographic test I was to perform on myself would descend certain Fate, but her hand on my chest, its pressuring my breast, was reassuring to the effect that I would entangle with Fate, religion, and knowledge, that I would entangle with the entity which had moved into A.E. Phrenology, and that it would not be a physical entanglement. It would be an entanglement of will and control. Life and death were separated by an essence—will.

Lena removed her hand from my chest and walked in through the sliding glass door, back into the house. For a minute longer, I sat at the table on the back deck. the skies returned my assuredness. The psychographic test tomorrow was to occur, the effects of which were untold. But, they would become evident. The hand that giveth and taketh away was not subtle. It was prideful. It was coy.

Nine o'clock turned to ten o'clock and I was readying myself for bed, having changed into my sweatpants and a tee-shirt. After brushing my teeth, I went into Lena's bedroom and watched her sleep. She breathed and was undisturbed by my presence. Looking at my six year old daughter, that little girl, Lena, the notion that life and mortality were hanging precarious above not only me but above many of those to whom I was closest was not realized. It seemed, as I hovered over the small single bed within which lay Lena, my logic, this connection between Tyra, Herbert Podrey, and the supposed fatal psychographic tests was delusional. It was all in my head. But, it seemed too obvious. Something stark pulled at my instincts. It was the notion of an imploding reality, a living, thriving organism revolving around me. This occurred to me, but also what occurred to me was the dichotomy, or rather the two components necessary for exacting the test, which made phrenology and psychographic testing feasible. There was the phrenologist and the psychograph. It was true a subject was also needed, but as far as tomorrow's test, the subject and the phrenologist would be one in the same. A question dawned on me as I watched Lena sleep: Who really was the culprit of such heinousness and inhumanity, the psychographic test or the phrenologist who exacted the test? I was damned. I knew it. It was I who was the instigator of this connected slew of fatalities; but perhaps the notion I was, in fact, guilty was incorrect, and the notion I was not the common denominator nor an innocent professional obliquely delivering men and women to their deaths was the case. That A.E. Phrenology was a preliminary checkpoint to death was soon to be criticized. If I survived, Tyra, Hebert Podrey, and A.E. Phrenology were not, in fact, intermixed in a fatalistic dance. If I perished, I would know within the void my practices were fatal; and if consciousness remained there in the void, if the prideful and coy entity and I converged, it would be deserved. I closed the door to Lena's bedroom and went into my own bedroom, where I lay in bed and fell asleep. Within minutes it seemed, I had awoken. The bedroom had infused its nighttime darkness with the hues of morning time, and within the hour I was driving towards A.E. Phrenology.

The purple and yellow carpet compelled me forward through the main anteroom towards my office, and once at its door I unlocked the deadbolt and stepped inside. The room, darkened by Venetian blinds, coated the mahogany desk, the bookcase and its books, and the psychograph with an opaque cognizance. In this room, in A.E. Phrenology, my thirty-five years of life would become marked as if by a cosmological bounty hunter. Flipping on the light switch, the opaque cognizance retreated, disappeared into non-space. The psychograph, mahogany desk, bookcase and books were now visible and lifeless. A second ago, A.E. Phrenology and the opaque cognizance that enshrouded it seemed to beckon me forward with sardonic intentions. Traversing the purple and yellow carpet, I noticed my feet were heavy and like the negative ends of magnets, the purple and yellow carpet the positive end of another magnet; with each step, fatigue rose through the soles of my feet into my knees. I walked around the mahogany desk and placed my briefcase beside my chair. For many seconds, I sat contemplating a glass of whiskey. It did not take long to make the decision and I removed the bottle and a glass from the bottommost drawer. I poured one and took it down. The chair had become comfortable, far too comfortable. The psychograph was miles away and I thought over, really thought over for the first time, my intentions in regards to the morning's psychographic test. There were two options. One, take the psychographic test and find out once and for all if A.E. Phrenology and I were the culprit of Tyra's and Herbert Podrey's deaths. Or two, hightail it out of A.E. Phrenology and never look back. The latter option was beginning to look enticing; the former option was turning my spine from the bottom up into an icicle. Lena came to mind, as did Yasmin, Lenny Amaranth, and Raleigh Durman. I had not even said goodbye and it occurred to me, if I were to perform the psychographic test, I could wreck on the way home, get into an accident and die, without saying goodbye to anybody, exiting this world without a hint of what had happened, taking leave without a speck of legacy. If this entity, this abstract and ethereal energy which killed, and which lived through A.E. Phrenology pervaded reason, I, Allen Earnhardt, would be thrown into the catalogue of people murdered by its malice. Allen Earnhardt would be forgotten. He would be buried, and the actual causation of his death would evade discovery. My intentions this morning were not only to test myself with the psychograph but to ascertain the fundamental ins and outs, the effectuality of Fate, knowledge, and even religion. It was then the psychograph increased in presence and demanded it be turned on and used. It was not tentative, the way I rose from the chair, which had become all too comfortable, rounded the mahogany desk, traversed the purple and yellow carpet to the psychograph, and activated it, knowing full well I had a death wish.

I activated the printout mechanism, too, which had spit out the results of both Tyra's and Herbert Podrey's psychographic test results and which would soon spit out my own. Beneath the archaic headpiece, with its moving parts haphazard and interweaving, the receptor of my head's undulations, the helmet in its entirety enmeshed and collecting at the top of the cranium like a poignant exclamation, I heard the results printed. The test had concluded. Through the miasma collected around my cranium, through the support column which connected the phenomenal receptor to the base of the machine, and through to the printout mechanism which was on my desk beside me, my aptitudes and mental faculties were transposed into signals, casted through the copper as epistemological ideas and inclinations of personality and man. The complex structures of thought—spirituality, time, destruction, mirthfulness, sublimity, sex, reason—were cascading elements, which together composed Allen Earnhardt; these structures of thought were being made discordant by the abstracted energy I was tempting. Reason, time, spirituality, all the faculties of man, no longer held consistency. They were paradoxical and voided. The logic behind the events which had taken place, and which would take place baffled the timeline, it accosted reason, and it did so with fatalistic tendencies. This fact was yet to be ascertained. Of yet, this discordance was a mere notion, a fabricated possibility I had conjured. The test I was now exacting upon myself was the fulcrum which connected possibility and inevitability, reality and actuality, probability and definitiveness. The printout mechanism had spit out the test results and I had risen from the small stool and contemplated the wisdom of reading the results. I tore out the test results from the printout mechanism and decided it was of no importance. I was preoccupied with the possible misfortune I may have descended on myself, and Yasmin and Lena, too. The test results, which may have been the catalyst to my death were wadded up and thrown into the trashcan. Briefcase in hand, the lights switch was flipped to the off position and the opaque cognizance once more dressed A.E. Phrenology. I clicked the deadbolt into place and walked through the sliding glass doors into what was becoming another cool and otherwise commonplace morning. It was, however, far from commonplace. I had exacted a psychographic test on myself, an action which, I premised, could have been the causation of two deaths. If this were true, my own death would be the last; for A.E. Phrenology following my own death would not exist. Nobody knew how to operate the psychograph and A.E. Phrenology would fall into the caches of unexplainable phenomena which occurred on Earth. A.E. Phrenology would pass unnoticed, undiscovered, like a camouflaged arachnid on a forest tree. I was the only person who conceived this parallel, and its evidence would become definite. The Chevy churned into liveliness. On the way back to the house, cars alongside me drove placated. The oak trees, which swayed in their extremities, stood anchored into the earth like marble columns, as if they were delaying an eventual cave in which was bound to take place. People walking their dogs, joggers, and bicyclists walked, jogged, and cycled to and fro unknowing of the primordial elements through which they walked, jogged, and cycled and in which they thrived. It seemed to me all too apparent that what had just occurred in A.E. Phrenology broke the bounds of logic. A.E. Phrenology and the happenings within it had before broke boundaries, those of life and death and what I once believed to be a linear and grounded timeline. The events which had taken place, Lenny Amaranth's words, *"He's going to jump out the window. He's going to jump out the window,"* and the successive suicide of Herbert Podrey had shaken this faith. Now, I knew something primordial was in action. That which was primordial, that which had taken the life of Tyra and Herbert Podrey and would, perhaps, take my own life, may have been all high, a conception above the frequency of the brain, an aptitude which the psychograph could not detect, and which took precise action through the psychograph. Or maybe the primordial energy, the entity which had evolved and varied from prior Paleolithic times, was that of the lower dominion. It seemed obvious to me. The energy, the opaque cognizance which lived within A.E. Phrenology was of a lower dominion; for the deaths were not subtle. They were violent and malevolent, asphyxiation and suicide. No, the energy which commanded life and death, and which cloaked A.E. Phrenology was not all high. On the contrary, it was a low and desultory manifestation. It was prideful. It was coy. Pulling into the driveway, I donned myself a man who had just marked himself for death.

That I had exacted a psychographic test on myself and instigated possible, even probable death by my own hand, I realized, was suicide. I had never been a religious man. The study of phrenology was the most religious I had ever gotten. My conception of phrenology could even be called spiritual. Phrenology was the dawn of psychology. It was the forefather of psychiatry and contemporary neuroscience. Once, slipping into the abode of what was now called ancient science filled me with self-worth and even spirit. Now, the very study, phrenology, instigated a very opposite effect in me, one of unease and uncertainty. My entire philosophy on the science had changed. I, in the months following Herbert Podrey's suicide, had discovered Franz Gall had got it all wrong. All aspects of man, his inclinations and aptitudes, his mental faculties and emotions; the perception of time, love and hate; his spiritual growth and destructiveness; his sexual preferences and disposition and even physical characters; his reason and decisions and resolve; his resilience and constitution, were not subjected to the cephalon, that was the head, but were rather the effects of one central node, housed below the cranium and caged, a manifestation with which I would compete over the next six months: the heart of man.

(Part Two)

Lena came down with a fever three nights later. It was late when Yasmin shook my shoulder and roused me from sleep. The three days prior had amounted to total eventlessness. No danger made itself evident. All was in order. The tragedies following the psychographic tests must have been coincidental, I mused; Tyra and Herbert Podrey had died soon after their tests and three nights following my own psychographic test, Yasmin was shaking my shoulder and telling me Lena had a 104° F fever and I needed to go out to the twenty-four hour pharmacy and get cough medicine to bring down the fever. Still, I lived.

"If it gets any higher," Yasmin said, "we may have to bring her to the hospital."

I told her I would be right back, swung my legs out of bed, and placed them on the carpet. The clock read quarter to one. Feeling my way across the bedroom, I could feel my feet tingling on the carpet with what felt like electricity. I blinked back haze and entered the hallway, following Yasmin to Lena's room. Yasmin then sat on the bed. Lena had a wet hand towel over her brow and I asked her if there was any pain. She groaned, and I assumed that meant yes, there was pain, and I told Yasmin to take care of her and that I would be back in fifteen, twenty minutes at most. Downstairs, I slipped a pair of slippers onto my feet, picked up the car keys from the glass table beside the front door, and stepped outside into the early morning. Silent and dark, the midnight moonlight consumed me in its cosmic and fluid ambience. The Chevy was in the driveway and, traversing the walkway, I sniffed the autumnal scents and the crisp Maryland air, listened to the whispering leaves which still remained on the trees and brushed against one another, and I thought about A.E. Phrenology and its supposed victims, that per chance all was just a coincidence, a freak accident no way related to psychographic testing. That Tyra and Herbert Podrey both died soon after their tests was not a supernatural occurrence. The tests which preluded the deaths, tests which I had administered, were not common denominators and they were not the precursors to death. After all, three days following my own psychographic test, I was still alive; and I thought myself quite mad thinking the two-fold deaths were somehow related. The heat was turned up in the Chevy, and a relaxed state descended upon me.

It may have been the heat coming from the vents having me feeling so comfortable and relaxed, or it may have been the calm before the storm, brought about by the opaque cognizance which was quite present and which I had dismissed as I drove down Binley Street towards the twenty-four-hour pharmacy as nonexistent.

The twenty-four-hour pharmacy was five minutes from the house. I thought of very little on the way there. Lena was foremost, and on the periphery was an alleviation of anxiety, the notion that my own death was not, in fact, imminent and I had evaded Fate.

The Chevy parked, I once again stepped out into the cool mid-night atmosphere and walked into the pharmacy. After checking out, cough medicine in hand, I for the third time, walked through the serene night and silver moonlight to the car, got in, and started the ignition. The heat was turned up already and the car had not changed much in temperature in the three minutes I was in the pharmacy. I turned onto the road, heading home. A long stretch from the center of town to Binley Street, which was a few streets inward of and perpendicular to the long stretch, was ill-lit and had only two lanes, both of which were narrow, and on either side of the road were wide stretches of grass.

It had been ten years since the foundation of A.E. Phrenology. Starting the company was an easy decision. I wanted to practice phrenology, no matter how extinct and shunned it may have been. The practice would be started, and I would practice phrenology, but the acquisition of materials—the psychograph for one—and subjects would be a different and more trying pursuit. Tyra and I had been together at the time I acquired the psychograph, which I had found at a small store of antiquities in New York City, called Guzman's Antiquities, *vis a vis* a connection, a scholar with whom

I had studied phrenology before deciding to start my own practice.

The travels to New York City were to be undertaken as soon as possible. The psychograph was about seven feet in height, as was your typical psychograph. I had called Guzman's Antiquities and a man who introduced himself as Mr. Guzman said he had been trying to rid himself of the old machine for what was now nearing a couple of years. It was growing dusty, he said, and he would give it to me for a cheap price if I did, in fact, come up to New York and purchase the machine. Mr. Guzman and I had made a date, Friday the following week, and I told him I would purchase the psychograph if all was in working order. He assured me it was, and days later I was driving a rented moving van northward towards New York City with the anticipation of my new business, my practice, A.E. Phrenology, and my subjects smartening my ears.

Guzman's Antiquities was rather hard to find. It was on a small back street in Manhattan, tucked in between a coffee shop and a shop which sold lines of clothing I had never heard of. It was nearing five o'clock P.M., and the sign on the glass door read Guzman's Antiquities closed at six. Once inside Guzman's Antiquities, the haphazard way in which the store was situated strained my eyes. Glass shelves with glass bowls, music boxes, crystal prisms on which were etched letters, and other items were along the yellow walls. In the center of Guzman's Antiquities was a wheelbarrow, the smokestack of a steam engine, and the psychograph. The counter, also made of glass, was across me in the small shop, and behind the counter was an aged man with gray hair, and he was wearing glasses; he took them off, cleaned the lenses with his shirt, and said, "Can I help you, sir?"

"I called about the psychograph," I said, now pointing to the psychograph with my thumb over my shoulder. "My name is Allen Earnhardt. I came all the way from Maryland to do some business with you. You must be Mr. Guzman."

"I am Mr. Guzman," he said. "Glad you could make it." He reached over the glass countertop and shook my hand, walked around the counter, and approached the psychograph. "I've been trying to get rid of it for a couple of years. It's accumulating dust. Nobody wants this thing, or so I thought, until you, Mr. Earnhardt, called."

I looked over the psychograph and traced my forefinger down its support column. Mr. Guzman was right. It had been accumulating dust. My finger was gray from the dust which had accumulated. I brushed my hands together to get rid of the dust on my forefinger, and said, "Is it in working order?"

"It is. We can turn it on."

"No matter."

"Working order," he said. "All is in working order."

"Very good," I said. We haggled over the price for a minute. Mr. Guzman was quite glad to rid himself of the psychograph after so long, and he did not put up much disagreement when I offered a number quite lower than the number tied to the psychograph. We shook hands, and Mr. Guzman helped me transport the psychograph into the moving van. I wrote him a check and was southbound by six o'clock P.M. The haphazard traffic of New York City was good to escape. The congested freeways turned into open highways bordered by oak trees which swayed in the evening wind. The scents of the city turned once more to clean air one could only find in rural areas. My window was rolled down and overhead the night sky was clear. The dark fabric lay over the hundreds of miles before me, a separation, a threshold for what was bound to occur to my subjects and I in the following years. In the moving van was not only a phrenologist but a psychograph which would be housed within his practice for the next ten years and which would be the device used to wrought untold devastation upon subjects and its operator. I did not know this at the time, of course, but the machinery I was transporting halfway across the country was material representation of death. It was, in the darkness of the moving van on the voyage home, quiet and patient, waiting for its time to take action. I drove the moving van with care not to damage or topple over the psychograph. I drove through the night and into the early morning, and arrived back into our hometown at around three o'clock A.M. I turned off of the main road and onto Binley Street that night with a silent killer in the cargo bed.

I was nearing Binley Street again, but this time I had in my possession not a psychograph but a bottle of cough medicine for Lena. This night was similar to the night on which I had driven halfway across the country, the oak trees swaying, the night clear, the crescent moon silver. I was nearing Binley Street, about one mile from the intersection, when the first and only other car I saw that night came into view, driving opposite me. At first, I was not sure if I were hallucinating. The car's headlights were bright and blinding and had glowing white, wispy circles around them. I squinted and focused my eyes. Then, I saw the car approaching from the opposite direction was not in his lane, not in the right-hand lane, but in my lane and was bounding headlong straight for me. I flashed my high beams, but the car did not change lanes. It was going to crash into me head-on, or so it seemed, and I swerved to avoid being killed by this madman who must have been drunk or high or both. Swerving into the grass on my right, I took out a yield sign and the Chevy spun out.

Facing again the twenty-four-hour pharmacy, I watched the car which had been driving on the wrong side of the road speed away and correct itself back into the right-hand lane. The Chevy hummed as if nothing had happened. On the ground in front of me was the yield sign I had run over. Shock overcame me, and it dawned on me I had been wrong in my assumption I had feigned the strong arm of Fate. It was evident. My life was in danger. What had just occurred was proof of that. I had been close to being killed in a head-on collision with a drunkard, and I realized A.E. Phrenology, the psychograph, or even my own self-inflicted, destructive practice of phrenology had brought to life the opaque cognizance, and the opaque cognizance was quite active. It was quite alive. And it was blood thirsty.

My thoughts of comfort and relaxation, my feelings of safety and triumph had disappeared. They were gone and all present now was fear, my heart racing as the knowledge overcame me that Tyra's death and Herbert Podrey's death were not coincidental, and that my own death was imminent. Why the opaque cognizance which was housed within A.E. Phrenology waited for the third night to take action was unexplainable. Though its actions were delayed its intentions were clear. It wanted my life. A.E. Phrenology, or rather the entity which had descended from unearthly heights, or maybe ascended from somewhere chaotic and preternatural, was now present. It was omnipresent. It acted through the filaments of human flaws, in their temporal caches, and capitalized on times when people were weak or vulnerable.

That was what had happened when Tyra asphyxiated on the scallop. That was what had happened when Herbert Podrey took the dive off the third story of his house on W Beverly Road. It had attempted the same action on me, as I, half-asleep, drove homeward to deliver the medicine to Lena, who was getting toasted by a 104° F fever. But, it had not killed me. I sat in the Chevy, looking back toward the town center and watching the taillights of a car speed towards home or the next bar, shivering with a sense of my own mortality coursing through me. I turned the car around and got back on the road. I drove slow. My trembling was not because of what had just happened. Not anymore. Now, my trembling was because of what was yet to come.

In what ways would that which resided within A.E. Phrenology make attempts on my life? In which way would it succeed? I was sure I was a dead man. But, as I pulled into the driveway, the familiarity of home casted out the shivers and enamored me with a composed nature and will power. If my life was in danger, so be it. If A.E. Phrenology and the psychographic test I exacted on myself wanted to toy with the strings of life and death, so be it. I would let it. But, I would not do so with listlessness. I would not do so with absentmindedness. The shroud which hung over A.E. Phrenology, its past victims, and I were not going to triumph without battle—a battle of will power and witticisms and good nature—and if the opaque cognizance did triumph, my goal would be accomplished. I, from the grave, would know A.E. Phrenology was, in fact, damned, and that there was no such thing as coincidence. If it did not kill me, if I did survive, I again would triumph. It was a win-win, and as I walked into the house with the bottle of cough syrup in my hand and as I put the car keys on the glass table beside the front door and as I slipped off my slippers, I knew before me was a battle of cosmological proportions. It, too, occurred to me I was at a disadvantage, for that which operated through my practice was supernatural. It was higher in terms of thought and perception. It was the quasi-living, quasi-lifeless being which coursed through human veins and flickered in the brain and kept grounded the personality, in its selfish, manipulative ways so it could kill. But, to course through the human and operate within him was to be a part of him, and this made it, the opaque cognizance, malleable. It made it apt for defeat. How I was to defeat it I had yet to ascertain, but I had one notion in my faculties now I did not have before: The knowledge that I was marked for death.

Ascending the staircase, my own mortality was forgotten. The events of the past week—Hebert Podrey's funeral, my own psychographic test, and the near head-on collision—faded from memory. Lena was the priority now and I was not going to let foolish, hellish games dictate my effectiveness as a father. Lena and Yasmin were still in Lena's room. Lena was lying on the bed and Yasmin was sitting at its foot.

"I have the medicine."

"Great," said Yasmin. "Give it to her while I wring out this hand towel and get a new one with fresh water."

"Sure."

Yasmin walked out with the hand towel which had been on Lena's brow. I sat at the foot of the bed and began reading the directions on the bottle. The girl was in pain, I saw. She moaned and groaned, and I tried to comfort her, telling her everything was going to be all right, but I did not believe it myself.

First, it was Tyra. Then, Herbert Podrey had died. What about all the other subjects on which I had performed psychographic tests over the course of A.E.

Phrenology's existence? A slew of deaths may have taken place as a result of the tests, my practice, A.E. Phrenology, and I. There was Isabella Inglewood who, following her test had asked if I had a copy of *Elements of Phrenology* so she could study and learn a little more about the science. I said I did but the book was at my home, and we made an arrangement to meet at a small diner called Lawrence's the following morning, so I could give the book to her. I went to Lawrence's the following morning, as we had agreed, but Isabella Inglewood did not show up at the agreed upon time. She missed the date. She stiffed me, I thought, but as I sat on Lena's bed it occurred to me what had happened, the reason she missed our date that morning at Lawrence's was for a more dire and terminal reason. There was Rich Ferguson, who had forgotten his checkbook on my desk following his psychographic test. I looked on the inside of the checkbook and saw his address in the top left corner of a blank check. The following morning, I went to the address, knocked on the door, and waited for a minute, but nobody answered the door. I rang the doorbell and knocked again, but Rich Ferguson did not answer. He was absent from the home or busy inside, I gathered, and slipped the checkbook into the slot in the door meant for mail. Rich Ferguson's inability to answer the door, it stuck me now, was because of something much more conclusive. There was Earl Klein, who had asked me if I knew of a Jungian psychologist who was competent with the Myers-Brigs Type Indicator. He was interested in partaking in the personality inventory questionnaire. I told him I would look into it and would call him the following morning with a psychologist's contact information. I did as I promised, called Earl Klein on his home phone. The call went to the answering machine. I called a second time and the call

174

went to the answering machine. An hour later, I tried again, but the call went to the answering machine. There were many more subjects on whom I had administered psychographic tests over the ten years I had been practicing phrenology. Their Fate may well have been the same as Tyra's, Herbert Podrey's, and soon my own.

I unscrewed the bottle of the cough medicine, pinching its edges and twisting off the plastic top. Lena had become quiet. I poured a dose of the cough medicine into the plastic cup and turned to her. Her eyes were wide as saucers and the whites of her eyes were not white at all. They were red and sweat glistened on her brow.

"Allen dies." The words came out of her mouth, croaked as if from a cold-blooded animal. "Why does Allen have to die?"

"I'm not going anywhere." It struck me Lena was talking about me. Her words, "*Allen dies,*" could only mean my time was near. It could only have applied to me, her reference to "Allen." It was quite disconcerting, first Lenny Amaranth's prediction of Herbert Podrey's death, "*He's going to jump out the window. He's going to jump out the window,*" and now Lena's prediction of mine, "*Allen dies. Why does Allen have to die?*" A shiver again coursed up my spine like a cold finger. It was Fate which was creating this maelstrom of non-chronological predictions. No, it was that which operated through Fate. It was that which controlled it and used it as a means to an end.

"You have to take this medicine," I said. Lena reached out a hand, I handed over the medicine, and like a big girl she downed it without a grimace.

Yasmin came in then, walked over to the side of the bed, and placed the damp hand towel on Lena's brow. "How is she?"

"She's just taken the medicine."

"Good," said Yasmin. "Good." Turning to Lena and stroking her hair, she said, "It'll all be over soon, dear. It'll all be over soon." And I could not quite avoid thinking Yasmin's words applied to me, too. "Go to bed, Allen, if you want. I'll stay with her a little bit longer."

I nodded, squeezed Lena's knee, and rose from the bedside. I kissed Yasmin on the head, turned out of Lena's bedroom, and went into my own bedroom. I lay down, recalling the taillights of the car speeding away towards town center, the Chevy facing in the backwards direction, a dead man in the driver's seat. I recalled Lena's words, *"Allen dies. Why does Allen have to die?"* and I recalled A.E. Phrenology and the psychograph within my office. Outside, the branches of an oak tree casted shadows which looked like old fingers onto the window pane. Once more, the chill of mortality and of danger and finality went up my spine. If those shadows on the window pane were old fingers, they were the fingers of the opaque cognizance which had come alive through my practice, and they had followed me home.

***

The following morning, the fingers on the window pane were gone and replaced with refracted sunlight. It looked cool outside, typical for an autumn morning, the air having a visible and transparent crispness to it. I swung my feet out of bed and performed my morning rituals—brushed my teeth, took a shower—and then I slipped on a polo shirt and pair of khakis. Downstairs, Yasmin had prepared a pot of coffee. I poured a cup and sat at the kitchen table. "How is Lena? Is she up yet?"

Yasmin said, "No, she isn't. She had a long night. I wouldn't be surprised if she slept until noon."

"Me neither." I took a sip of coffee. "Could you be a doll and fix me up some toast?"

Yasmin said, "I'll fix you up some toast under one condition."

I raised my eyebrows from behind my coffee cup.

"Replace these tiles within the week and I'll do more than just fix you up some toast. I'll grow the wheat and make fresh bread myself. It's been too long. These tiles have been broken for months."

She was right. In the corner of the kitchen there were quite a few cracked tiles. Yasmin had been asking me for months to replace them, but I never got around to it. Now, she was putting forth an ultimatum, and I was not upset. The tiles needed changing and I did want some toast. "It will be done."

"Thanks," Yasmin said, and she went over to the bread box, took out a couple slices of bread, and put them in the toaster oven.

"You don't have to grow a wheat field, though."

She smiled, went to the refrigerator, and took out the butter. I sipped my coffee and thought about Lena, not so much her words of the previous night, but more so of her fever. That today could have been the last day of my life did occur to me, but I was not going to let it show. I was not going to be afraid. My theory was the following—whatever it was that was killing off my subjects fed off of fear, or insecurity in some form. For that reason, I pushed the notion to the peripheries of thought and stuck to what was happening at present— the toast in the toaster oven beginning to smell up the kitchen, the steaming cup of coffee in my hand, Yasmin washing a dish, Lena upstairs sleeping like a foal—and I circulated throughout these elements, avoiding the one which, by any logical state of mind, should have been occupying my thoughts in full: mortality. The toaster oven popped and brought me out of my reverie. Yasmin went over to the toaster oven in the corner of the kitchen with the broken tiles, took the toast out of the toaster oven, and put them on the plate she had been cleaning. Then, she smeared some butter on them and brought over the plate.

"More coffee?"

"Sure."

Yasmin took my cup, which was now emptied of coffee, and went to the coffee machine to fill it up. I took a bite of toast and relished its earthy and dark flavor with the butter making it a bit sweet, a perfect conglomeration of flavors which made it a hearty breakfast around the world. Yasmin came back, put the cup of coffee on the kitchen table, and sat down. She, too, had a cup of coffee, and slurped on it like she always did, until it cooled off.

"I'll look into those tiles today."

"Good, Allen. Thanks. It'll give me some peace of mind."

"I'm glad." I took the last bite of toast and downed my coffee. A mom and pop, do-it-yourself store called Elver's Hardware Emporium was close by town center where, the night before, I had picked up the cough medicine. It was there I would ask Elver, who owned the place and with whom I was acquainted, what would be the best option in terms of retiling the kitchen floor. He seemed knowledgeable the time I went in to ask about paint for the bedrooms. That was four or five years ago. How he had managed since who knew? Things had a way of changing in a matter of seconds. Life, its momentum, turned on a dime. And, sometimes, people did not even know it. "I'm going to head over to Elver's to check out tiles and get an estimate."

"Don't make any decisions," said Yasmin, and I knew this was coming. "Don't make any decisions. I want to be there when you choose the tile. Just get an approximate number. We'll take it from there."

"Sure." I got up, put my dish and coffee cup in the sink, and gave the kitchen a rough estimate in terms of its square footage. At a glance, it was fifty, sixty square feet. A good size, which would cost some coin, but that was a non-issue since the inheritance from Yasmin's side of the family and some good investments which had panned out. We were sitting pretty. "I'll be back in an hour at most." I kissed Yasmin on the head and was out the door.

The Chevy took me past the place where I had skidded out the previous night. Four skewed, uneven marks made by the Chevy's wheels looked like outlandish calculus parabolas, overlapping and crossing each other. The yield sign was still lying on the grass. Nobody had picked it up and I doubted anybody would until some conscientious policeman or other authority figure put the word in that somebody had taken down the lone sign out toward town center, right around Binley Street. Passing by the spot, my eyes caught the fuel gauge and the needle was at a quarter tank. I would stop and fill up the tank before going to Elver's Hardware Emporium. The twenty-four-hour pharmacy was on my right. I passed it and went into the gas station beside it. I pulled up to the pump and got out of the driver's seat. I took out my debit card, unscrewed the gas tank, and put the card into the slot and waited. Nothing happened. I slid the card into the slot again and the machine was not responding. Something was wrong with the magnet on the inside of the card slot or something was wrong with the magnetic strip on the back of my card. I hoped the former was the case. I screwed the cap back onto the gas tank and went inside the gas station. There were few people inside the gas station—a man in line paying for a case of beer, a woman looking at the lottery tickets inside the plexiglass countertop, a boy and girl and who must have been their mother perusing the candy aisle. I got in line behind the man paying for beer and the woman looking at the lottery tickets. Behind the cashier's shoulder, on his left-hand side, behind the checkout counter—the counter was an island around which was more candy, newspapers, postcards on a rotating rack, and buckets of ice containing beverages—something caught my eye. Opposite the side of the cash register, behind the island checkout counter, a small shelf was chalk full of cups, coffee cups nobody had any interest in, not until today, not until I walked in and saw a coffee cup, light brown in color, and it had something written on it in white letters, which seemed to call to me from across the entire gas station. I left my spot in line, knowing the boy and girl and who must have been their mother were going to go ahead of me, but what was the rush? I walked around the checkout counter, past the rotating rack of postcards, over to the shelf, which was about chest high, and looked at the coffee cup which had gotten my attention by some form of gravitation. It read:

2nd Law of Thermodynamics
Energy in the Universe available for work is
Decaying
"Cosmos to Chaos"
Laws are Meant to be Broken!

The words shone from the light brown coffee cup with ambience, the white lettering taking on a fourth dimension which seemed to escape the bounds of simple depth-width-height, taking the cup's significance to a new level. I picked up the coffee cup and it was smooth, almost weightless in my hand. I retraced my steps, crossing again the gas station, went past the rotating rack of postcards, and got back in line, the coffee cup in hand. The boy and girl and who must have been their mother were finishing up at the counter, getting their change. Then, they turned and exited the gas station, and I took their place in front of the cash register.

"Pump 5 is out of order. It isn't taking my card. Can we try here?"

"Sure, how much you want to put in?"

"Put in twenty bucks. And I want to buy this coffee cup, too."

The cashier took the cup, scanned it, and handed it back to me. I swiped my card and the twenty dollars for gas and the price of the coffee cup showed up, itemized on the screen. It read accepted, I thanked the cashier, and went outside back to pump 5. I put the coffee cup which read **"Cosmos to Chaos"** in the front seat and put twenty dollars' worth of gas in the car, then headed towards Elver's Hardware Emporium. Elver's Hardware Emporium was a short drive from the gas station, right across the street, in fact, diagonal, and I thought how many ways I could die in such a short distance. Collision, explosion, brain aneurism. But, nothing quite caught ahold. Nothing quite instilled fear in me. In fact, I felt quite invincible pulling out of the gas station, the coffee cup in the passenger seat beside me, which also read **Laws are Meant to be Broken!**

Elver, it turned out, was sharp as a tack, and he helped me out, gave me an estimate on retiling the kitchen floor. Yasmin was a stickler for quality products and so was I. The estimate turned out to be less than expected, however, and that added even more to my confidence. Two cups of coffee in me, a couple slices of toast, my new acquisition, the coffee cup, had me feeling elevated. Almost foolish, I thought. Perhaps, rather than bad composure, like Herbert Podrey had had upon learning of his low sublimity result; and rather than absentmindedness, as was Tyra's flaw on which Fate had fed; perhaps rather than these traits, traits which were blatant and easy to capitalize on, Fate or the opaque cognizance would capitalize on my over confidence. It seemed all too the case. I needed to check myself, have composure, relax myself so I could avoid falling into some trap, like a lumbering bear stepping on a wrought iron jaw set by the shadowy hand which had followed me home from A.E. Phrenology.

My nerves settled as I passed the tire marks again, the tire marks I had put there, and the leveled yield sign. The estimate with a number not too staggering was in my pocket. With luck, Lena would be up and about. With luck, she would be better. With luck, it was just a twenty-four-hour thing, the fever having abated, Lena back up and running like nothing had ever happened, like she had not, the prior night, spoken words which may have been a nail in her old man's casket, *"Allen dies. Why does Allen have to die?"* and my response, *"I'm not going anywhere,"* as if I had any control over the situation, as if my composure or my over confidence even played a part, as if the events of the next few months were malleable. In fact, what was happening was far out of my reach; it was far out of reach for any man. The uncontrollable force which sped onward, unbound and unabated by anything, was sovereign. What was going to happen was going to happen, and my own cognizance of its schemes as a mere observant, who had no control of the future and who had no control of the present, was ineffectual. I was swelling with the waves, dipping into the troughs and peaking at the crests of living, moving Fate. What I had planned was not taken into account by the opposing cognizance, the cognizance which wanted my life and had already threatened it. What I had planned was a non-issue. What did matter and what would happen was the will of the opaque cognizance which resided within A.E. Phrenology. I, unbeknownst to me at the time, was powerless.

Back at the house, I got out of the Chevy and locked the doors. It was noon and, once inside, I could hear Lena talking to Yasmin in the kitchen. She seemed healthy. The fever must have been a twenty-four-hour cold because her voice was sharp as a trumpet. She was saying something about the trees in the backyard as I walked into kitchen, and I could not help but think about the gnarled, black hand outside the window last night when she was in bed sick with a 104° F fever, having just intuited her old man's death.

"Photosynthesis, it's called. That's how the trees grow. It's everywhere. It's how they eat."

"Good afternoon," I said, and Lena was startled by my entrance.

"Daddy!" she said and came over and hugged me. I did not know if she remembered what she had said the previous night and decided I did not care. Better off she did not remember, and I would not reminder her.

"How did you sleep?" I asked.

"I slept normal," she said. I patted her head and went over to the cupboard which held all the coffee cups. I put the coffee cup which read "Cosmos to Chaos" inside of it and shut the cupboard.

"That's good," I said, and I took a seat beside Yasmin. "Feeling better?"

"Yeah," Lena said.

"That's good," I said, and got up and grabbed the newspaper from the countertop. Lena—she had become interested in science, earth sciences, biology, and chemistry—went on talking to Yasmin about school as I flipped through the newspaper pages to the sports section. An article was on the front page of the sports section and read of a game between the Baltimore Orioles and the New York Yankees taking place that very night though it was off season and the proceeds were going to research. I decided to call Lenny and Raleigh and suggest we go to the game. It was not the game I was interested in, however. The Yankees could have won, and I would have felt just as well as if the Orioles had won. The reason I wanted to go to the game was because I wanted to tempt the tempter. I wanted to put myself in closer reach of Fate and see if it would squeeze. That I was powerless had not occurred to me. The confidence I had felt at Elver's Hardware Emporium was driving me onward, and I wanted to see what was in store for me. I wanted to be sure I, in fact, was marked for death, and as of yet I was not convinced in full. The drunkard had almost hit me head-on the night before, but that was not a reason to consider oneself destined for early death by some supernatural hand. I wanted to know without question. And going to the game where anything could happen—I could be murdered, shot or stabbed, I could have an embolism, the foul line light fixtures could fall on my head and shatter my cranium—seemed a way to tempt the tempter, a pompous way to establish dominance. It occurred to me, while I was sitting at the kitchen table beside Yasmin, Lena's words somewhere in the distance talking about sunlight and leaves and chlorophyll, I was playing a game not too far from devilry. Within myself, the compelling notion to compete with something ethereal as Fate pushed me towards a boundary, which would be breached by the new year. It was present yet subtle, repressed and evasive. It was coy. I said, "The Orioles are playing tonight." Lena stopped speaking. "They're playing the Yankees. I'm going to invite Lenny Amaranth and Raleigh out to the game, if that's okay with you."

Yasmin said, "I don't see why not."

I got up, put the newspaper in the trashcan, and placed a phone call to Lenny Amaranth, then to Raleigh Durman telling them of the off-season matchup and the charity cause. Both said it would be fun, and I told each of them I would pick them up at six-thirty and we would head into Baltimore.

Three o'clock came and then five o'clock did, and I could not stop thinking about Herbert Podrey's funeral, his house with its hydrangeas and his desultory wife and the geometric patterns his son had painted, on the refrigerator door. If tonight was my last night alive I would go out in style and in good company.

Six-twenty came, I kissed Yasmin on the head, kissed Lena on hers, and made way over to Lenny Amaranth's. I did not go to his house often, and I realized the last time I had been over to Lenny's was when I dropped him off following Ebberfield Hospital South and his bout with retrograde amnesia. I was knocking on his door, in recollection of Lenny Amaranth's sobs and his face in his hands, having just intuited Herbert Podrey's death, and I felt sorry for Lenny Amaranth and for Herbert, too, thinking I was the culprit or rather the device the opaque cognizance used to deliver the mark upon my subjects, or its victims.

Then, Lenny Amaranth opened the door and my angst and my pity evaporated. Lenny had on his New York Yankees baseball cap. He clapped me on the shoulder and we were off to Raleigh's, which was toward the freeway.

"I was going to watch the game on the T.V., but watching it in person is even better," Lenny said, and I agreed. "Ballpark dog, beer. It's better than Gretchen's cooking. Sometimes I don't know why I'm marrying her."

I shot him a glance.

"I'm just kidding. Really. Her cooking is actually pretty good. You should come over sometime."

"I don't see why not," I said, and I thought I would if I made it through the next few days. "Yasmin would want to come, and Lena, too. Yasmin and Gretchen always hit it off."

"That's true," said Lenny Amaranth. "By all means, bring them along." By then we were pulling into Raleigh Durman's house and he was standing outside waving a Baltimore Orioles cap over his head. Raleigh got in the backseat of the car and within ten minutes we were on the freeway headed towards Baltimore.

Raleigh said, "We'll buy tickets from some guy who's scalping them. We could haggle and if the guy's dumb we'll get 'em cheap. We could save five dollars at least. Five dollars saved means an extra beer by the end of the game."

We cruised by exit ramp after exit ramp, and with every passing minute the significance of my decision to bring Lenny and Raleigh out to the game only to tempt whatever it was that was systematic and killing my subjects to kill me became all too intense. The Chevy coasted over blacktop and the white lines which differentiated lanes passed by speedy and methodical.

Lenny and Raleigh had quieted down. They had been talking, but I had not been listening. I was too wrapped up in my own thoughts, my fearlessness of Fate, or the opaque cognizance. But, it occurred to me I was afraid. Somewhere deep down, as the shallow, fluidic sound of rubber wheels on blacktop serenaded me, I knew there would be pain. I knew another attempt on my life would be made. But, I did not know when and I did not know how.

"That's our exit, Allen," said Lenny.

"Oh, yeah," I said, and turned sharp into the right-hand lane and onto the exit ramp. Oriole Park at Camden Yards was not far off. We would pick up some cheap tickets and we would have beer and ballpark dogs. I knew that. But, I did not know if this strange sensation of somebody over my shoulder would abate. As I walked up towards the ticket booths, the Chevy parked and locked, Lenny Amaranth and Raleigh at my sides, the presence was felt more than ever. It was dark and hanging over my head like wool from a black sheep. Raleigh bought three tickets from a guy close by the ticket booths and we walked into the ballpark. It was a calamity. People were filing onto escalators, lining up at concessions, and coming in and out of the gift shop where they sold tee-shirts, baseballs, and foam hands you could wear and wave when the Orioles got a hit or a run. The coffee cup I had picked up at the gas station in the morning surfaced in thought—"Cosmos to Chaos"—and I thought whoever had invented the 2nd Law of Thermodynamics had got it right. They may even have had Oriole Park at Camden Yards in mind, but I doubted it, and stepped into line with the rest of the fans who were here to see the Orioles win, save Lenny Amaranth who would give away his last rights to see the

Yankees go through another dynasty like they had in the 1990s and who was a Yankees fan to his stark, yankee bones. Our tickets were on the upper level, but I had no qualms with that. Neither did Lenny, I presumed, and Raleigh had been the one who bought the tickets, so he had no problems sitting in the nose bleeds as long as they had a guy yelling "Cold beer, here. Cold beer," without end and selling wet cans of the stuff out of a cooler full of ice. We ascended the levels until we got to the uppermost level where our seats were located. Then, we walked around the oblong walkway which surrounded the baseball field, seven hundred feet skyward, and found the section which matched the section on our ticket stubs; we walked through into the open-air ballpark. The baseball diamond was down far below, crisp in the distance. The crowd had begun to assemble and the clock, which also read the run count when the games were in full swing, was ticking backward from the fifteen-minute mark. Lenny was in front, and then it was Raleigh and then me. Lenny took us even higher into the nosebleeds and we took a seat five rows from the uppermost. Looking down at the field from this height was spectacular and made me think about the sheer numbers of people who watched this sport all over the country. It made me think about the motivations of these people, why they came here and why they were so happy to watch the Orioles play. It seemed to me it was something along the lines of contentment. The people came into Oriole Park at Camden Yards night in and night out and watched the Orioles play baseball because it made them feel alive. It made them feel significant, taking part in something larger than themselves, larger than life. Then, I reflected on my own motivation for coming to Oriole Park at Camden Yards, and it occurred to me it was not far from suicide. I knew full well I was tempting the tempter, but the cool air at this height was brisk, and the chattering crowd was thrumming with high expectations, and I did not know if it was the temperature this evening, the bounding and rebounding chatter of the crowd making me apprehensive, or if it was the subconscious notion I was in danger, sitting fifth from the top row at Oriole Park at Camden Yards and thinking about Fate, Lenny Amaranth's words at Ebberfield Hospital South, and Lena's delirious, foretelling words of the previous night.

"Allen?" Raleigh said, beside me. "Allen?"

I turned to him. "What?"

"I said we really lucked out this time, don't you think? Nothing but bird shit and dust up here."

It occurred to me Raleigh was being sarcastic. What else was new? "You bought the tickets," I said. "This doesn't bother me, though. It's rather pleasant." Raleigh clapped my shoulder and smiled, and I tried to smile back. Then, he turned to Lenny Amaranth who was on his right and they started talking about something I could not hear. But, that was all right. I wanted to stay quiet. The drive in, the number of people present, and the height at which we were sitting had taken away the over-confidence I had had in Elver's Hardware Emporium, the over-confidence which had followed me around all day. It had been replaced with an ominous shadow, a foreboding notion that coming here was foolish. I knew in my gut this entanglement with the opaque cognizance or A.E. Phrenology or even myself, or all three components as one omnipotent entity, was far from over. I mused just how long I would stay alive and how long I would retain breath in my lungs. The night had cooled off quite a bit and the starless night shone dark through the clouds. The music started. The game was underway.

Raleigh bought the first round of drinks at the beginning of the first inning. He handed me a beer and then drank his down to about the halfway point. In this way, Raleigh, Lenny Amaranth, and I watched the top of the first become the bottom of the first, the first inning becoming the second inning, then the second the third and so on until the seventh inning stretch, when "Take Me Out to the Ballgame" came on, and everybody stood up and pulled their arms behind their backs, their elbows up in the air over their heads like chicken wings, and stretched their hamstrings, too. At this point, we had gone through four rounds of beer and it was my turn to buy the next round. I flagged down the guy yelling, "Cold beer, here. Cold beer," at the top of the eighth inning and bought a round of beers for Raleigh, Lenny, and I. Again, as the beer was drank, I thought of the coffee cup—"Cosmos to Chaos"—looking down at the baseball diamond and thinking if the American pastime were something so well ordered as baseball, intuited by some revolutionary in the sporting macrocosm, what was really happening when a 102 mile an hour fastball was pitched and the batter swung and made contact, hitting it up into the stands, when the crack was heard all the way up in the nosebleeds, the ball and bat making contact and a split second later you heard it. In that space, in the millisecond between what your eyes told you was real and what your ears told you was real was where it resided, the force which was claiming lives, one after the other, following their visits to A.E. Phrenology. Somewhere in between the law of gravity and the speed of sound, in between the electrostatic law and the speed of light, it resided; and I thought of the remaining line on the cup of coffee, the bottom most line—Laws are Meant to be Broken! I would try. There was an underlying force at work, a force which had killed Tyra and Herbert Podrey, and I would try to break its cycle. If I failed, I died. But, if I triumphed, A.E. Phrenology and the coincidental occurrences which had taken place following the goings on within A.E. Phrenology would be just that—coincidental and not supernatural. As the ninth inning came to a close, I looked up at the scoreboard and saw the Orioles had come out on top of the Yankees 9-8. And what was even better was I was still alive.

Raleigh, Lenny, and I got up from our seats and went down to the escalators. It was all very disorienting, the calamitous filing out of well over seven thousand people, everybody shimmying onto the escalator and into elevators, and somewhere in the miasma Lenny pulled on my shirt sleeve and got my attention.

He said, "I didn't want to ask you while the game was going on. We were having so much fun." We were descending level after level, riding the escalator down to the exit of Oriole Park at Camden Yards, and I wondered what Lenny was talking about. "I didn't want to ask you up there, but now that the game's over I wanted to ask you." He leaned back onto to the escalator's moving hand rail. "I want you to be the best man at my wedding. How about it?"

I would be lying if I said I was not taken aback, but, at the same time, his asking me to be best man at his wedding was not at all surprising. Lenny and I had a closer relationship than Lenny and Raleigh had, and being the best man at Lenny's wedding was an obvious yes. His asking me was inevitable, and it made sense to assent to the request even though by default, if something were to happen to me, Raleigh might well have to step in and assume the role. I made the decision to be his best man, however, knowing I would stay alive at least until the wedding, which, as Lenny had told Raleigh and I at Johnny Hovan's the Friday before the Herbert Podrey appointment, would take place in December. "Lenny, it would be my pleasure. I would have it no other way."

Lenny Amaranth clapped me on the shoulder and laughed. "Great," he said. "Great. I knew you would say yes." We were off the escalators and walking out of the ballpark when Lenny said, "Everybody's invited, of course. I wouldn't be surprised if Gretchen chooses Yasmin as one her bridesmaids."

We were off, headed northbound towards home. Lenny and Raleigh were quiet and so was I. The radio was off, and I was listening to the fluidic rushing of tire on blacktop again. This time, it was not so foreboding. That Lenny wanted me to be his best man had perked me up. It gave me a reason to combat that which was threatening me. Good thing, too, because neither of us would relent. I took the exit ramp and made a right to go towards Raleigh's house. He was in the back seat with his eyes closed. When we were on his street, I woke him, and it seemed as though he had forgotten where he was.

Then, he said, "Home. Thank you for the ride and the invitation to the game, Allen. I'll see you at Johnny Hovan's on Friday?"

"You bet."

"Good," he said. "See you there, Amaranth." He got out, shut the door, and Lenny and I were off to Lenny's. Lenny's was past my house, so I would have to double back to get home, but it was all right. I enjoyed Lenny's company even in a small car like the Chevy and learned to appreciate times with him. Deep down I knew Lenny had some intuition. It was evident in his words while he was a patient at Ebberfield Hospital South; and I thought maybe if I kept my ears open he would say something that could save my life. But instead, he said, "Thanks for the ride, Allen. Have a good night," when we got to his place, and I felt rather sheepish.

"No problem, Lenny. You, too. See you on Friday."

Lenny Amaranth nodded his head, shut the door, and walked up to his front door. I backed out and drove off before I saw him enter his house, not knowing the exchange we just had was damned well close to being the last exchange we would ever have. "See you on Friday," I had said, thinking the three of us would meet up at Johnny Hovan's at eight-thirty like we always did, but that was not the case.

Yasmin was in bed by the time I arrived home. She was lying in bed on her back and was covered with the sheet. The coverlet was bunched beside her on her right-hand side. She lay undisturbed as I looked on and I watched her chest move up and down and her hair maintain the eternal movement it had. She sighed, her eyes fluttered open, and her irises, which were brown and sedative, looked upon me with ease.

"You're home," she said.

"I'm home. I'm taking a shower."

"Don't," she said. "Come to bed."

I lay down on the bed beside her. She turned toward me, her bosom almost spilling out of her cotton nightgown. She started to caress my arms with her fingernails. My hair stood up on my arms.

"I've been waiting for you to come home," she said. She gave me a little kiss on the corner of my mouth and asked me if I wanted to get naked. Within seconds, Yasmin was lying on top of me. We had each other late into the night. Once in the shower, I mused this may well be the last night I would ever have sex with her.

The night of the Orioles-Yankees game took place on Tuesday, and Yasmin and I went down to Elver's Hardware Emporium to pick out tiles for the kitchen the following day. At around nine o'clock the following morning, she and I went down to Elver's Hardware Emporium, and by noon she had picked out a tile, and we placed the order. By one o'clock, we were back home, and I was having coffee out of my "Cosmos to Chaos" Laws are Meant to be Broken! coffee cup.

"I hope we made the right choice," said Yasmin, talking about the tiles. She had picked a sanded white which would contrast the blue countertops.

"You made the right choice, Yasmin. Don't second guess yourself," I said, and then drank a bit of coffee. Elver had a connection just outside of town who had a stockpile of tiles, and Elver said the tiles would be delivered tomorrow morning, Thursday morning, and then they would start to tear up the old kitchen tiles to replace them with the sanded whites ones. I was elated I was not the one who had to lie the tiles, but I kept the elation to myself. In two hours, Lena would get home from school and the three of us would have dinner around six. My foresight did not go past dinner time and that was for the best. I had it figured out that thinking too far ahead opened avenues for defeat when dealing with mortality. You tended to lose sight of what mattered when you looked too far ahead, and you started to lose rationality, too. But, as I sat drinking my coffee, I thought I was already there. My hypothesis that a cosmic murderer had been unleashed *vis a vis* A.E. Phrenology, I mused, was rather irrational. There was no foundation on which to base the assumption, other than an observation—the correlation between Tyra's and Herbert Podrey's deaths and the psychographic tests—

making it plausible. There was no concrete evidence. All conceptions regarding the supernatural were insubstantial, but still I remained in between believing and unbelieving as a skeptic. I was not convinced in full my theory was correct. Anybody who would be convinced it was with so little actual evidence may well be called psychotic. For this reason, I kept my convictions to myself and waited for reality to unfold.

I finished my cup of coffee and went outside onto the deck. I sat down in my usual chair, the same chair in which I was sitting when Lena approached me, handed me the photo of Tyra at the Niagara Falls, and then placed her hand on my chest, insinuating Tyra lived on within me, all hours following Herbert Podrey's funeral, the day before I exacted a psychographic test on myself. Now, rather than night, it was day, and the oak trees swayed in the wind and there were sparrows dipping and diving from limb to limb. There was a wakefulness in the light green grass and in the trees' viridian leaves, too, which made me attentive and thoughtful. It was as though an observant were observing the observer, who was I, and I could feel manifold eyes on me. There was the tempter, the observer, and I, and I mused I embodied the tripartition. I was tempting the tempter and I was observing the observer and likewise the tempter was tempting me, and the observer was observing me. It was all very simplistic like the way the breeze courses through the tree canopy and moves the leaves or the way a notion or ideal can be contagious as laughter. The yard behind our home was very quiet and there was no laughter. There was only the systematic convolution of the elements and the beating of my heart.

***

The following morning, at nine o'clock, the doorbell rang and a man in a blue jumpsuit was standing on the porch. "Name's Frank Enberg. Is this the Earnhardt residence?"

"It is," I said. I had already had a cup of coffee and breakfast and was expecting the deliveryman to show up with the tiles we had ordered the day prior at Elver's Hardware Emporium. "You're from Elver's Hardware Emporium?" I said, already knowing the answer.

"Yes, from Elver's Hardware Emporium," said Frank Enberg. "We have a delivery of sanded white tiles. Come on outside, take a look, see if they're the tile you ordered."

"Sure," I said, and went outside, closing the door behind me. Frank Enberg took me to the van across the side of which was painted Elver & Enberg Inc. in blue letters. We went to the back of the van and he opened the barn-style doors.

"Sanded 10x10 tile, quantity one hundred tiles, coming to the grand total"—he checked his clipboard which had been under his arm, and then told me the price.

"That's right. Sanded 10x10, one hundred tiles. That's right."

"Good," said Enberg. "I'll unload these tiles into—where?—the garage?"

"Sure," I said. "Let me open it for you." I went into the house and into the garage, and then pushed the button which opened the garage door. Sunlight slipped in under the garage door as it was opening, and then Enberg and the Elver & Enberg Inc. van came into view. I went outside and approached the van. Enberg was already in the back of the van readying himself to pick up the stack of tiles and transport them into the garage. The tiles looked heavy. I could see it in his face it was no small feat picking them up. He took five tiles into his grip and walked towards the garage. Then, I, too, picked up five tiles and headed towards the garage. Frank Enberg was lowering himself, using his knees to lower himself, in order to place down the tiles. I was right behind him and followed suit. Bending at the knee, I placed down the five tiles and felt a bead of sweat already course down the side of my face. We had to do this a few more times, carry the hefty load of five tiles to the garage, bend at the knees, and place down the tiles, and then begin the installation process. Enberg was to rip up the tiles already inside and without help. I thought to myself how long this process would take and decided it would not be finished by sundown. Enberg was carrying another five tiles in towards the garage and I took five in my own grip. Then, Enberg, bending at the knees placed down the tiles, and I did the same. His phone rang, and he stepped aside to answer it. He was muttering something to who must have been a client or maybe Elver. I went behind the van to take the next five tiles and bring them into the garage. Picking them up, I noticed this immediate stack of tiles was heavier, or maybe it was heavier only to me. I thought it was just me because as I took my first ten steps towards the garage I felt as though I had been stabbed through the arm. My head became hot. There was pressure in my chest, and as I bended at the knees I felt all the blood rush to my head, the pain on the inside of my left arm was more than ever, and I started losing consciousness. My head started to spin; and I collapsed onto the garage floor and blacked out.

All I recall was black. It was a boundless space in which thought was only the electrified circuitry of the brain. I did not exist. My thoughts, identity, my name, profession, family, the names of my wife and child, where I was and what I was doing, were not recalled. Sensations in my arms, legs, and body had dissolved. The only part I remember was the black, boundless space becoming filled with the colorful internal electric firings off of the brain, and they were disorienting. The geometry which was drawn by Herbert Podrey's son and which was taped to the refrigerator door in the Podrey household on W Beverly Road I had seen the day of Herbert Podrey's funeral surfaced, and the vision of the exact shapes escaped me just as they were taking on definition in my eyes.

I woke to Yasmin standing over me. Frank Enberg was on the phone. Yasmin had splashed a glass of water in my face. I was soaked. The cold water and my hot skin were charged with sensitivity. Steam was not rising from my skin, but if it were I would not have been surprised. I grumbled something supposed to be words.

"He's alive!"

"He's alive," I heard Enberg say into the phone. "Okay," he said into the phone, and then hung up. He walked over to us, Yasmin hovering over me and I, lying on the garage floor, burning alive like I was being cooked over an open flame; and then Enberg said, "They'll be here in a few minutes."

He was talking about the ambulance, but I could not comprehend that, not after the pain and the heat, the sharp yet dull pain and the searing heat which was licking my forehead. I lay on the garage floor, knowing another attempt had been made on my life. That which was within A.E. Phrenology, call it Fate, call living, breathing death, had once again struck. "Water," I tried to say, but only a grumble came out. The water was not to drink. I was not able to swallow water. My throat was burning like hot coals and had closed up. It wanted to splash it in my face, which was still a frying pan lying

198

on a burner set on high. The pain had receded. Then, I heard the sirens in the distance.

Yasmin said, "Water?"

I nodded. She came back with a glass of water and I sat up, taking the glass and splashing the water in my face. The heat, too, was receding. I licked my lips and swallowed a bit of the water. My throat opened up and the pain was gone. I was anxious, nervous, and rather angry. I took a deep breath. The lungs inflated with autumnal air. The sirens were closer now and I attempted getting to my feet, but it was too trying. I sat on my hindquarters with my forearms resting on my knees, and I thought I was going to die. My time was limited. I might as well start saying my goodbyes. I should make a call to White Egret Funeral Home and buy a plot nearby Herbert Podrey. We would be two victims of a cosmological, anomalous murderer. Goodbye sweet world, goodbye Yasmin, goodbye Lena, Lenny, Raleigh. Goodbye Cathy, faithful barmaid at Johnny Hovan's. It's been good. Then, the ambulance pulled up in front of our house, two EMTs came out on either side of the ambulance, dressed in blue scrubs, and the EMTs took a stretcher out from the back of the ambulance. They came over to us, lowered the stretcher, and transferred me onto the stretcher. They raised the stretcher and began taking vitals. My blood pressure was high and so was my respiration. My pulse was good, however. They asked Yasmin if she would like to come back to the hospital. "Yes," she said. "Yes, I do. Ride in the back?"

"Yes, ride in the back, Mrs. Earnhardt." The two EMTs transferred me over to the ambulance and lifted me in. Yasmin was talking to Frank Enberg. Then, she got in and we were off. The EMT in the back with us hooked me up to a heart monitor and set an IV. I listened to the tone, which repeated, and which was the very action taking place within me, keeping me alive, transposed into harmonics. "I'm no doctor," he said. "But, it looks to me you may have suffered from a heart attack." The words did not affect me, "*You may have suffered from a heart attack,*" but what did affect me was not knowing what would happen next, or where or how. My life was coming to the end of the line. I knew this, but I was powerless over the knowledge. I knew that now. The confidence I felt inside Elver's Hardware Emporium was a delusion of grandeur. In the back of the ambulance, mortality was present as ever, more present, in fact, than it was at Herbert Podrey's home, following his funeral, and the only reason it was more present here than it was there is because when mortality happens to you, you feel it, you know it; when it happens to somebody else you only empathize but it does not hit you in the gut, it does not pull at your heart and lungs begging for your attention. It was all around me, mortality that was, coursing through my veins and bounding and rebounding in my brain and circulating within me. It inflated my lungs and deflated them. That which had originated as an abstract and temporal entity had become material. It, spatial, operated within me. It took the improbable and made it probable.

The ambulance jolted as it went over the gutter into the parking lot, and I knew we had arrived at Ebberfield Hospital South. The EMT drove to the ER entrance and I was taken out of the ambulance. The harmonics chimed, incessant. They took me into the hospital and into a room. I was rather disoriented, but I had a vague understanding of where I was in terms of the layout of the hospital. The room in which Lenny Amaranth predicted Herbert Podrey's death was down the hall, the cafeteria was in the opposite direction of that room, and it occurred to me I was hungry. A nurse came into the room, checked my vitals, and then looked at my chart. "Dr. Oliver will be in shortly," she said, and I nodded and thanked her. Yasmin was sitting on a chair and asked me if I was thirsty.

"No," I lied. Really, I was thirsty, but I did not have the energy to drink. I did not have the energy to do anything but lie on the hospital bed and think. What was I supposed to do? My life was nearing its end. I was a dead man. But, how was I supposed to tell everybody I knew I was dying soon because a cosmological hand I had instigated was taking my life, killing me, without sounding delusional? It was then I decided I would not tell anybody. When I died, I died, and people would think it was surprising, but they would not know I had known all along. They would not know I had died by my own hand, having made a death wish.

Presently, Dr. Oliver came into the room and he, too, looked at my chart. "Long time no see. You missed me that much, Mr. Earnhardt? Forgive me. I shouldn't joke in such serious circumstances. How do you feel?"

I wiggled my hand, making it look like a see-saw. "So-so."

"I expected as much. What were your sensations upon losing consciousness? Upon waking up?"

I told him of the pain in my left arm, the pressure in my chest, and the burning.

He hummed, then said, "We're going to take an EKG to check your heart spindles. I would like for you to stay here for the next two days, at least, so we can gauge how serious this is and prevent any future problems. Until then we don't know exactly what happened, but if I were to take a guess I'd say, Mr. Earnhardt, this morning you have experienced myocardial infarction, in layman terms a heart attack."

I was not surprised, and yet I was. I was not surprised for the sole factor of A.E. Phrenology and my theory that it was damned. I was surprised because I was a young man, thirty-five years of age, and healthy. If there were a dichotomy which separated the spirit and the body, this was evidence it existed. The ethereal being taking lives *vis a vis* the non-space, the space between sound and light and gravity and electrostatics, was eternal and omnipresent. The body, my body which had just fallen victim to a heart attack, as Dr. Oliver presumed, was small and ephemeral. As I lay on the hospital bed, the dichotomy, the delineation between cosmology and the material was present more than ever. I was thirsty now for something, but what I was thirsty for was not water. Really, I wanted the bottle in the bottommost drawer of the desk in my office, and I had the intention when I was released to go back to A.E. Phrenology and show the opaque cognizance, the black fingers which had followed me home, and Fate, how I felt and what I was thinking. It was not afraid, but I would make it afraid. If it wanted to take my life, it would. But, it would be taking a man who was, too, fearless. It would be taking a man who already had thrown its murderous intentions into the light, a man who had already made it vulnerable. As I lay on the hospital bed, my head throbbing, I knew somewhere the cosmic killer, too, was feeling the pain, because twice now it had failed.

Yasmin came to the bedside and stroked my hair. "Oh, Allen," she said, and I knew she, too, was thinking of mortality. I knew this very well could be one of my last moments with her. Death might have struck at any second. "Oh, Allen." She continued stroking my head. She looked at me, plaintive. "I'll get you a cup of water, Allen. That's what I'll do. And then, I'll call Lenny and

Raleigh." She said this, and for the first time since losing consciousness I was glad.

(Part Three)

For two days I lay in the hospital bed, eating fish and chicken and ham sandwiches, defrosted and prepared in mass amounts for the patients of Ebberfield Hospital South. They were tasty, but I felt as though every meal could be my last, and the notion gave the meals a tastelessness which was not tastelessness but emptiness and misfortune. Yasmin was with me throughout my time at Ebberfield Hospital South, and her presence gave me a bit to go off of in terms of morale. Lenny Amaranth and Raleigh came to the hospital the day of the heart attack and also each of the two days following the heart attack, Friday and Saturday, which were ingratiating and slow. At about three o'clock the day following the heart attack, Friday, which had me questioning the basis of humanity—how could a man wait so long for a EKG and not have tachycardia out of suppressed rage in the process?—I was taken into the room within which was the EKG, a nurse hooked me up to the machine, and suction cups were placed all over my chest and ribcage. The electrocardiograph test lasted three minutes, the nurse spoke very little, and I was wheeled back into the hospital room—they had moved me up to the third floor and I shared a room with a man who had undergone surgery, an appendectomy, I overheard—where Yasmin was waiting for my return. They wheeled me in and Yasmin got up from her chair. This time, it was her turn to kiss my head.

"How'd it go?" she said. She sat back down in her chair, I got up, and lay on the hospital bed. I could walk and moving was not painful.

"It went well. Was fairly quick once they got me in."

"Lenny and Raleigh are coming at about six o'clock," she said, and I knew they would be with me for about two hours, and then jump over to Johnny Hovan's for the usual drinks at eight-thirty.

"Good," I said, and I hoped they would bring whiskey, so I could drink with them at least in spirit. They had not and, really, I was glad. Drinking in a hospital, in front of your wife, who was worried halfway to death herself, was not appropriate behavior for somebody who had had a heart attack not forty-eight hours ago. Lenny, Raleigh, Yasmin, and I spoke a little and sat in silence, like people do in hospitals when they visit their loved ones, as if they were watching flora bloom. But that was hospitals. It took forever for something to happen and when it did you were so much closer to death. Eight o'clock rolled around and Lenny and Raleigh left for Johnny Hovan's. Yasmin stayed around until about nine o'clock, and then she went home.

Lena, Yasmin had organized, was with a classmate while the two of us were sitting waiting for the grass to grow and would be picked up by Yasmin on her return trip home. Then, the lights would turn off and I would lie in darkness waiting for the following day, a Saturday, the day on which I was to be released. As I lay there a subtle shutter of anger went up my spine—anger toward A.E. Phrenology, anger toward phrenology as a science, anger toward Fate and my seeming helplessness. I lay awake in bed, listening to the man snoring beside me who had had the appendectomy, and decided I would think of this from a more scientific basis, not on a spiritual level, not on a cosmological level, but from a literal, grounded level. Two people had died as a result of psychographic tests, and there was bound to be a third. Rather than some shadowy hand, exacting death from lofty heights or stony depths, perhaps the culprit of the twofold deaths, bound to be threefold, was faulty machinery. The psychograph itself may have been the relayer of death *vis a vis* unbalanced and unilluminated psychographic feelers, which were supposed to take the readings of mental faculties of subjects by adjusting to the subject's cranium. By some inconsistency between the brain, its electromagnetism, and the very fundaments of mechanics, the psychograph and its seeming faultiness was affecting the brain with erroneous anti-brainwaves, so to speak, and redirected one's thoughts, aspirations, and in effect Fate, bringing out the subjects' fears, insecurities, and vulnerabilities. The subjects, as an effect of this tainted machinery, were falling victim to aberrations in science and religion, that was if the brain was a proponent of science and death one of religion. I knew what I would do following my release from Ebberfield Hospital South. I had known the second Dr. Oliver presumed I had a heart attack when I lay in the hospital bed, having told him about the pain, pressure, and burning. I fell asleep with the emptiness of unknowing and the anger of helplessness.

The sun was out, piercing the blinds, and sunlight was in my eyes. Yasmin had awoken me the following morning. Breakfast was being served. I ate the breakfast of pancakes, orange juice, and coffee. "I talked to Dr. Oliver," said Yasmin. "You're being released today." I was glad but repressed my feelings of anger toward the psychograph and A.E. Phrenology. I was not going to let my anger show, and if I did people would start asking questions, and I would end up in another type of hospital if I started answering them.

"Good," I said. "Good." I had finished my pancakes, orange juice, and coffee, and my eyes were closed. Somewhere in the blackness dwelled death, but I did not know where. I did not know how to capture it and defeat it, smother it like a grease fire.

At noon, Dr. Oliver came in and looked at my chart. "You're healthy," he said. "As far as I'm concerned. You're being released today."

I said, "I know. Yasmin told me this morning."

"Your EKG came back negative. All is well. You'll be out of here by three and if all goes well I won't see you again. Regarding the same issue, that is."

I nodded. "Thank you, Doctor."

"I'm prescribing some medication called Tenormin. It's standard following heart attacks. Take it as prescribed and all will be well."

I hoped he was right. I thanked him again and he went out of the room. I lay back and hours passed, the sun reaching its zenith, its light no longer in my eyes. And then, three o'clock came and I changed into the clothes Yasmin brought from the house. I said goodbye to the man who had gotten the appendectomy—he grumbled something inaudible—and then, Yasmin and I were going down in the elevator.

"Lena's been worried about you," Yasmin said. "She's been asking about you. 'Where's daddy?' she's been saying. 'Where's daddy?' I didn't want her to see you in that condition. I told her you were on vacation."

"That's all right," I said. We stepped out into the autumn afternoon air, which had a nip to it, and went across the parking lot towards the Chevy. "I'll drive," I said, and Yasmin did not protest. I would drop her off, wait an hour, play off my apprehensiveness as if I had none, and then go to A.E. Phrenology. Once there, I would end this cycle of fatality, this slew of death once and for all. We picked up Lena from her classmate's house and she screamed as if I had been away a lifetime.

"Daddy, where were you?" she said.

"On vacation," I said, and she believed me. We were home, pulling into the driveway when Yasmin asked me what I wanted for dinner. "Steak and green beans," I said, but I did not really care. I was too preoccupied in thought by my intentions for this afternoon.

"Great," she said.

"I'll go to the store and pick up steaks and green beans," I said.

"Okay," she said, and we went inside.

I made a pot of coffee, and then I took down the "Cosmos to Chaos" coffee cup. I read the words on the cup again.

2nd Law of Thermodynamics
Energy in the Universe available for work is
Decaying
"Cosmos to Chaos"
Laws are Meant to be Broken!

The white letters were a different texture than the cup. I ran my finger over the text, which was smoother than the rest of the cup. The words seemed to relate to me and to my present situation. It could not have been more relatable. This descension of Fate was an aberration in logic and was called cosmology. What had been happening made no sense to the logical and grounded man. But, it was happening. The cosmic conception of phrenology had actualized itself into a device for death, at least in my predicament, or so it seemed. Somewhere deep down, I hoped the causation of these deaths was a malfunctioning psychograph. That a cosmological and omnipotent being was exacting wrath upon my subjects *vis a vis* the test was an idea too hard to swallow. It hurt my head thinking about it, but my head was not the ultimatum in this exchange. The ultimatum was my heart. As long as it kept beating, the cosmic death bringer had failed. This was the way I wanted to keep it. This was the ultimate goal. The coffee machine beeped. The coffee was done. I poured coffee into the coffee cup which read "Cosmos to Chaos." The coffee was drunk quick. I looked at the clock on the stove. It read 4:27. I would be a little early. Yasmin would not mind. And neither would Fate.

"I'm going out to the store," I said. There was no response. I went outside and got into the Chevy. The grocery store was not going to be my first stop. I would pick up the steak and green beans on the way home. First, I was going to A.E. Phrenology.

When I got there, the parking lot was quite empty. I got out of the Chevy and locked it. Then, I went up to the office building and walked in through the sliding glass doors. It had been weeks since I had walked across the purple and yellow carpet and into A.E. Phrenology. I had been avoiding A.E. Phrenology perhaps out of fear, perhaps out of disrespect, perhaps both, and as I walked across the purple and yellow carpet towards my office door, beside which read A.E. Phrenology in black letters, I was quite fearful, and I did feel disrespect for the place. I felt disgusted, the way two people had walked into this office and left it dead, for all intents and purposes. Now, as I unlocked the door and opened it, I was dumbfounded I was still alive. Shadows were draped over the objects in the room. I flipped the switch and the objects were illuminated. The shadow was gone,

208

but I still felt discomfort. I felt the eyes once more watching me—the tempter and the observer as individuals, my own mirror image. The psychograph was on my left. I walked across the carpet and went behind the desk. Now, the psychograph was on my right. I reached down and got out the whiskey and a glass. I poured myself a drink and downed it. It must have been the psychograph killing my subjects. There was no opaque cognizance. There was no conscious being with the intention of killing my subjects. It was scientific and logical. The psychograph was faulty, the electricity was throwing off brainwaves and sending its subjects helter-skelter towards their own Fate. Fate was not conscious. How could it be? It was only an ethereal conception brought about by the human mind and its yearning to understand the universe at large. It was not alive. It was not bloodthirsty. I poured another drink and then downed it. Then, another. The shutter I had felt in the hospital bed after Yasmin had left went up my spine again. The anger centralized in my head. I grew hot and flushed. I got up from my chair and went over to the psychograph, looking it up and down, thinking this archaic machine, its kinked wire, feelers, and locater, was pretty damned close to extinction. Phrenology was nearing its end. And I would expedite the process.

I took the psychograph from its bent support column and threw it to the carpet. It sounded like a bucket of nuts and screws when it fell, and I stomped on the helmet with great force, the wire and feelers and locater scattering across the purple and yellow carpet under my weight. The psychograph was destroyed. It lay devastated across the carpet in a hundred pieces. The metallic device was a piece of wreckage, a shattered antiquity which was now a defeated symbol of science and mind-body progress. If it was not extinct already, it was now. At least to me. As of that day Allen Earnhardt was no longer a phrenologist. As of that day Allen Earnhardt was a vigilante.

Before going to the supermarket, I decided to pay a visit to White Egret Funeral Home, but I went to the florist shop beforehand to get some flowers for Herbert Podrey's gravesite. There was a florist shop nearby the town center. I was not going to be picky. A simple bouquet of flowers was all I wanted. But, I did have in mind a specific flower I wanted to put on Herbert Podrey's gravesite. Amaranth. Walking into the florist shop, the scents of fifty different carnations mixed as one and entered my nose. It quelled the angst in me. It was like a dense mist one had to push through yet was carried through by some airy stream.

"Can I help you?" said the florist.

"Yes, you can," I said. "I hope. I'm looking for a bouquet of amaranth. Have any amaranth available?" I held my breath.

"Yes, Mr—"

"Earnhardt."

"Earnhardt. Yes, Mr. Earnhardt. I do have amaranth, in fact. One bushel is all you need?"

"Yes. And thank you," I said, and the florist went into the back of the microcosm one could call a paradise and got some amaranth together. Then, she wrapped it up in some plastic, tied a string around the amaranth, and came back over to the counter. "Thanks," I said. "What'll that be?"

"Immortality for whoever you give it to." The florist laughed. I could not laugh. Mortality was not a laughing matter anymore.

"I meant how much will that cost?"

"Oh, fifteen dollars even ought to cover it," she said.

I pulled a twenty out of my pocket and gave it to her. "Keep the change," I said. "Goodbye." I went out of the florist shop, got into the Chevy, and headed towards White Egret Funeral Home. My inhibition was low. I no longer scanned the road for dangers. I was quite sure I was a dead man, and I had embraced the fact. White Egret Funeral Home had a gray stone at its entrance and an iron gate, which resembled a headstone and the gates of hell. I was convinced I was headed there within the next twenty-four or forty-eight hours. My body, otherwise known as Allen Earnhardt would end up buried somewhere in White Egret Funeral Home, close by Herbert Podrey, but my mind would be damned in a circuitry which perpetuated Fate, and which was not my benefactor. Fate was working against me, but for how much longer nobody could tell. If what I surmised was true, I would be, in the circuitry, perpetuating Fate to claim others like me. I thought this as I walked across the grass towards Herbert Podrey's gravesite. Once there, I read the headstone.

Herbert Podrey had been about thirty when he died, when A.E. Phrenology changed his life course. He had been about thirty when he jumped out of the window. I was thirty-five, and nobody could know the method primordial Fate would use to kill me. I only knew it would be ugly. But, for the time being, the amaranth in my hand was wet and cool, and the exchange I had had with the florist surfaced in mind.

"What'll that be?"

"Immortality for whoever you give it to."

But, Herbert Podrey was already dead. I surmised his Fate was much like mine, almost identical. His body was buried six feet beneath my feet and his mind was in perpetual revolution in the depths of hell. I had not noticed the sky had clouded over. It would rain. I felt a drop of rain on my face, and then put down the amaranth on the gravesite. If he were somewhere else, still alive, still thinking, still feeling, Herbert Podrey circulating as a memory or notion, perhaps the amaranth would grant him immortality. It was an ambivalent thought to leave on, and as I turned my back the sky clattered lighting and thunder, and the rain started coming down. I hurried to the Chevy, turned it on, then went to the supermarket to get food for dinner. That was my last visit to White Egret Funeral Home for some time. As it turned out, Herbert Podrey's and my own Fate were not identical. No, I was not to be buried at White Egret Funeral Home, not this week, not until I was an old man. As it turned out, Fate had other intentions for me.

***

December came, and it was the day of Lenny Amaranth's wedding. The day I visited Herbert Podrey's gravesite was two months prior. I had not visited his gravesite again, nor did I have the intention to. I focused on the present, what was before me, and before I knew it, Lenny, Raleigh, and I were standing at the altar of the Second Coming of Christ Protestant Church in our tuxedos and waiting for Gretchen to come down the aisle, escorted by her father. The Second Coming of Christ Protestant Church was much like the Church of Heavenly Saints where Herbert Podrey's service had been. Both churches had stained glass windows with the images of saints staring transfixed back at you. An organ was to the right of the alter of the Second Coming of Christ Protestant Church. In the Church of Heavily Saints, the organ was on the left of the alter. Both churches had marble alters and carpet floors where the pews were situated. Lenny, Raleigh, and I were standing on the marble before the altar. Many people were standing in the pews. The most significant difference between the Church of Heavenly Saints and the Second Coming of Christ Protestant Church was, in the Second Coming of Christ Protestant Church, this time around, not everybody was wearing black.

The priest and I had been introduced before the wedding ceremony had begun. Lenny Amaranth had introduced the two of us. We shook hands and the priest had said the angel Gabriel would look lightly upon the ceremony. On the marble, waiting for Gretchen to come down the aisle, the priest's words surfaced. He had mentioned angel Gabriel and had struck a lost memory in me of my childhood, one I had forgotten by means of the mechanism the mind used to block out unwanted memories. It was a memory of the family cat, who was named Gabriel. Gabe had been in our family for years, and the gray cat spent most of his time outdoors catching mice and rats, and survived by his own means and by his own natural instinct. He was a good cat and was loved by our family, that was Mom, Dad, and I, for the time we had him. We lived in Newbury, Maryland—I had no intention even as a child, of moving away from Newbury, Maryland—and on warm summer days I went outside, called for Gabe who came to me whenever I called him—we had a kind of chemistry only a child could have with a cat—and I fed Gabe cheese. It was, in the summers, a ritualized exchange. I had a ham and cheese sandwich and brought out a slice of cheese for Gabe when I was finished.

On one warm summer day, Gabe did not come when I called him. I called "Gabe, Gabe?" but the cat did not saunter in my direction like he always did. I looked at the slice of cheese in my hand, quite defeated. The lot was spacious and green, and I walked further out into it, calling, "Gabe, Gabe?" but still he did not make himself known. Our street was small and narrow, a side street further westward than our house at present. It was dusty and brown, and people almost never walked down the road, beside the Hedmon's child who every so often walked to the river to fish, and if somebody did walk down the small street they never escaped without a significant amount of dust on the hems of their pants. Three vultures crowded around a fresh find down the road, their plumage black as soot yet radiant in the afternoon sun. I started to walk towards the vultures, then I picked up my pace to a jog, and then I was in an all out sprint towards the vultures who were disemboweling a carcass. Drawing near, I frightened the vultures and they flew off six yards distant. Entrails had been dragged over many feet of dusty ground and I saw they were Gabe's entrails. The gray cat was flayed open underneath the beating sun. I dropped the slice of cheese, picked up Gabe into my arms, and ran back to the house as fast as I could, the cat's head lolled to the side and innards dangled as I ran. I kicked open the door and went into the kitchen, where Dad was sitting and drinking juice. The cat was lifeless in my arms and tears were in my eyes.

"The devil?" said Dad, standing up.

I cried, Gabe in my arms. "They got him, daddy. The vultures. They got him."

"Take him outside, Allen, now," my Dad said, and I did. We buried Gabe in the backyard where the oak trees separated our property from the forest. We had tied two sticks together with twine, making a cross, and put it into the ground at the head of Gabe's grave. Now, the same geometry found itself casted throughout the church, only now it was not made of sticks tied together with twine. It was carved into the marble. The priest's declaring angel Gabriel would look lightly over the ceremony and the crosses carved into the marble roused the memory in me after so long a time it may as well never have happened. But, it did happen and my recalling the incident made a parallel between what had happened to Gabe the warm summer day at my childhood house and what was happening in regards to A.E. Phrenology quite substantial. There was a dominant and an inferior contender at work and I could not help but make the connection that my subjects and I were the inferior contenders and the opaque cognizance, the black hand on the window pane which had followed me home the night of my own psychographic test, was the dominant contender. It was so clear in mind, as clear and as vibrant as were the vultures' black plumage the day I found Gabe lying on the dusty road.

The organist went into "Here Comes the Bride" and everybody turned their heads to face the precession of bridesmaids, the flower girl, and then Gretchen herself, arm in arm with her father, come down the aisle. Her belly was bulging.

"She's beautiful," I said. Lenny was silent, then looked at me.

"She is. She always will be." Gretchen and her father were about halfway down the aisle when Lenny turned to me and said, "I have good news. I'll tell you at the reception." The ceremony was very beautiful, and I knew Lenny and Gretchen would stay together until the end.

The reception was in full swing right from the beginning. It was an open bar, which was good, and Raleigh and I headed straight for the bar, got drinks, and sat at the table with Lenny. They had hired a band to play at the reception. As I drank my whiskey, the band picked up into "Twist and Shout."

"I have good news," Lenny said. He had been talking to one of Gretchen's family, and then had turned to me, his face lax and pink. "You know Gretchen's pregnant."

"She shows," I said.

"Right. She shows." Lenny laughed. "If the baby is a boy we're going to name him Allen, after you. Allen's a good name, strong. And if I had anyone to pick to be my son's namesake it would be you. So, drink up and hope that baby has nuts."

"Very good, Lenny, very good." I was glad, but somewhere in my gut a dark pretense was making itself known. It was subtle, but it was as if I did not want the baby named Allen if it came out a boy. "Nothing would make me happier."

"Good," said Lenny. "Good. And make sure Raleigh doesn't make a fool of himself. You know how he gets."

"Sure."

The chatter of the people was broken by an announcement by the band. "If we could have everybody clear the dance floor and have Mr. and Mrs. Amaranth come to the dance floor, we can get this party started."

"That's me," said Lenny. He and Gretchen got up from the table and went onto the dance floor. The band started up "When a Man Loves a Woman" and Lenny and Gretchen Amaranth danced. They danced, and it was as if the outside world did not exist. They were in their own world now. All the hardships of the past few months were a non-issue. What lay ahead for them was only hope and goodness. I could only hope a similar goodness lay ahead for me. The band went from "When a Man Loves a Woman" to "I've Got a Rock 'n' Roll Heart." The people rushed onto the dance floor. Everybody was happy and gleeful, but a discomfort had

216

been roused in me. It was the notion that Lenny's firstborn child, if it was a boy, would be named after me. It would be named Allen.

***

At Johnny Hovan's, Lenny, Raleigh, and I were sitting at our usual booth and drinking beer and whiskey. Three weeks had passed since the wedding. No attempts had been made on my life. I was alive, sitting in Johnny Hovan's, drinking my third glass of whiskey, and listening to the chatter of the bar patrons, the cracking of billiards balls, and the jukebox.

Lenny was talking about marriage and the honeymoon he and Gretchen were going to take after the baby came. "And then we'll shoot over to Bucharest for the weekend," Lenny said. Lenny had been talking for quite a while, telling Raleigh and I about the itinerary. They were leaving to Copenhagen after the baby was born, and then heading east, were visiting Hamburg, and then heading south to Bucharest. The baby would be with them. "And then we're heading home via London but we're not going to do anything in London. It's just a layover. We'll stay at an airport hotel and arrive home Friday afternoon our time. Just in time for our usual rendezvous at this lovely establishment."

"That's great," said Raleigh. "Colleen and I should have done something to that extent. We just went down to the Bahamas for a week and I lost most of my money at the casino. She didn't mind, though. She was there all the while, drinking every drop of vodka she could get her hands on."

"We're keeping it low key," said Lenny. "As low key as one can keep it. We'll have the baby along with us."

The dark foreboding filled my belly again. I took a drink of my whiskey, finished it, and then flagged down Cathy for another. "It will be great for the three of you," I said.

"It will be," Lenny said. "One more thing I forgot to mention earlier. Get this, Allen. This past Monday, Gretchen had a sonogram. We wanted to be surprised by the gender of the baby at first, but we couldn't contain ourselves. The baby is male. It's going to be named Allen. Allen Leslie Amaranth. What do you think about that?"

Lenny had said, *"The baby is male. It's going to be named Allen,"* and I just about sunk into the overstuffed cushion of the booth. The dark foreboding was in my belly again, and it was stronger and darker than it had been at Lenny's and Gretchen's wedding reception. I did not know why the baby being named Allen was so terrible. But, it made me feel as though a storm cloud had manifested in my belly and was traveling up my oesophagus. "That's great, Lenny. Allen Leslie Amaranth. All the best," I said, and I felt guilty and loathsome. The loathsomeness was not because of the baby or Lenny or even the events which had followed the psychographic test I had performed on myself, nor was the loathsomeness directed toward the psychograph. The loathsomeness was directed toward me. "When's Gretchen due?"

"She's due next month, February 2nd."

Lenny said this, and I recalled the night Lena had come down with a fever, the night three months ago when I almost got into the head-on collision with the drunkard driving on the wrong side of the road.

"Allen dies," Lena had said. *"Why does Allen have to die?"*

As I sat on Lena's bed, pouring a dose of cough medicine into the plastic cup, I was under the assumption she was referring to me when she said *"Allen dies. Why does Allen have to die?"* I was under the assumption I was the one Lena said would die. But, as Lenny, Raleigh, and I sat at our booth in Johnny Hovan's one Friday night, three weeks following Lenny's and Gretchen's wedding, I knew who Lena had been referring to was not me, Allen, her father, but Allen Leslie Amaranth, Lenny Amaranth's unborn child.

The clock at Johnny Hovan's struck nine-thirty, and I decided to leave. Lenny's child being named Allen was taking its toll on me. I was tired and needed to get home. And I wanted to talk to Lena. I said to Raleigh and Lenny, "I'll be off," and I got up from the booth. "You two drive safely."

"Leaving so soon?" asked Raleigh, to which I nodded in assent. I slapped his back and told him to take care. Then, I went outside, got into the Chevy, and went home. The dark foreboding never left my stomach. It grew darker and heavier the closer I got to home, and when I arrived home, opened the car door, and stepped out into the January night, the crispness of winter and the hot forbearance mixed in my gut. I exhaled, and I could see my breath. Once inside the house, I put down the car keys and went upstairs to shower and change into something more comfortable. Yasmin was lying in bed, flipping through a magazine. "Home," I said.

"How was the bar?"

"Same as always."

"And Raleigh and Lenny?"

"They're well. Lenny and Gretchen's child is male. Gretchen took a sonogram last Monday. The baby will be named Allen, Allen Leslie Amaranth."

"That's great," Yasmin said. I did not agree, but I kept my mouth shut and went into the bathroom to take a shower.

Once out of the shower, I got into a pair of pajamas and a tee-shirt, then went into Lena's room to say goodnight. Lena was lying in bed with her eyes closed, but I could tell she was not asleep. She was tapping her fingers at her sides. "Hi, Lena," I said.

Lena's eyes fluttered open. "Hi, daddy."

"You're not sleepy?"

"No," she said, and then yawned. "No, I'm not tired."

I sat on the edge of her bed where I had sat when I poured the plastic cup full of cough medicine for Lena, the time Lena had said, *"Allen dies. Why does Allen have to die?"* I squeezed Lena's knee, recalling the exchange. "Remember when you had a fever months ago, Lena? When you were sick? And I had to go out and get you cough medicine?"

Lena hummed yes.

"Do you remember what you said to me before I gave you the cough medicine?"

Lena shook her head no.

"You said, 'Allen dies. Why does Allen have to die?' You don't remember that?"

"You're dying?" she said. She had choked out the words and sounded scared.

"I'm not going anywhere."

"You're not going to die are you?"

"No, I'm not, Lena."

"Good. Okay." Lena rolled over on a side, and I squeezed her knee again.

"Good night," I said.

"Good night, daddy."

It was apparent she did not remember having said those words the night of her fever. I was confident, however, the Allen she was referring to in the exchange was not the Allen who had just wished her goodnight. I was sure of it. It was all too obvious considering the way she had referred to "Allen," using a proper name, "Allen," rather than "daddy" or "you," as in "daddy dies" or "you die."

I had a headache. The past few months were catching up to me. I was fatigued and anxious to see how this played out. What if Allen Leslie Amaranth died instead of Allen Earnhardt, as Lena had predicted? Would it be a cosmic screw up? Had Fate made a mistake and would take the wrong Allen? Or was it a sort of compromise, a silent and secretive compromise made between Fate and I, to take Allen Leslie Amaranth rather than Allen Earnhardt? After all, the opaque cognizance was coy, and it was prideful. It would be cruel, too, to end on such a witticism.

January passed, and February came in along with a cold front. The temperature dipped to 15° F. The oak trees in the back yard had shed all their leaves. The blades of grass were frozen like miniature, icy stalagmites. The ground was hard as stone. Stepping outside was like being bitten all over. It was too cold for anything but coffee, liquor, and heavy clothing. The cold front moved in on January 31st and rescinded on February 4th, the day Allen Leslie Amaranth was delivered. On February 4th, at about four o'clock P.M., the doorbell rang, and I answered it to find Lenny standing on the porch with his New York Yankees cap in his hand. He was twisting the baseball cap. "Can I come in?" he said.

"Sure, Lenny, sure. Come in." I shut the door behind Lenny. "Can I get you a coffee?"

"No, thanks. I just want to talk."

"Sure, come into the kitchen."

"I was thinking we could go to Lawrence's, the place out towards the train tracks. I'm hungry. I haven't eaten since morning."

"Sure," I said. "Let me get my jacket." My jacket on and my shoes on my feet, I went outside with Lenny Amaranth to the Chevy, and we drove off westward towards Lawrence's where Isabella Inglewood and I had planned to meet the morning following her psychographic test as per the copy of *Elements of Phrenology* I was giving her and where Isabella Inglewood failed to arrive, all those years ago. The Chevy cut through the cold February afternoon and took us towards Lawrence's which was over the railroad tracks, a few minutes west of town and rather close to the Podrey household and W Beverly Road. The parking lot, when Lenny Amarnath and I arrived, was empty for the most part, an R.V. situated along the side of the parking lot parallel the curb and taking up three adjacent parking spots, a pickup truck a few spaces away from the R.V., and a couple of motorcycles leaned on their kick stands in front of the diner, which was a small, glistening, and metallic diner, a trailer three feet off the ground and perched upon iron scaffolding like a diner one would visit in a typical fifties late night out after a high school prom and drinks. I pulled the Chevy into a spot close by the motorcycles. I twisted the ignition towards me, the Chevy ceased vibrating, and it was silent. Lenny Amaranth had been quiet the entire ride out to Lawrence's and I could already tell something was not as it should have been. "Shall we go inside?"

"Oh, yes. Yes, Allen. Let's go inside." Lenny was caught up in some daydream which had taken away his usual gaiety. He opened his car door, and I opened mine, and we stepped outside onto the gravel parking lot at Lawrence's, the parking lot churning in the way gravel parking lots churned when walked upon. I walked up the aluminum stairs which went to the front door of Lawrence's, took the horizontal door handle, pushed it open, and held the door open for a rather sullen and gray Lenny Amaranth.

He walked to the podium at which waitresses received customers for seating, and said, "Two of us today. Thank you."

The waitress, a middle-aged woman whose blonde hair was beginning to show signs of gray took us to a booth in the corner of Lawrence's, which was empty save those who arrived in the R.V., the pickup truck, and on the motorcycles, the time being as it was, quarter past four P.M.

"Thank you," said Lenny, sitting down at the booth. I took the seat across him as Lenny Amaranth picked up one of the menus which were upright in the metallic stands underneath the window.

"You look down, Lenny. Is everything all right?" I said. Lenny Amaranth did not respond. He did not speak for an entire minute until the same waitress came over, the one with the blonde hair beginning to show signs of gray, and she asked us what we would like to eat.

"Short stack," said Lenny. "And coffee and orange juice."

The waitress wrote down Lenny's order of pancakes, coffee, and orange juice in her pad, and then said to me, "For you?"

"Just a coffee. Thanks."

She smiled a crooked smile, which showed her uneven teeth, and walked behind the bar and poured two cups of coffee and a glass of orange juice. I did not want to push Lenny into talking or saying anything he did not want to. He looked devastated. I could tell he was. I had not seen him look so aged and disheveled ever in my life; and I knew there was bad news he was going to tell me, and I knew it regarded his son, Allen Leslie Amaranth. We sat in silence and the waitress who had taken our order brought over the coffee and orange juice and set them in front of us. "The short stack will be right out. Do you want jelly?" she asked Lenny, who shook his head in dissent. Lenny Amaranth sipped his coffee, and then he sipped his orange juice, and then his coffee again. Minutes passed in the small diner called Lawrence's across the railroad track, west of town and close by the Podrey household and W Beverly Road, like swatches of cloth being clipped off a bolt of fabric. They were soundless and eerie. The waitress came to our table and placed Lenny's short stack in front of Lenny, who thanked her and took the maple syrup from beside the menus in their metallic stand underneath the window, poured a copious amount of maple syrup on his short stank, more than I had ever seen before on a short stack four pancakes high, and then smeared butter, which was in a small cup the waitress had brought over with the short stack, on each pancake. Lenny Amaranth ate with fury. I said nothing, watching him devour each pancake like a man who had found nourishment after three days in the wilderness. He sure looked as though he had been in the wilderness for three days. His eyes were dark and baggy. His skin looked sallow, wrinkled, and cracked. As he finished the pancakes, I could see Lenny's skin take on a bit more color, his eyes looked more alert and sharp, and he looked like the Lenny I was used to, the same Lenny with whom I met at Johnny Hovan's every Friday night at eight-thirty for drinks, the same Lenny with whom I went to see the Oriole-Yankee game at Oriole Park at Camden Yards, the same Lenny

Amaranth who had told me if his and Gretchen's child were male they were to name him Allen.

Lenny looked up at me, we made eye contact so intense I thought there was a serious crisis in the head of our good friend Lenny Amaranth, and he took a sip of his coffee, finishing it. Lenny flagged down the waitress for another coffee, who came over and filled up his coffee cup. Lenny said, "Gretchen went into labor this morning."

"What's the matter, Lenny?"

"It was a still birth, Allen. The baby came out gray as wet concrete. It happened this morning at around nine o'clock."

"Oh, Lenny."

"You know what was strange?" he said.

"What was strange?" I said.

"After the baby came and the doctor was holding the gray thing, Gretchen said, 'Cosmos to chaos. Laws are meant to be broken.' Does that mean anything to you?"

"No," I said.

"I didn't think so. How could it? I was stupid to think it might have." Lenny Amaranth was silent and sipped his coffee. I flagged down the waitress and asked for the check.

"I'll pay for the pancakes, Lenny, and the coffee and the orange juice." It was a way to redeem myself in my own eyes. That Allen Leslie Amaranth had died per chance by my own actions could not be conveyed to Lenny even if I wanted to convey such an idea. It would make no sense to the man and neither would my telling him Gretchen's words, *"Cosmos to chaos. Laws are meant to be broken,"* made sense without an absolute conveyance of the sequence of events which had occurred since Herbert Podrey's psychographic test. It was a perplexing sequence of events, one which I had trouble understanding in fullness, and I would not bring Lenny Amaranth, a friend and now a childless father, into the sequence of events, which, I presumed, may well take on a more direct and violent effect on him *vis a vis* the opaque cognizance which tended to be at work. The waitress came to the table and took the check and a ten dollar bill I had stuck into the plastic clasp in which the check had come.

Lenny said, "I'm ready to go if you are. Gretchen is waiting for me back at the hospital."

"Sure, Lenny. Sure. let's go." I stood and so did Lenny Amaranth. We walked back to the entrance of Lawrence's and I took the horizontal door handle and this time pulled instead of pushed and held the door open for Lenny Amaranth, who walked out into the February afternoon followed by myself. The gravel lot churned under our footsteps like it had when we walked towards Lawrence's half an hour ago. Now, we were walking away from Lawrence's, only now I knew my apprehensiveness in regards to Allen Leslie Amaranth had been correct and warranted.

We drove eastward towards the house, crossed the railroad tracks, and found ourselves back in the residential area of Newbury, Maryland. I pulled the Chevy into the driveway, in which Lenny's pickup truck was parked. He and I exited the Chevy, and we walked towards the front door, Lenny Amaranth following me into the house. I put down the car keys on the glass table, and said, "Are you going to the hospital?"

Lenny Amaranth said, "Yes, I am. But, I just wanted to come in, say hi to Yasmin, and spend a little more time with my buddy Allen Earnhardt."

"Sure, Lenny. Sure. Come on in. Can I get you another coffee?"

"No," Lenny said. "I've had enough coffee this afternoon."

I led him into the kitchen where there was a pot of coffee. I poured a cup for myself. "You're sure you don't want coffee?" I asked.

"No," he said. "No, thanks."

"Everything will be all right" I said. "Everything will turn out all right." I was apprehensive. My presumption regarding Allen Leslie Amaranth and his death had been accurate and Lenny had confirmed it at Lawrence's. I was devastated and so was Lenny, but I was devastated because of my seeming hand in the matter whereas Lenny was devastated, damned near broken, as a result of his child's death.

Lenny had begun to sniffle. "I know," he said. "We—we had such high expectations." Lenny walked to the sliding glass door which went out to the backyard, opened it, and stepped outside. I followed him outside, the cold biting my skin in the way February afternoons in Maryland did. Lenny sat down on a chair and I sat down on one beside him. Lenny Amaranth was crying.

Lenny Amaranth took off his New York Yankees cap and placed it on the table. I sat in silence, watching Lenny, his face in his hands, wiping the tears from his eyes. It was so cold I was surprised his tears did not solidify and freeze into ice.

Lenny Amaranth was looking out into the oak forest. Lenny hummed. Lenny and I both sat in silence, each breath visible in the winter air. Lenny said, "Amaranth is supposed to signify good luck and immortality," he said. "Who was I to think that were the case?" Lenny rubbed his hands together and blew into them. "I guess we're lucky, Allen, to be alive. Having amaranth is like a big 'you win.' What more could you ask for?"

I said, "I've got my amaranth right here," and squeezed his shoulder.

"I guess—I guess you're right," said Lenny. "I've got to get back to the hospital." He stood up and went back into the house. I followed him in and led him to the front door. "Come on over to the hospital tomorrow," he said. "She needs all the support she can get."

"I'll be sure to come over tomorrow," I said. "Yasmin and I will be there around ten A.M."

Lenny Amaranth nodded and put on his New York Yankees baseball cap. He turned and walked back to his pickup truck, and I shut the door. I walked into the kitchen, opened the cabinet where all the coffee cups were located, and took out the one which read, "Cosmos to Chaos" Laws are Meant to be Broken! went outside, and shattered the cup on the deck. I'd be damned if Lenny or Gretchen saw this cup, on which was written a premature eulogy for their son. I had been hopeful, positive, and ambivalent when thinking about Allen Leslie Amaranth the past few weeks. The notion of him dying was morbid but over the past few weeks I mused perhaps the notion was untrue. It turned out to be true, however, and as I swept up the shattered bits of ceramic I mused if the cyclical, murderous attempts on my life had ceased. I mused if Fate and I had reached a compromise. If, in fact, we had, the weight of child murder would cling to me for the rest of my life, perhaps ever for eternity. But, if the notion, a compromise, was not reached, and attempts on my life were still made, it was evident I had far underestimated the bloodthirsty nature of this cosmic killer. I loathed myself for thinking I had overcome the opaque cognizance, but I clung to the notion I had overcome it, too, because what was a life half lived? What was the point of unveiling a secret just to be killed once you apprehended its intimacies?

This, I felt, was the case insofar as A.E. Phrenology and the phenomenon which had been killing subject after subject. I had unveiled its malicious, cosmological intention, and had broken its weaponized circuitry. A.E. Phrenology had within its walls a psychograph, which was quite destroyed, and which was a degraded killer and also within its walls was Fate, which had failed time after time in its attempts to kill me. It had settled on Allen Leslie Amaranth, but the question remained, who or what was the cause of such violence? Was it the desultory psychograph? A cosmic entity who had become conscious and murderous, having found a route into our world through the psychographic tests? Or was I the culprit this whole time? Was I the damned embodiment of death or a bystander? The truth was yet to be unearthed. As I deposited the shattered coffee cup into the trashcan, I mused if answers would ever surface.

I stepped outside to take a last look at the deck, to see if I had missed any fragments of ceramic. I had not. I looked up in the same direction Lenny had looked when he was sitting here, out into the oak forest, and I thought all of us—Lenny and Gretchen, Yasmin and Lena, Raleigh, and I—were mere puppets exacting a dance, playthings for the sublime.

(Epilogue)

The following day, Yasmin and I went to Ebberfield Hospital South where Gretchen was recovering. Lena was with us. Before we went to the hospital, we went to the florist shop, the same florist shop where I had gotten amaranth for Herbert Podrey's gravesite, and got the same flower for Gretchen. It cost fifteen dollars. I gave the florist a twenty and told her to keep the change. We arrived at Ebberfield Hospital South and asked the receptionist where Gretchen Amaranth was located.

"Room 313," the receptionist said, and she gave us stickers to put on, so people could identify us as visitors.

Then, we went up to the third floor, found room 313, and went in. Gretchen was hooked up to an IV and was lying on her back. She turned to us when we came in and gave us a wan smile. "Hi, guys," she said. "Hi, Lena."

"Hi, Gretchen," said Lena. She put the amaranth on the table beside the hospital bed. "We got you flowers."

"They're beautiful," Gretchen said, and everybody embraced. Lenny was sitting in the corner. We shook hands and kept silent. Yasmin and Gretchen were talking about the incident—the contractions, labor, the delivery. Gretchen had begun crying and I thought what I had thought while in Herbert Podrey's home following his funeral, walking among his friends and loved ones, walking through his house with the intention of talking to his wife.

(You are a murderer. You are a murderer.)

It all seemed a dream. Gretchen and Lenny Amaranth, two parents without a child, Yasmin, Lena, and I standing in a room at Ebberfield Hospital South, standing in the white room, room 313 within which hung a curtain from a sliding track on the ceiling. When closed, the curtain divided the mourning and the external world. When closed, the curtain divided the dream scape in which all the events of the past six months had occurred from the actual loss found within it. It occurred to me, as I stood beside Lenny Amaranth, all I knew and everything I had ever known, was not actual. My childhood, my parents, my first wife, Tyra, were all conjured in memory like phantasms. They did not exist, not anymore. Memories, people, and all else you remembered were like the muscles of the human body. They died and regenerated, they oscillated anew, the muscles which comprised your body as a child were no longer yours. Your skin, your hair, your nerves and bone marrow had been replaced since then. You were not you.

(You are a murderer. You are a murderer.)

I thought this again as I stood beside Lenny Amaranth, listening to the tears of a mother cheated out of motherhood. This time, I was among my own friends and loved ones, and I decided I really was an indecent son of a bitch. I decided I was the culprit, the instigator, the cause of all this death. It was not the psychograph but me, its operator, who was the murderer. Gretchen cried into the bed sheets and Lenny just watched on. We all just watched on as Gretchen Amaranth mourned the death of her firstborn son.

Standing there beside Lenny, and, too, beside myself, I felt a sense of curiosity rouse in my gut. Months ago, I exacted a psychographic test on myself. I recalled it with clarity. I had been sitting on the stool beneath the psychograph's helmet which months later I had destroyed, and then the printout mechanism had spit out my test results which I had disposed of without even taking a glance. I was not interested in the results at the time. I was interested in the effects of the psychographic test in terms of death. I was interested in unveiling the similitude between Tyra's and Herbert Podrey's deaths, and seeing if there was a parallel between them and psychographic tests. No, I was not interested in the results of my own test. But, now, I was. I wanted to look at those results, examine them to see if I was, in fact, destructive or mirthful. I wanted to see if I scored high in these faculties. If I did score high in those faculties, it would not be hard to believe I was the culprit, per happenstance peripheral culprit, of these unfortunate events. Gretchen dabbed her eyes with the bedsheets. She was done crying for now. I doubted it would be the last time she would cry about her son's death—it was tragic—and as she gave us that wan smile again, anxiousness was mounting in my gut, an anxiousness to examine those test results.

Yasmin, Lena, and I stayed in room 313 for an hour or so before Lena said she was hungry and we decided to go home. Yasmin kissed Gretchen on the head, Gretchen patted Lena's head, I shook Lenny Amaranth's hand, and we were off, back in the elevator heading downstairs. I tore off my sticker which indicated I was visitor. Yasmin did the same, then tore off Lena's. We were home within fifteen minutes, but I would not stay long, just long enough for a quick bite to eat, and then I would be off to A.E. Phrenology and would retrieve the test results from the trashcan beside my desk where I put them months ago, and I would examine the results. I put on my shoes and told Yasmin I would be back in an hour at most.

"Where are you going?" she said.

I said, "A.E. Phrenology."

"You haven't been to the office in quite some time," she said. "Is everything all right?"

"Never better," I said. "In fact, I'm closing down A.E. Phrenology. It's over. It's not something I want to practice anymore, phrenology, that is."

"Really?" said Yasmin. "You're done?"

"Done, and I'm going to terminate the contract binding me to the office right now."

Yasmin was silent. "Good for you," she said.

"Thanks," I said, and I was out the door. The cold front had rescinded. Yesterday, the day Lenny Amaranth came over and delivered the news about little Allen

Leslie Amaranth, was the coldest day of the year. Its coldness would be felt a long, long time.

The windows of the Chevy were rolled down as I drove towards A.E. Phrenology. It was still cold but not below freezing like it had been the past week. I was shivering nonetheless, but it was a good chill, the kind which voided out any anxiety and replaced it with anticipation; it chilled my bones and energized them, too. The parking lot was half empty and spacious. I parked and walked into the office building, but I did not go straight to A.E. Phrenology. I went to the landlord's office first—I knew he would be there; he always was— and I knocked on his door, beside which was a plaque which read Mr. Owen Clark. I heard Mr. Clark say, "Come in." I went inside and saw Mr. Clark sitting behind his desk, glasses set low on his nose. He was looking through some paperwork. "What can I do for you, Mr. Earnhardt?" Mr. Owen Clark knew me well. I had been renting the office out of which I ran A.E. Phrenology for quite some time.

"Sorry to bother you, Mr. Clark. I have a request."

"By all means," said Mr. Clark.

"I'd like to terminate my contract for the office. I can't run my business anymore. Something's come up."

"You're sure?" said Mr. Clark.

"I'm sure. I'd like to pay this quarter's rent and then void the contract."

"Okay, Mr. Earnhardt, okay. Do you have your checkbook on you?"

I tapped my breast pocket. "No," I said. "It's in my office. Care to join me?"

"Let's go," Mr. Clark said. He got up from behind his desk and we went to the door to A.E. Phrenology. I unlocked the door and turned on the lights. The psychograph littered the purple and yellow carpet in a hundred pieces. "What happened here?" said Mr. Clark.

"Gehenna."

"No matter. It must be cleaned up before you leave."

"It will be clean as when I moved in," I said, and sat down behind my desk.

Mr. Clark sat in the chair opposite me. "Do you have the checkbook?"

I opened the desk drawer, took out the checkbook, and wrote a check for the quarter's rent. "There you are, Mr. Clark. I appreciate your business and patience in this request. But, really, it's time I closed down A.E. Phrenology."

"We all have our reasons."

"Indeed, we do," I said.

"Take care, Mr. Earnhardt."

"This mess will be cleaned up by tomorrow night. Rest assured."

"Not a doubt in my mind." At that, Mr. Owen Clark exited A.E. Phrenology. He closed the door behind him and I sat back in my chair. The bottle of whiskey was in the bottom most drawer where it always was. I took it out and a glass, too. The bottle was almost empty. I poured a glass of whiskey and downed it. Then, another. I finished the bottle and turned to the trashcan. The wadded-up test results were there where I left them. I took the results out of the trashcan and replaced them with the empty bottle. I unwrinkled the paper and looked at the results. What was printed out on the paper were not psychographic test results at all. In fact, what was printed on the paper was far from what I was expecting. I was expecting to read high numbers beside the words destructiveness and mirthfulness. Instead, what was printed on the test results were as follows:

Amativeness: LIVE
Tune: LIVE
Philoprogenitiveness: LIVE
Calculativeness: LIVE
Adhesiveness: LIVE
Constructiveness: LIVE
Combativeness: LIVE
Comparison: LIVE
Destructiveness: LIVECausality: LIVE
Secretiveness: LIVE
Vitativeness: LIVE
Acquisitiveness: LIVEIdeality: LIVE
Self-Esteem: LIVEBenevolence: LIVE
Approbativeness: LIVEImitativeness: LIVE
Cautiousness: LIVE
Generation: LIVE
Individuality: LIVE
Firmeness: LIVE
Locality: LIVETime: LIVE
Form: LIVEEventuality: LIVE
Verbal Memory: LIVEInhabitiveness: LIVE
Language: LIVEReverence: LIVE
Coloring: LIVEConcientiousness: LIVE
Hope: LIVEWeight: LIVE
Marvelousness: LIVE
Order: LIVE
Size: LIVE

What I saw left me dumbstruck. Not a single sensical result was on the paper. Every aptitude was followed by the word LIVE. I blinked to make sure I was not hallucinating, shook my head, and looked again at the results. LIVE followed every aptitude. Six months ago, I had exacted a psychographic test on myself to prove the deaths following the test, in this office, using this psychograph, by this phrenologist, were coincidental. I had wadded up the results, uninterested, and threw them into the trashcan, the very results I was now holding in my hand, the results which read LIVE following every aptitude. I had not looked at the results back then, months ago when I tested myself, but if I had looked at them and saw the illogical printout of the would-be results, would the attempts on my life have been made? Would I have almost gotten killed in a car accident? Would I have had the heart attack? Would Allen Leslie Amaranth still be alive? I thought no, I would not have almost gotten into the car accident and I would not have had the heart attack. I thought yes, Allen Leslie Amaranth would still be alive.

Yet, I thought the opposite—it did not make a difference—and I thought my rash decision to throw away the results was preconceived by this opaque cognizance which was, as it turned out, quite coy and prideful. It had played a game with me from the very beginning. It knew I was not going to look at the results. It knew I would survive the random dangers it put before me. It knew I would check the results months after I had exacted the psychographic test on myself and the results were printed out, curiosity flittering in my belly. It had made a compromise, Allen Leslie Amaranth instead of Allen Earnhardt. The whole while, I was speculating. It could have been a cosmic killer or a malfunctioning psychograph or a cursed phrenologist, but there had been no physical proof this parallel—the out of chronology predictions, Lenny Amaranth's outburst at Ebberfield Hospital South, Lena's words regarding Allen Leslie Amaranth, the deaths which had followed the non-linear predictions, correlating with the psychographic tests—existed. I had been speculating for months, thinking many times I was psychotic when the entire time the physical proof lay in the trashcan. I thought again of the coffee cup I had bought at the gas station, "Cosmos to Chaos," and I thought of what Lenny had said when he visited me the final day of the cold front, *"Gretchen said, 'Cosmos to chaos.' Does that mean anything to you?"* I looked again at the test results in my hand, and it became apparent; a candid strike through logic had occurred, an erroneous fissure in reality had skewed reason. The psychographic test results reading LIVE after each aptitude gave the impression of a conscious being at hand. It was commanding me yet releasing me. The test results were proof of this. It all added up to this instance, a phrenologist sitting at his desk, soon to be retired, an empty bottle in the trashcan beside him, the crescendo of six months of looming death, and then the document which had proved an aberration in time being examined and in his hands, the script of a cosmic killer, a tip of his hat.

I folded up the results and put them in my pocket, and then I started taking books out of the bookcase. I made a stack of books on the desk. *Principles of Neuroscience*, *Interpretation of Dreams*, *How to Read Character*, and many more, stacked, one on top of the other. I unplugged the printout mechanism connected to the psychograph. The stack of books I had made on my desk was tall and heavy, but I would manage. I opened the door of the office before picking them up, and then went to the desk, picked up the books, and walked out of the office. Traversing the purple and yellow carpet, the stack of books in my arms, I realized this was my last day walking across this carpet. I had told Mr. Clark the office would be empty by tomorrow, but I would clean it out by dinnertime.

The stack of books were in the Chevy and I walked back towards A.E. Phrenology to continue emptying the office. The purple and yellow carpet would be traversed many times, back and forth with stacks of books in my hands, old folders regarding past subjects who may or may not be alive today. I mused they were not and this was unfortunate to a very obtuse degree, so obtuse, in fact, that not only my feet grew heavy as I exited and reentered A.E. Phrenology, but my chest also did, and it was not physical strain making me so fatigued; it was an emotional and even moral fatigue which was slowing me down and perplexing me. I traversed the purple and yellow carpet with books in my hands four or five times, I emptied out my drawers full of the old folders, and then I began removing items from my desk like the brass all-seeing eye, pens, and a photograph of Yasmin, Lena, and I. When the office was voided of all personal items, what remained were the desk, the bookcase, the two chairs, and the devastated psychograph which littered the purple and yellow carpet. There was a maintenance closet down the hall and I went to it, looking for a broom and dustpan. The door on which was stenciled Maintenance opened when I twisted the knob and pulled on the door. Inside were a bucket, a mop inside of the bucket, cleaning supplements on a metal and wood storage shelf, and in the corner of the maintenance closet I could see a broom and a dustpan. I grabbed them and took them back to A.E Phrenology. This was one of the last times I would ever be inside A.E. Phrenology. I was sweeping up the screws, metallic plates, and copper wires, the remnants of the psychograph which I had gotten from Guzman's Antiquities in New York City all those years ago and which had been crushed under my foot. They were the remnants of an extinct science. After all which had occurred over the past six months within and because of this office, I had no problem saying goodbye to the science as a whole. In fact, I sent it my regards with blunt force. The trashcan, which had held the psychographic test results now in my pocket and which held the empty whiskey bottle, was full of the psychograph's feelers, locater, and wire. The skeletal psychograph, voided of its essential components which made it operable, lay on the purple and yellow carpet awaiting disposal. It was a gangly and flimsy looking object now that it had been destroyed. I tied up the trash bag, took the psychograph in both hands, and made my way outside to throw the bag and the machine into the dumpster, which was beside the office building a ways, and then I would go to Johnny Hovan's for a double cheeseburger. It was nearing noon and I was getting hungry. Following lunch, I would call Raleigh Durman and tell him to get over to A.E. Phrenology with his pickup truck, so we could transport the desk, bookcase, and chairs back to the house. The Chevy took me to Johnny Hovan's with smoothness, its tires driving over the blacktop of the Newbury streets with ease and confidence. It was as if the angst of the last six months had been extinguished, the fluidic weight of the Chevy across the Johnny Hovan's parking lot and its unkinked stillness when the ignition was twisted into the off position an assurance the travesties of the past six months were, in fact, over; and the neon lights of Johnny Hovan's were, too, a reassurance that all was going to settle down, smoothen out like it had been prior the conflagration which had arisen within A.E. Phrenology.

Johnny Hovan's had a different atmosphere in the day time. I had not been to Johnny Hovan's for lunch in years. It was the usual Friday evening rendezvous which brought me to Johnny Hovan's, but today the bar had a translucent quality one could almost see through with clarity and apprehend something not there before. As I sat down at our usual booth, the booth with torn upholstery and stuffing pouring out like faux snow, I mused what was clearer and unearthed was me.

Cathy came over to the table, and said, "Allen. Good to see you here in the afternoon. And it's not even Friday."

"Good to see you, Cathy," I said. "Bring me one of those double cheeseburgers you guys are always talking about and a scotch."

"Sounds good, Allen. That will be right out," she said, and as she walked away I turned to the television which had on a polo game. The ponies were controlled by men who, I knew, were small and who were wielding mallets to shoot the ball into the goal. Allen Leslie Amaranth came to mind and I thought of Lena. Allen Leslie Amaranth and Lena would have been good friends if Allen Leslie Amaranth had survived and grown into a young man. The ponies on the television screen roused the memory of Lena's conception in mind. Yasmin and I had gone to a small ranch west of town, much farther west than the Podrey household and W Beverly Road, and had rented two horses to ride through the forest. It was a riveting ride, Yasmin and I riding through the dense forestry of Maryland, the oaks and ferns coated with moss and the red earth which rose into our noses like incense, the imminent and unforeseen conception of our first and only daughter lying before us in a clearing within which were yellow grass and yellow irises, which swayed, metronomic. Yasmin and I stayed in the small yellow clearing for hours, the two horses who were named Ajax and Thetis nibbling on the yellow grass and occupying themselves in the blissful way horses did in paradisal forests, such as the one in which Yasmin and I resided until sunset. When the sun showed

240

signs of its descent towards the earthen line, which separated the heavens and the terrestrial, Yasmin and I mounted Ajax and Thetis and rode back towards the stable where we had first acquired the horses for our short but all-important excursion. Yasmin and I did not know, in the small yellow clearing with the yellow irises which inhabited the clearing like earthy exclamations, a child had been conceived. I did not know about our impending parenthood for a month until Yasmin approached me one morning while I was drinking coffee on the deck, looking out at the oak forest which bounded it, and told me I was going to be a father and she a mother. "Think about a name for her if she's a girl and name for him if he's a boy," Yasmin said, and I told her I would. The small yellow clearing was full of suggestions for the name of our child. There was the sunset, the flora, the forests and its trees and fauna. Then, I thought of the names of the horses, Ajax and Thetis, Ajax a Greek warrior in the Trojan War and Thetis the immortal mother of the Greek hero Achilles. We named the child who had turned out to be female after Helen of Troy. We named her Lena, which meant ambience, temptress, and light. We named her after Helen of Troy who, I mused, as I sat at Johnny Hovan's eating my double cheeseburger, had been in the wrong place—she had been displaced—at the wrong time, and a war had started over her. A.E Phrenology and what I had donned the opaque cognizance also was displaced. The deaths which had followed the psychographic tests were fissures in logic. There was no indisputable evidence holding the theory together, but it was blatant and obvious the psychographic tests and the deaths were correlated if only for the test results in my pocket, the test results which read the ominous word LIVE after every mental aptitude testable by a psychograph.

It was as though predestination were the foundation on which the opaque cognizance functioned. The test results with the single, imploring command—LIVE— had been printed and seen, attempts had been made on my life by the cosmic, or haphazard force, and Allen Leslie Amaranth had been killed in my stead. It was not chronological, the way the events of the past six months had occurred, and that was perplexing. It was as though my survival was inevitable all the while, and Fate was being entertained.

I finished my double cheeseburger and scotch, put a twenty dollar bill on the tabletop, and went outside to the Chevy. The drive back to A.E. Phrenology was as smooth and unkinked as my ride to Johnny Hovan's. This being my last time driving to A.E. Phrenology may also have been the reason it was so blithe and unconfined. Once back inside of an empty A.E. Phrenology, save the desk, the bookcase, and the chairs, I sat down on the chair behind the desk and called Raleigh Durman. He said he would be right over with his truck, and I sat back and waited for Raleigh to show up so we could remove the furniture from A.E. Phrenology and call the day, as well as A.E. Phrenology, closed.

Raleigh Durman walked into A.E. Phrenology without knocking on the door. "Greetings, Allen," Raleigh said. "You're calling it, huh? No more A.E Phrenology?"

"No more A.E. Phrenology, Raleigh," I said, but I was not going to expound on my reasoning as to why I was, as Raleigh had said, calling it.

"That's all right," Raleigh said. "That's all right. Shall we take this stuff to the truck?"

"Yes, let's do it. Let's get it over with." Raleigh and I carried the bookcase out over the purple and yellow carpet into the February afternoon and put it in the bed of the pickup truck. Then, we went back inside and took the desk, which was quite solid, and managed to put it, too, in the bed of the pickup truck, and then we did the same with the chairs, the test results all the while in my pocket. "Follow me back to my place," I said to Raleigh, and as I drove down the road on which I had almost gotten into a head-on collision days following psychographic testing months prior, he remained right behind me. We passed the section of road off of which I had swerved to avoid being killed. The churned grass was still there and still looked like parabolas in a calculus problem, but now they had some grass growing in the troughs of the tire marks. I made a left onto Binley Road and so did Raleigh. Raleigh pulled in behind me as I twisted the ignition towards me, extinguishing the Chevy's engine. Raleigh was out of the truck and opened the tailgate, I went inside and opened the garage, and then Raleigh handed me the chairs, which I brought into the garage. Raleigh and I transported the desk and the bookcase into the garage and I did not fall victim to a heart attack this time, and for a good reason, too, because I intended to make short work of what was in my pocket once Raleigh Durman left with his pickup truck. "Thanks very much, Raleigh. I appreciate it."

Raleigh Durman left, and I went inside, said hello to Yasmin, and poured myself a glass of scotch. The fireplace in the living room had not been ignited in many years, but that was about to change. I went into the kitchen and got a matchbox, and then I went outside and got two logs of wood, kindling, and tinder from the side of the house. The tinder went into the fireplace. I struck a match and lit the tinder on fire. The fire spread, catching on the tinder, making it brown then black, and filled up the entire living room with a good and hearty smell. The kindling went into the fire, and then the two logs were deposited into the fireplace. The flame ran its way onto the logs. The flame grew in size and heat, and I used the bellows to instigate the flames into growing even bigger and hotter, so the two logs would be aflame in entirety. I sat before the hearth, drinking my scotch, a phrenologist no longer pursuing the mysteries of the mind, a phrenologist no longer interested in the cranium, its interpretations, and the aptitudes its dimensions suggested, a phrenologist pursuing and having ascertained and even triumphed instead over the mysteries of the heart, willpower, and Fate. The flame grew and licked my ankles, arms, and face with tenacity.

Yasmin had come in, having smelled the smoke, and so had Lena. Yasmin said, "A fire? What made you start a fire?"

"It is cold outside," I said.

"It is," said Yasmin. "Why did you close down your practice?" she said after a silence.

"Call it intuition," I said. "Something wasn't right about it." That was the most I had ever mentioned or insinuated regarding the travesties which had originated because of A.E. Phrenology, and I would not say any more. I would not bring Yasmin or Lena, Lenny Amaranth or Raleigh Durman into the maelstrom that was my practice, A.E. Phrenology, any more than I already had.

"That's all right," said Yasmin. "If that's what makes you happy." She turned around and walked into the kitchen.

Lena came over to me and sat on my lap. She watched the fire for many minutes, its orange

and red wisps licking upwards and expelling smoke into the chimney, its dry heat ensconcing her. The flame

244

was rather large now and Lena could have sat and watched the flame all night in

her mesmerized state. I kissed her on the head and told her to go into the kitchen with her mother. She did and once she was in the kitchen, I reached into my pocket and removed the test results, opened them and looked them over one more time. It was unexplainable, the repetition of the word LIVE throughout the entire document, a sure prediction of the events which occurred in the six months following the results' being printed, my survival and apprehension of something quite paranormal. It occurred to me, as I held the wrinkled test results in my hand, what I was holding was the only actual proof making my hypothesis correct. Without this document, one might have thought me mad, deluded, or outright lunatical. Nobody could have had the same insight into the sequence of events following Herbert Podrey's psychographic test even if they tried. It was too disassociated from reality, but the document I held in my hand gave subtle if not definitive proof that an invisible murderer, killing my subjects, was, in fact, the case and at hand. The flame crackled in harmony with the test results when I wadded them up a second time and threw them into the flame. The flame began to dematerialize the document. A single word, superimposed in vision, hanged and was suspended from whence the divine casted its wit: LIVE.

The Auk

Clark Bennington did not believe in omens. Dispersing of the wine and bread to the people of his church, a zealous belief in divinity had him shun the concept. The people were lined down the aisle, receiving the Eucharist. Each held the cloth to their chins and stuck their chins out and drank the wine from a golden spoon. Clark Bennington, on this morning, regarded divinity as the will of Yahweh, through whom humanity's course pursued its iconoclast path through the Earthy and the divine. Putting on his regalia for the Sunday mass, Father Bennington felt in his gut His calling to save the sinners, who attended his church. He was doing so now; the housewives and hardworking men, the boys and girls of all ages collected before him as a unified host of His will, which Clark Bennington reciprocated through communion, and he believed he was saving the congregation. No, Clark Bennington did not believe in omens, but that would change.

The Eucharist was finished, and mass was over and Father Bennington, on his way home to have lunch before making his rounds to the ill, recalled the words his father had spoken when he, Clark Bennington, was a boy. Clark Bennington bore a striking resemblance to his father. Both had a strong jawline and protruding brow. Clark Bennington could still hear his father's voice. He, Clark Bennington's father, had been the one who instilled religiosity in him. "God is the only way to salvation, Clark. Pray like it is your last day, everyday, and you'll go straight to Heaven when the reckoning comes." Clark believed it. He believed his father's words with such sureness that, at the first opportunity, he went to school and became a priest, a Father. He abstained from sex. He believed it was the theatre though which the devil prospered; and with modern day explicit sex in the movies and on the television, he decided he was quite right. The men with which Clark Bennington was attending school, who were, too, pursing priesthood, abstained from sex, alcohol, and hereticalness of all kinds, which was omnipresent in New York City, where the school was located. Clark Bennington, if not hated the city, much disliked it. It was a cesspool of drugs, leather-wearing criminals, and prostitution. It was a subtle taint, but it left him trembling. The dormitories, shutting off the lights for the night, the warm day turning into a cold night, and the air from the open window, striking Clark Bennington, had him feeling at home and good; but as he closed the window and turned around to face his bunk, primordial mortality waited for him, sitting on his bed, adorned in black, and ready to envelop him. The pajamas Clark Bennington wore, and his youthful gait went only so far as to sustain his vigor. It was striking and preternatural when Bennington closed his eyes and talked to the darkness behind his eyelids. Generation after generation of priests dwelled within the walls, but Clark mused, here, in his darkness, lay the actual mystery. It was factual. Clark Bennington had seen the opalescent eyes of religion before him and then they had vanished. Lying on the bed, he felt a shiver course up his spine. Clark Bennington, following his graduation from school, left New York City and arrived in the small town of Little Boat, where he now lived. The small town of Little Boat was all he needed. The small church was by no means the most glorious of churches, but it was satisfying to worship there. Today, following mass, he was to visit a young man named George Gray, who was dying of leukemia. The boy had been fighting it for almost five years now and was just now starting to slip away. George Gray needed Bennington. Bennington knew he needed him. Clark Bennington finished his lunch and got into his Lincoln and headed south, towards George Gray's home.

The boy was tired, said the mother, and he looked as so. Clark Bennington took a seat beside the boy, and touched his forehead, which was glazed with sweat.

"My son, how do you feel?"

"I'm ill, Father," said Gray. "I fear my time has come."

A pause. "It may as well have, but, you know, Earth, where we are now, is only the beginning. There is a whole realm of splendor and goodness awaiting you. You know that, don't you, my son?"

"I know," said the boy, and he closed his eyes. "I haven't lived long enough to commit sin. So, I don't think I will descend."

"Indeed, there is room enough for one as you."

"Thank you, Father. Thank you." The mother came in at that moment with a glass of water for George Gray.

He drank the water, and turned to Clark Bennington, saying, "I've heard of trails before access to Heaven can be granted."

"Life is the trail," said Bennington. "There is no more trail than life itself."

"Nevertheless, I feel I will be tempted."

"That may be so," said Bennington. "That may be so."

"Have you ever been tempted, Father?" asked the dying boy.

Clark Bennington remembered an oblique image, an image from youth. Before he was ordained, Clark Bennington had attended a school in a small town in New Jersey. It was said a boy in particular took girls behind the maintenance shed and had his way with them.

"Have you ever been tempted, Father?"

I shouldn't have come, Bennington thought.

Young Clark Bennington once followed this boy and saw the boy had taken a girl against her will to the shed. There had been screaming, but the shed was too far for any adult to hear. Clark heard. Clark heard the screaming. He turned the corner of the maintenance shed and saw the boy's face up the girl's dress. He had pulled him out and struck him half a dozen times in the face, bloodying him up. That day, he was tempted. He was tempted to kill the boy.

"Have you been?" said George Gray.

"No," Bennington said. "No, I haven't been."

At this, he rose and blessed the dying boy, who thanked him; and Clark Bennington said good-bye to the mother and went to his car. The car started with a sputter, and Bennington drove northwards.

Evening had come. Bennington, as was his habit, went to a nature reserve to admire the animals, deer and squirrels, and walk a bit. He pulled into the gravel lot and shut off the car. George Gray was still in mind. Gray did not have much longer.

Clark Bennington had lied. He had lied about ever having been tempted, and the time with the boy behind the maintenance shed was not the only time he had been tempted. Perhaps the worst of all temptation, Bennington thought, was the temptation of knowledge. It was by that temptation Satan had seduced Eve into eating of the forbidden fruit. Bennington, to a degree, had fallen to the same temptation—for he had begun reading books, not heretical in their entirety, but books which deviated from common Christianity. He started contemplating the basis of morality and found himself on both ends dismissing the good and evil deeds as His will. Following New York City, Clark Bennington considered all deeds natural. The streets of New York City, each time he went for his walks during his time in school, were small, snide-looking fissures within which heretics dwelt, and it was then Clark Bennington decided morality was out of context, the filth and intoxication and sin versus purity and benevolence and the church. Bennington with infrequence looked at the establishment which was the church, without a dark streak. He saw women and men and children basking in messianic blood. The people were performing an act to which Clark Bennington was central. The observation of such phenomenon—the rallying of people around a single man, searching for the absolution of their sins— could not but alter Bennington's life course as he continued towards priesthood and went to bed and thought again of the darkness before him, shivering and falling into a deep sleep. He had read, in the school's library, a book which read when a person is open enough in belief, belief and reality begin to meld as one, the outside realm and the internal realm becoming one's own. Often times, Bennington thought of this. On walks through the nature reserve, he most times forgot such notions, but on this night, he was all too reminded by the finality of George Gray's life on Earth. He recalled the young boy at his school behind the maintenance shed and he recalled the darkness behind his eyelids and he recalled the totality of religion, and in this miasma, he mused if there were a polar opposite to faith. Yes, he decided, and the answer was knowledge. For that reason, Clark Bennington felt his faith slip away. He felt confident George Gray would go to Heaven, but he did not feel confident in his own ascension. Clark Bennington stopped walking, a sense of shock coursing through him. He heard a shattering squak! from overhead and looked up. A bird was perched on a branch. It fell and struck his face. The black and white bird lay on the ground lifeless. Yes, Clark Bennington would believe in omens. Indeed he would, and this was just the beginning.

Creighton

Through dark mahogany doors, people once walked into the home of Randall Creighton. Cathedral high ceilings and high bay windows were on both sides of the entrance portcullis. The dark purple curtains fell tumultuous down to the floor and were embroidered with golden and scarlet stitches; the candles shone bright in the dimmed corners of the halls and brightened the darkened corners. No cobwebs formed on the chandeliers or in the black corners of the ceilings.

The grand hall gave way straight into the sitting room—which was a fitting name, for in that room Randall Creighton's time was spent. There were the East and West Wings, which broke off, symmetrical, from the sitting room.

The small pieces of pleasure—fruits, wine, and caramel candies—and the pristine home, however, did not bring solace to Randal Creighton's mental fragility. Time and time again, Randall Creighton's thoughts receded back to a few choice times: Clarice, Beatrice, the war. He found himself, with mysteriousness and with frequency, amidst those memories, which worsened his appetite, swiped away peace of mind, and, as time wore on, accounted for physical sickness.

***

Randall Creighton, when he grew tired late in the evening, lay down to sleep in the East Wing. Randall Creighton ate in the East Wing, read in the East Wing. He many times thought somber of the other side—the West Wing—which housed not only choice keepsakes, but the past. The West Wing was not menacing. On the contrary, it was pleasant. Reliving those times with his daughter and wife instilled infinitesimal feelings of joy, vaporous and one-dimensional thoughts, which lived in his mind and which he had not seen with his physical eyes for years.

Leaving those clouds, those gaseous thoughts before dropping into the depth of night, he felt a void or an omnipresent sense of isolation.

Creighton thought of the inside of the human brain.

She never relearned to move or speak. Clarice, his daughter, had cracked her head on a rock while horseback riding. Nobody had entered Creighton's safe-haven since. He did not let anybody in, nor did he leave. He wanted to be alone ever since the accident, alone to contemplate the basis of reality. The fabric that was Creighton's reality began interweaving with a quasi-reality over the recent years, for he had begun to open doors, doors he had not opened in over a decade.

Creighton placed an empty wine glass on the table beside his armchair and stood. He ran his gnarled fingers through his hair. The house was in perfect condition.

Creighton walked west. Determined, through the halls to Clarice's bedroom he walked, the clicks of his heels sounding sullen against the hard wood flooring. The door was the same. The same wood, the same golden doorknob, and he stood in front of the door and turned the knob.

Sunlight is glaring into his eyes as he steps onto lush green grass. Gurgling, the sound of a stream finds his ears and he, on the bank of a stream, follows the bright water and black rocks with his eyes up to the horizon. He sees Clarice, and she has picked up her trot to a canter, and she is close to the rocks along the bank and in danger, squatting, flying towards him faster than an albatross, and Creighton has begun to run, waving his arms, but she does not slow down. Only ten feet in front of Creighton, the horse has taken a nasty spill and Clarice is soaring into a somersault, smacks her head on a rock and cracks her skull, finishing her life. Randall Creighton's voice shatters. He is about to pick her up, kneel before her. A pallid version of Clarice has risen from her body and stands before him, the color sanguine matted on her face. He tries to speak but cannot; he can only manage a whimper. Clarice, expressionless and wondrous, leads him back to the freestanding doorway and walks through, back into his life.

He shut the door behind him and watched his daughter walk east down the hall. He followed his daughter into the sitting room, where she wandered, looking at trinkets and books and furniture, touching the walls and the books of the house in which she had blossomed. For days, he followed the apparition around his home, gladdened again to see her young face.

Letting her back in, however, made him feel like he was slipping. Like he could not take hold and possess rational constitution. He begged Clarice, pleaded with

Clarice, and cried to Clarice, so that she could speak. She never returned a word.

He had formulated a plan. After reliving Clarice's death, he had immersed himself in the memory of her birth. He found her crib, her toys, her highchair and spoon, her clothing and baby shoes. He found a way to manipulate his past! There was balance. All he had to do was relive what had happened, and then immerse himself in the relating positive memories, and it was working!

He felt inflated, loved. He felt his chest, felt his hair, which felt thicker than ever. Color began to fill in his hair. It was working. He had vanquished the memory of Clarice's death, and now it was time to vanquish the needless death of war.

As a hero, he had been rewarded; medals and ribbons had been given to him, and he had shaken the hands of many an older gentlemen, whose names escaped him, and he had been named a war hero. His medals and ribbons were kept in a small cupboard, deep in the West Wing. It was time to banish the fear that had chewed a hole in his self-confidence and respect.

Clarice's death to the fallen soldiers' was different. The soldiers' death had been seared into his mind, forming an everlasting amalgamation, forbearance, his resignation. Mustiness filled Creighton's nose as he stood before the cupboard, a polygonal doorway. He bit his lip again and touched the round knob and caressed the wood with his thumb. He turned the knob, pulled the door, and entered the cupboard.

Again Creighton's eyes meet light, constrict, by moonlight this time. It has soothed him, this soft blue, this breeze and warmth, and heard is the ritualized pat! pat! in the distance. An all too familiar sound, gunfire, and there! The wounded soldiers. He can remember what happens next. The Vietcong are close. Creighton—the four soldiers, wounded, are lying in the wet soil; Creighton can see himself, younger, taller, wearing fatigues—drawing straws with the two healthy soldiers who are still standing. He sees himself drawing the straw shorter than the others. The two healthy soldiers, who can walk, run into the bush, leave him and the four wounded men behind. Creighton, watching, re-lives the moment, sees himself putting a gun to a wounded soldier's head and pulling the trigger. Two bullets to make sure the job is done. Then the next, and the next, and the next, eight bullets. Creighton has turned away as he hears himself finish off the last three soldiers, hears himself run into the jungle. Creighton has bowed his gray head before the four dead soldiers and has uttered something; and he sees them, as if what he has said had worked, lift out of their chests, and the four men, who are wearing fatigues and bullet holes, look at him clement and pull him with their eyes back through the cupboard doorway, back into his home.

The musky air of the hallway refilled his nostrils. He was in shambles. Every step each of the four soldiers took chipped off a piece of his sensible state of mind. He had not only seen himself, the murderer, run back into the jungle, but he also felt those emotions mixing with those at present. He felt his run through the jungle and was pleased, relieved, and thankful those had passed rather than he.

As the days bore on and as the dead soldiers stood and walked in the living flesh, he began to notice the paint inside the house was peeling. Cobwebs began accumulating on the chandeliers, candles flickered then burned out. He looked out of a window from the grand hall and noticed a thick fog had descended down onto his villa, obscuring his vision.

He needed to revisit the times when he first befriended these soldiers, when the relationships were fresh. Only he had no photos, no pieces of them, nothing. Only the notion existed, and, of course, the four dead soldiers. The memories and the actual soldiers traveling through his home walked through walls as if the walls did not exist, as if they held no weight.

Creighton toyed with the idea of going back into the cupboard, searching there for something, what? He did not know. All he knew was that he needed to gain perspective on who these men were, where they came from, where they would have gone, and still, a strong sense was preventing Randall Creighton from entering the cupboard. Instead, he approached a single soldier.

This man, excluding the two holes in his temple, was the best-looking man, the man who looked most like a soldier, the man who had taken strong residence in Creighton. The soldier had a long, bony jaw line and pouting lips, which created dark traces around his mouth. His lips had turned gray and grayer still over the weeks. Creighton pulled at the soldier's vest. "Excuse me," Creighton said. "Excuse me, private. Who are you?" The soldier flickered, a small twinkle in his eyes, slight recognition and the soldier batted his eyelashes and shifted his vision, brief, and turned back to his inward glare. "Soldier," said Creighton. "Who are you?" The man flinched. "Soldier, Goddamnit? Who are you? Who are you, soldier? Talk to me, Goddamnit!" The image shifted like a hologram, as if the man shone through a prism and the soldier backed away and came forward again.

Creighton, exasperated, eased into an idea of his daughter who was washing in and out of the walls. Randall Creighton turned to the soldier, the man with two bullet holes in his head, which Creighton had put there, Creighton the war hero, the decorated soldier, the one who had made it home. He turned to the faded soldier, hardened his face and saluted. The chiseled man stood, slow, straight at attention and returned the somber gesture and a tear perhaps had fallen. Creighton could not tell. The man's face was as translucent as a tear, and again the soldier backed away and walked east into the good wing.

A scabbard. Creighton felt like a scabbard. He was a bag full of trinkets, of age. Still he felt, with slightness, haphazard upon walking to his armchair and sitting down and lighting his pipe. He eased into a trance, smoke filling his sinuses. He closed his eyes and immersed himself in clarity. He felt the walls around him breathe, his home, and upon opening his eyes he noticed some of the cobwebs were gone, the paint had grown a little more vibrant, and the candles, which had burnt out, were flickering once again, ignited, miraculous. He breathed and remembered.

Loneliness was no longer a factor. Creighton had his family and friends in the house with him. He did feel euphoria, joy, though, not the type of euphoria one felt when triumphing over hardship (although he had triumphed; he had conquered his past). This was the type of euphoria one experienced with delusions, a delusion of grandeur, for Creighton had delved into memories and had made them his own. A detachment from reality. A third-prong grasp. An acceptance of this. The giddiness he felt fueled his behavior. He had made the time, made the decision to now relive his Beatrice's death, the only memory binding him tight.

He needed to see the woman. With the hair of an angel, she should have been a goddess. He cherished her. He had lived in complete love and togetherness with her, for she carried with her control, and she had mothered his daughter, Clarice, whom he had saved, brought

back to life. To give that gift back to Beatrice, to give the gift of life—her own life and her daughter's—back to her had him feeling completed.

He needed to find out how she had died. Her body was found with the others', underneath the ocean, buried by a day's sand.

The bedroom. The eye of life, where his life and Clarice's had been created.

Long and empty years had passed since he walked down that corridor, in the West Wing, the corridor, which held only that bedroom, the master bedroom. Creighton turned the corner and walked placated, and in entirety, across the lavender carpeting to the door.

He takes a deep breath and pulls open the door that leads to their old bedroom. At first, the darkness has veiled his eyes. Pure black, reaching out and touching his eyes, Creighton notices he is in the ocean, eighty feet below water level. A gelatinous membrane. He extends in and feels cold water, gurgling. He pulls out his hand and tastes the salty reaches. He has ventured, and there! He has felt with his hand five slender fingers. A hand. He, with all his strength, is pulling out the hand into visible light. Fingers, nails! He recognizes them. A ring. He is pulling, pulling. There is resistance. With all his strength he pulls at Beatrice, to pull her back into his life. As her arm comes out dripping, the membrane stretches.

And then, it pops!

Creighton was blown back from the doorway, water gushing out onto the carpet and his face, soaking the walls. Sprawled onto the carpet are a dozen, well-dressed men and women, inside his home.

The water slopped through the halls, ran through the fibers of the carpet, and Creighton ran. He ran into the living room, where dust covered the floor, holes accentuated the walls, roaches scurried across the floor and ceiling. Beatrice and the others were walking beside him like a shadow. No features held any difference or substantiality. Everybody was the same. Creighton was aghast when the men and women, the soldiers, and Clarice began hemorrhaging others into his home. As each new entity flooded out of the phantoms that were Creighton's past, the ocean splashed and, eager, encroached onto the sitting room floor, rolling and receding. More personalities spewed out of the walls, and more phantoms, and Creighton felt his train of thought explode into the corners of his psyche. The puzzle pieces that made up his rational mind, the nuts and bolts, shattered into millions of tiny picture-esque, oblong pieces. The windows shattered, all the candles blew out, extinguished, cabinets and drawers opened and slammed shut, chandeliers swayed, violent, and fell, crashing to the floor, bugs disgorged from the cracks in the ceiling, swarming Randall Creighton.

He heard whispers in his head. He lost everything that kept the minute features of his cognition wrapped up so tight. He ran, ran away from the bugs, ran away from the voices, ran away from his villa. For the first time in his life he ran. He ran straight for the door, and out of his house, ran into the thick muggy fog that surrounded his once humble home. He ran far, far into the distance.

He was out.

Finally out.

Finally out of his mind.

Fire!

Throughout my studies in the cosmological components of our world, I, Theodore Taylor, have come to notice a peculiar setting, in which the five elements—fire, earth, air, water, and consciousness—come together and dictate the mortality of our Earthy bodies. In people, a single element reigns supreme, and differs from person to person. The theory of this cosmological placement has been symbolized by the pentagram, which, in its five points, has symbolized the five elements. The flow of the cosmic elements through the central nodes of the human body do render one talented in their respective behaviors; and I do think it customary to state not all are talented in the ways of the supernatural. What met my eyes, on that rainy night, so many nights ago, could only be set into motion by those portentous and affiliated with the supernatural, as not my eyes nor my mind ever thought of such things as plausible. Maintaining faithful to the fact that human beings are grounded on the Earthy level of existence cannot be sustained, as the storm which presided that night was something of a lower cosmic force. Whether upper or lower, as the case may be, the occurrence took me by its innocuous and foretelling zeal, which has become an obsession. Nights, now, I look into the flames of a candle, musing on what really sustains the fire, and what really composes the light, which we all know and take for granted. That it is something far beyond the human mind's capacity to understand I, assured, think is so; and as sure as Prometheus stole the element from god, I do think of the element of fire such that it, perhaps, is something secret, and should not have been taken to the Mortals. For the Mortals are now under the influence of something so malevolent and sardonic their Fates are sure sealed and locked up in the box above the clouds, or, perhaps, deep within Earth, so none can escape absolute pain upon leaving the Earth; as I am sure, now, after seeing the man perish by means of the sinister element, the epitome of all elements will be experienced, felt, and recognized upon our inevitable deaths. Being such that fire, in its dormant states, such as flickering on the wick of a candle or in the safe rotunda of a pit of fire, cannot and will not change my mind, in that fire is the element which makes us fear and fire is the element which makes us paranoid and delusional, and fire is the element which the humble servants of Hades use upon collecting the Souls of the damned. Therein do I find myself horrified, as I have witnessed the apex of the element; and do find myself assured and under the influence of the element, which, with wholesomeness, controls Mortals at will. Take from this what you will, but by the end of this tale, the listener, whomever they may be, may rest assured that Fire! breathes in their lungs, and that Fire! is the sole perpetrator of all hate, anguish, and adversity experienced by any and all, and that Fire!, as peaceful and enlightening as it may seem, is in fact murderous, vengeful, and wicked into its very physiology; this is so much the case that I, upon this warning, feel the licking of the flames of Hades in my chest and the uneasy fumes, filtering into my skull.

Nights ago did I see a man burn to death before me. It was no natural fire; and it could only be brought about by the entities who controlled the element, that is to say practitioners of the occult. This man was my brother; and as I stood above his ashes I thought upon the world what travesty this was, what kind of man could do this to a boy of twenty years of age? It was not a spontaneous occurrence, however, and many events led up to his eventual combustion.

Nights prior the terminal incident, I was skirting along the bounds of sleep, half conscious and half in dream state, when I heard, from the conjoining room, cackles, which came from my brother; and I was awoken by the sheer vivaciousness and rambunctiousness of this cackling that I rose and went to his door and knocked. The scent of fire was omnipresent outside the doorway, and he refused to answer. I heard, every thirty seconds or so, another volatile cackle and the eruption of flames. The roaring of the element, beyond the doorway, was unmistakable; and I thought of he who lay beyond the doorway an arsonist, letting forth flame, spitting and rending throughout the apartment, by means of some juvenile prank. This, of course, was farthest from the truth; and as I crept back into my quarters I heard the shrieking of the poor boy, a sound painful as the Earth-shattering throat could unfold. I slept not that night; and when I rose the following morning, at twilight, I ventured into the living area to find my brother perched upon a chair, sipping a cup of coffee, with bright red burn marks on his arms and neck. I questioned him on the matter; and yet he denied any sort of usage of fire the preceding night, and presently left me alone in the living area to mull over my thoughts and observations of the preceding night and the morning. He had fallen into the camaraderie, and invited into the apartment on one event, a man adorned with black raiment, a bald man, with a head pale as a moon in full. The man, I saw at a glance, had nails longer than a big cat's and eyes emblazoned with fury. Brief, I acknowledged the man; and before long he took his leave of our apartment, leaving my brother, reclusive, in his sleeping quarters. The man I never once more saw, until the evening of my brother's immolation. My brother returned home late in the evening, with bandages on his arms and neck, and a grin on his face, which told not of the impending doom, in which he would find himself, in less than forty-eight hours.

The time of pacifism had elapsed, discord taking its place. Eleven o'clock P.M. commenced, two days prior the relaying of this tale, and the man, with hooded raiment entered the apartment, with notable fervor. He stormed into my brother's locale and began spitting words, which sounded hoarse and distended, and quick. He spoke: "Dare you use the power of Baël for selfish reasons? You have damaged your body with his Spirit, and you have shamed the order of Psilolexia! You are no longer a Brother! I will burn for this, you blasted boy. Learn! Learn your place here, tonight, as you are no longer admitted in this Kingdom!"

The man, I heard, stormed from the room, slamming shut each door as he exited the vicinity. I ventured out into the common area, and was met by my brother, who in one hour would fall victim to the element, which was so wholesome and revered. He cooed me and reassured me all was well and that the man in black raiment would never once more appear. I retired; and before long I was awoken by the shrieking gasps of a man having begun to smolder. Once more, I exited my room, and the harrowing sight before me had extended into the reaches of my heart; so much so that before throwing a blanket over the boy, I let out a shriek of my own. The blanket was, with bitterness, burnt through; and from the open mouth of the boy came balls of orange and black fire, which gravitated towards two spikes on my brother's head. They accumulated there and traveled down his face towards his throat. His face was terrible and burnt; and he threw me aside and ran outdoors into the cold rain. I followed; and upon seeing his entire body, his throat spitting forth embers of distinct red color, his arms waving, leaving behind them tracers of light and smoke, burning, I, with my own eyes, felt the welling of those infernal embers within me. That is was like osmosis of flames is not far from the truth; for as I watched my brother burn, my eyes felt emblazoned with hate and vehemence, as if something dæmonic were attempting to escape from them. The thermogenisis lasted thirty seconds before the boy was covered in flames. I was unable to watch and closed my eyes. Opening them once more, I saw the heavy, cold suburban rains could do nothing against the conflagration. Wooded areas surrounding instilled only further dreadfulness; and a waxing upstate New York moon split the storming clouds in two. Two more minutes passed by with excruciating cries of pain and stunning visuals. He, by the third minute of the inferno, was breaking up, like the Tectonic plates of Earth. He, slow, discontinued living, and fell into clumps of ash and residue. The rain thickened up the remains of my brother, and I had not a single bit of flesh to redeem. His body was burned, in entirety; and it was, in its finality, the moment I knew mortality was assured and Fate of human kind, and no man living, occultist or regular denizen, could penetrate the realm of immortality. It seemed too evident, so evident, in fact, I only retreated back into my apartment, and decided to file a document with the morgue the following morning. I, morose and inept, incapacitated, slept in tossing rhythms the entire night. While I was fearful of the events, which had taken place, I was not as mystified as the following morning, following a strange sequence of dreams, in which I was swimming in water, water so vast it took my eye in full, and so I saw nothing other than water, water everywhere; and what shook me the most was I had awoken drenched in sweat, moisture, so I thought my Fate, my end, would be nothing apart from the death element of water. I escaped my sleepy prison and went into the shower, where I enveloped myself in the element. I know not if it is my Fate, death by water, but, if it is, I know now the phantasmal swooning of water cannot be contended with, as the expanse, in which I found myself, curious while dreaming, was only the beginning of my Earthy transience. I redoubled my efforts, in spirituality, hoping god existed and that there may be a benevolent protector of our realm, as what I saw the night prior was only of the dæmonic and of the hellish dominion of the devil.

Now, I speak, for there seems to be no other escape. When I sleep, I dream of water. When I wake, I wake in cold sweats; and when I shower I feel fear pulling at my ribcage, as if it were a chewing toy; and when I write, as I have stated, I feel the power of the element, which took my brother—Fire! Not for any reason, but for a reason I have not yet actualized, I find myself more and more yearning for the knowledge of the element. The mystification, which connected my brother and the element was apparent, to say the least; and, as I believe in pedigree, there must be some inherent talents in me. I will not pursue the origin of such myths, nor will I pursue the art of fire bending; and yet, implored do I feel to look into the burning candle, if only to find a shred of humanity.

The Brothers Leibowitz Incident

Upon arriving at the Schlien and Klondike offices, Ezekiel Leibowitz felt as if somebody was following him; he knew it was not the case. The presence he sensed behind him was dread. That Mordecai, along with Mr. Schlien, was awaiting his arrival was not helping his morale. He took to long steps over linoleum flooring, beige and gray, to the last door in the corridor, which was the entrance to the Schlien and Klondike offices.

He twisted the brass doorknob, which was cold and hexagonal. Save a few chairs with yellow upholstery and wooden frames, an azalea in the corner of the waiting room, and glass tables beside the chairs, the room was empty. Ezekiel Leibowitz knocked on the sliding glass window, opposite which was a black silhouette; and the window opened and a blonde woman with horn rimmed spectacles looked back at him, her mouth a horizontal line and expressionless.

"Can I help you?" she said.

"I'm here to see Mr. Schlien regarding the inheritance of Mrs. Lilly Leibowitz," said Ezekiel. "They should be waiting for me. I'm a little late."

"Sure, yes, they have been waiting for you," said the blonde secretary. "I'll buzz you in."

"Thanks," said Ezekiel, and the wooden door buzzed, and he twisted the knob, and then entered another hallway. Purple carpeting felt static beneath his feet. The walls were paneled with wood. Ezekiel continued down the corridor until he saw the plaque, which read Carl Schlien. He let himself into the office and saw Schlien and the back of Mordecai's head. Diplomas on the walls, a crystal ball, a brass pyramid, pens, manila files, and family photographs had the office looking professional yet warm. Schlien stood and gesticulated to the leather seat beside Mordecai.

"Sit down, Mr. Leibowitz, sit down. We've been expecting you for ten minutes now."

"My apologies for my tardiness," said Ezekiel, and he sat down and exchanged glances with his brother.

Mordecai had not changed much. He still possessed a face with undulating features. He wore spectacles with a stronger prescription, Ezekiel noticed, since their last reunion, which was upwards of ten years ago. "Brother," Mordecai said. "It's good to see you."

Ezekiel wished he thought the same. In fact, he was repulsed by Mordecai's presence in the office, Mordecai having not visited their mother once throughout her sickness. Mordecai had called, Ezekiel reflected, maybe twice. "Glad to see you're happy," Ezekiel said, and returned his gaze to Mr. Schlien, insinuating his desire for the meeting to commence.

"Shall we begin?" said Schlien. He opened a file and leafed through a few pages. "Your mother made things very simple," he said. "There is the storage unit, which

269

may hold items of significance. There is the jewelry. There is the house. I presume you have hired me to supervise the dispersion of these properties, and if all involved do not create unnecessary problems and tribulation, there will be no difficulty in exacting a smooth transition of funds."

Mordecai said, "We thank you. You are correct and there will be no difficulties."

Schlien nodded and continued, "I suggest we put the property on the market as soon as possible. The jewelry, as per your mother's request, will be split evenly between the brothers. As per the storage unit, she has not specified. Which brings me to the question: What is it you want to do with the items in the unit?"

Mordecai said, "Let Ezekiel have the storage unit. To me, it is a hassle, and, as I live on the West coast, I am unable to sift through endless antiquities."

Ezekiel, as was his demeanor, said nothing, and felt the dread once more behind him.

"It's settled," said Mr. Schlien. "Ezekiel gets the storage unit. The house goes on the market. The jewelry gets halved. Are there any questions?"

Ezekiel shook his head is dissent.

Mordecai said, "No questions."

"If that is so, I will need your signatures." Mr. Schlien flipped around a document, which was the agreement to the dispersion of the inheritance.

The brothers signed their names on their respective lines, shook hands with the attorney, and exited the office. They went down the tawdry hallway, Ezekiel with angst in his gut, ahead of Mordecai, who, Ezekiel noted, had become in age ostentatious.

The brothers, having exchanged heady and perturbed silence, exited the Schlien and Klondike offices and went out through the electric sliding doors into the parking lot, where there were brittle oak trees and scattered leaves.

Mordecai, in this laconic middle ground, this foreboding no man's land, broke the silence. "It's too bad Ma's gone," he said.

Ezekiel was taken aback in that Mordecai, back from his perpetual roost on the West coast, had the gall to say anything at all about their mother's death. "You never were there," Ezekiel said. "Now, you want to show sentimentality when you're required to be present. It's ingratiating."

"I wasn't able to visit her. It was like I was being slammed with bilge in the workplace. I wasn't able to get away."

"Not even a phone call."

"I called," Mordecai said.

"I have more fingers on my right hand than the number of times you called."

"I was being slammed," Mordecai said.

"I hate you," said Ezekiel, and unlocked his car door and drove away from Mordecai, who was standing by the curb, senseless. Ezekiel did not know, and neither did Mordecai, that this was their final exchange.

Aboard the plane and headed towards the West coast and San Diego, Mordecai opened a bag of peanuts and sipped his coffee. He had not expected the reaction from Ezekiel, though he did know how Ezekiel felt about him ever since their father had died. Where did he get the courage? Mordecai asked himself, and decided it was the well water.

Mordecai had seized the opportunity in getting a window seat on this short but grueling flight from Cleveland to San Diego. He enjoyed watching the cirrus clouds pass and their uncanny topography. It was not that he did not love his mother—he did—but an obdurate fissure, which was Ezekiel, kept him from visiting or calling. Maybe, he thought, as he threw another peanut in his mouth, he did not love her at all and he only told himself he did, to fool himself into believing he was human. Mordecai closed his window and shut his eyes and began feeling disoriented. The pilot woke him in what seemed minutes later. They were nearing San Diego International Airport. The airport, a haphazard and skittering debacle, neared debauchery. Passengers and aircraft, luggage and pretzel stands and leaflets, entered and exited one another, and they overwhelmed Mordecai.

His carry-on luggage in his hand was all he brought with him to Cleveland. He stayed only one night in a lackluster establishment and ate only from the snack bar. He was famished and walked outdoors into the familiar Californian air, and then went to the long-term parking lot, where he had parked his car for the weekend. The aging Jaguar was in good order and present. Upon arriving home, he took off his loafers and jacket and went into the office, where he intended to sift through the accumulated documents and shred the unneeded ones. Rustic, the office was Mordecai's preferred place to rest. A shelf was full with an outdated Encyclopedia Britannica and books regarding real estate. Newton's Cradle ticked perpetual on the desk. A gargantuan chunk of petrified wood, above the desk, was anchored to the wall by hooks. Mordecai, fatigued, for five minutes shredded documents, and then he sat back in his leather chair.

Ezekiel kissed his wife and kids and prepared a cup of rosebud tea. His eldest was toying with his handheld; his wife was lulling the young one to sleep. Subsided, the anger towards Mordecai was tolerable; when active it was detrimental. Drinking his rosebud tea, Ezekiel watched his four-year-old son. The boy, with his fleshy, watery face, glanced back at him. The boy never had met his own uncle and never would. Ezekiel, for that, was somewhat thankful. There was, however, an irrevocable notion relations between he and Mordecai should have been better. They had been split, diverged like two halves of a blade of grass.

Ezekiel's wife entered the kitchen. "How was it today?" she said.

"Miserable and humiliating."

"That bad?"

Ezekiel finished off his rosebud tea, got up, and set the cup in the sink. "Mordecai is Mordecai," he said, and sat back down at the kitchen table.

Ezekiel's wife said to the boy, "Finish up the game and it's time to do your homework."

Ezekiel, his wife and son were silent. The clock ticked, a tree's branches and leaves tapped the window pane, the boy's fingers punched the buttons of the handheld with deftness, and the air conditioning thrummed into life—all these composite and infinitesimal sounds descended Ezekiel Leibowitz into trance, and all at once, he was alone in the kitchen and the boy and his mother had gone into the boy's bedroom to commence homework. On Ezekiel's tongue, the residual flavor of rosebuds clung, tingling and sweet. The kitchen table was clean, but he cleaned it off with a paper towel anyway. He dusted off the countertops, cleaned the sink, and moved into the living room to dust the shelves. He wadded up the paper towels, threw them in the trashcan, and decided to lie on the couch. Ezekiel strode into the living room and one toe stubbed the edge of the end table and Ezekiel lost his footing and collided into the coffee table with his head. He was unconscious when his wife and son found him. Crusted on the rug beneath Ezekiel's head was a large purple blot.

A linear strike through logic, an imperceptive syncretic had conjoined the Leibowitz brothers by an anomalous encounter with hate. In the seconds, during which Ezekiel Leibowitz lay on the floor in a purple globular crust, an earthquake 5.5 on the Richter Scale in the state of California had occurred, and Mordecai Leibowitz, ponderous and sitting at his desk, was readying himself for lunch and preparing for an afternoon sleep when the tremors shook the office, the Encyclopedia Britannica fervent in the bookshelf, Newton's Cradle faulting out of time, the tremors growing in violence, and pens and documents on the desk had begun to oscillate and move across the desk; the chunk of petrified wood, too, which hung over Mordecai's desk was jostled, and the hooks in the wall had come loose and the wood, with great force, dropped. That which followed was an aberration in reason. It was a harmonious inconsistency to natural order. The petrified wood had crushed Mordecai Leibowitz's cranium.

That Which Was Buried within Mount Kilimanjaro

The cave, dug out of the fossiliferous rock, was very small and stifling hot. Quinton Dudley could not fathom how the cave and the relic he found had not been found earlier by the locals or other tourists; he gazed at the discolored cranium and marveled at the barred teeth and wide, black eye sockets and sunken temples, and he picked up the skull. Quinton Dudley, a man of humility and integrity, ran his fingers across the fissure which separated the parietal lobes. It weighed little—nine or ten pounds at most—the optical centers, brain and muscle tissue having disintegrated over the recent epoch. Steady and increasing in altitude since the Precambrian eon had been this volcanic formation, in which Quinton Dudley, a tourist in Kilimanjaro Region, Tanzania, now stood. This was his last day on the African continent. His plane back to New York departed nine o'clock A.M. the following morning. Quinton, resolute and gladdened by the three-fold occurrence—the trip to Mount Kilimanjaro, the decision to break away from the tour group, and the unearthing of this, it seemed to him, ancient skull—was not embittered at the finality of his African experience. On the contrary, he was quite looking forward to seeing his wife, Annalise Dudley, whose idea it was for him to escape the American white-collar confines and go someplace he never had gone before. She had even proposed of his going alone, so the pressurized boundaries in Quinton could disseminate. Seven days later, Tanzania had a heady and perturbed Quinton Dudley in its borders.

He sped back to his rental, a small, manual transmission Renault, with the skull under his shirt, and returned to his hotel room and set the skull on the night stand. He was dehydrated from the hot excursion into the Tanzanian wilderness and he took a bottle of water out of the mini fridge and drank it. He looked again at the skull—preponderance and unbelievingness. He picked it up again and traced his thumb over the zygomatic bone and it glared lifeless back at him, evidence of a pre-historical people, a progenitor of the human race, a collagen manifestation which had survived unfound through the expanse of perhaps thousands of years until two hours ago. Quinton Dudley smiled, toothless and tight-lipped, but he was not happy; somewhere a sensation which left him scared had become manifest. Setting down the skull, he stripped of his clothing and got into the shower.

He knew he had acquired something he should not have. He should have given the skull to the Tanzanian government and scientists, but he was not going to give up his find. Instead, he would deposit the skull, wrapped in t-shirts and pants, in his suitcase, and bring it back to the States. It was better than any other souvenir store trinket. He had already gotten a SAVE THE LIONS t-shirt, a cotton tapestry, and a plastic tumbler, but none of these souvenirs came close to the timeless skull. How would Annalise take the induction of the skull into the home? He would have to preconceive an argument for keeping it, but Annalise was accepting of many of his quirks. That was the reason he married her.

He dried off with a hotel towel and slipped on his briefs. The mirror was foggy, but he combed his hair in it anyway. He put on his khakis and a button-down shirt, and then went downstairs for dinner at the hotel restaurant. In the elevator, a woman wearing heavy furs commented on the soccer game between Tanzania and Ethiopia. She had a heavy British accent; but Quinton Dudley could not stop thinking about the skull. He returned her formalities but did not hear himself speak. All he wanted was a dinner of rabbit and green beans and a good sleep, so, tomorrow, he was rested for the return flight to LaGuardia Airport.

When he was finished with dinner and two English pints of stout, he ascended to the sixth floor using the elevator and walked down the hallway to room 615, inserted his room key into the slot and entered the hotel room; he stripped of his khakis and shirt, and then got into his pajama bottoms and a white tee-shirt. He turned on the television to watch the final few minutes of the soccer match but was not interested. He turned off the television with a static-electric punch of a button and rolled over on a side. He woke to the blue Tanzanian morning penetrating his curtains. The skull was perched on the night stand. Quinton noticed the archaic brow and angular chin, got up from bed, took the skull in his hands, and began wrapping articles of clothing around it. Then, he tucked the package into the corner of his luggage and zipped it up. He checked out of the hotel and got a bottle of water from the gift shop. He got into the Renault and drove to Kilimanjaro International Airport. Quinton checked his bag before going through security. The ornamented Air Tanzania employees took his suitcase and put it on the conveyor belt. He went through security without a hitch. Nobody bothered him or questioned him. Nobody hassled him. He walked through the metal detector, put his belt and shoes back on, and pocketed his cell phone and money clip. Then, he went to the gate and sat down on the faux leather bench. Boarding call was in forty-five minutes. Quinton Dudley watched the people walk by—children, boys and girls, and their parents, a tall blonde with what must have been 6 BMI, and an African clergyman. He went to the gift shop and bought a bottle of water for the long flight. When he got back to the gate the plane was boarding. An Air Tanzania employee scanned his boarding pass, he boarded the aircraft, shimmied down the aisle, and took his seat. The screen on the headrest in front of him played a montage natural Tanzania—lions, gazelle, and grasslands—traditional dance and metropolises. The flight attendants closed the doors and the screen on the headrest began with the safety demonstration. Twenty minutes later, the aircraft was in flight and the flight attendants were dispersing pretzels and drinks. Quinton Dudley shut his eyes, his ears pressurized, and he flexed his jaw to let out the air. In eighteen hours, they would be landing in New York.

Quinton Dudley exited the aircraft and made his way towards immigration. The line was lengthy, but in twenty minutes Quinton Dudley was talking to a man behind a plexiglass window who asked him if he had anything to declare.

"Nothing to declare," said Quinton. His passport was stamped, he exited the terminal, suitcase rolling behind him, and he found Annalise outside the terminal.

"Welcome back to the States," she said. Annalise had flaxen hair which she most times wore in a bun. Now, her hair was down and, at the sides of her full head of hair, were two expressions, which were her ears. She wriggled her nose and kissed Quinton.

"Thanks," he said, and they strode towards the parking lot where Annalise had parked.

"How was Tanzania?" she said.

"Tanzania was good. Hot, but comfortable."

They got into the car and drove South. The Bronx was not like Tanzania. Instead of hot, pollenated air, one breathed quite the opposite in an American metropolis. Annalise drove on the congested freeway with deftness and, though Quinton missed her, he found himself already missing Tanzania. He had been there for two weeks, which was enough time to instill certain bonds. Annalise pulled into their driveway and into the garage. She turned off the car, both got out and went into the house. Pinewood floorboards and Persian rugs, bookcases filled with Annalise's college textbooks and porcelain bowls painted in geometrical patterns, sponged walls and granite countertops were the outcome of Quinton's and Annalise's hard work and life savings. They did not have children, nor did they want any, both reserved, private, and unwilling to contend with the tumult of parenthood. Quinton went upstairs and unpacked his suitcase. He unraveled the skull and placed it on the bed.

Annalise came into the bedroom, saw the skull, and screamed. "What is that? A skull?"

Quinton smiled. "Yes, it's a skull." He picked it up off the bed and bounced it in a palm. "I found it in a cave, on Kilimanjaro. It's all right. I want to put it downstairs in the living room."

She said, "Downstairs in the living room," rather mocking.

"If that's okay with you," he said.

"I—I don't see why not. You found it on Kilimanjaro and I'm sure it means a lot to you."

"Thanks, sweet," he said, and he planted a kiss on her mouth, the skull in his hand, and then he went downstairs, put the skull on a shelf, and phoned his friend, RJ Samson. "RJ," he said, when RJ answered. "I want to show you something. Come here as soon as possible." He hung up and an hour later the doorbell rang, and RJ Samson was shown a Paleolithic skull found within Mount Kilimanjaro.

"That's horrendous," he said. "Aren't you kind of grossed out having that in your house?"

"Not at all," Quinton said. "It's a piece of history and I found it. I'm glad to have it. It should be the damned center piece. I'm overjoyed."

"How much do you think that thing could go for in auction?" said RJ. "Probably thousands, hundreds of thousands."

"I'm not interested," said Quinton.

"You should get an estimate," said RJ. "I know somebody who knows somebody."

"I don't want to know how much some floozie would pay for it."

"You should get an estimate."

"For shits and grins, I may as well," Quinton said. "Call your guy. Not that I would sell it. I would never sell it."

"I'll make the call tonight and I'll let you know about the date."

"Thanks, RJ; but what a find, huh?"

RJ Samson shrugged. "I've got to get going," he said. "I'll call you in the morning."

"Very well," said Quinton, and Quinton walked him to the front door and they shook hands. He went into the kitchen, where Annalise was having a cup of coffee. "We're going to get an estimate on the skull," he said.

"Oh, yeah?" she said. She seemed distant. "It could be worth something."

"I'm not selling it," Quinton said.

Annalise, too, shrugged; and Quinton went outside to get some fresh air. Oak trees dispensed of their green and yellow leaves over the stone table in the center of the Dudley's yard. They did not sit at the table; it was for show, a circular stone table which had corroded in time and was covered by moss. He would not sell the skull. It was too rare. He knew scientists and collectors all over the world wanted pieces like this and paid big coin for them, too. It made no difference to Quinton. The skull would reside in the living room until they sold the house, or it burned down. It was the best piece he could have gotten from Tanzania and it was almost as if the skull were the very reason he went to Tanzania in the first place. He would be damned if anyone else got their hands on it.

Annalise was in the kitchen, cooking dinner. It was getting late. The sun was coming down and Quinton was starved. When the sun was set, and the dishes were washed and put away, Quinton and Annalise went to bed and had each other unlike it ever had been. Quinton woke at nine A.M. to Annalise over him, the cordless phone in her hand. "It's RJ," she said.

Quinton took the phone and said, "RJ?"

RJ, having the night before made contact with a specialist of African antiquities, said the meeting was arranged and tomorrow evening they would get together to examine the skull. Quinton agreed and hung up the phone. He doubted a specialist in African antiquities knew anything about a Paleolithic skull. He wanted breakfast and he wanted to see the skull. It could be worth millions, he thought, getting up out of bed and going into the kitchen to have a couple over-easy eggs. The eggs finished, he washed and put away his plate, and then went into the living room. The skull with its vacuum eyes and perforations looked ensconcing back at him. Really, he wanted to talk to this African antiquities specialist. He wanted to know about the man, or the remnants of the man, he had found in Africa.

The evening in which RJ, the specialist, and Quinton Dudley were to meet arrived. Presently, the doorbell rang, and RJ entered along with a bespectacled African-American man. "Let's see the piece," said the specialist, who introduced himself as Jerry Papa.

"Right this way," said Quinton. He led the specialist and RJ into the living room, where the skull was located.

The specialist looked at it and picked it up. "I've never seen something like this," he said. "And really it's out of my league."

Quinton was not surprised.

"If you want to know what I think," said Jerry Papa, "I think you should go to the papers and let someone who knows their stuff find you. Not many people know about ancient bones or fossils. Go to the papers, Quint. Someone will find the story and enquire."

RJ said, "That's a good idea, Quinton. You should go to the papers."

Quinton turned the thought over in his mind. It was not a bad idea. He did want to know about the skull and he wanted to know how much it would go for; he wanted to know if he had landed solid gold. He said, "I'll go to the papers, but only because there's no other way to find someone who can tell me about this. Really, I want to know what it's worth."

Jerry Papa replaced the skull on the bookshelf. Annalise, who had been making coffee, came in and announced the coffee was ready. The four—Quinton and Annalise Dudley, RJ Samson and Jerry Papa—went into the kitchen and drank coffee, a vacancy suspended which nobody could quite place.

Quinton Dudley, after a day's deliberation, sent word to the Daily News he had found a most peculiar piece in the wilderness of Tanzania, Africa, Kilimanjaro Region. An editor, after two days, got back to him, asking when they could meet to discuss the piece more personally? Quinton and the editor of the New York paper decided to meet the following evening and discuss the piece over coffee. What made you decide Tanzania? How long were you in Tanzania? Where and just how did you find the skull? Are you nervous regarding legal troubles? The final question was the editor's personal curiosity and was not mentioned in the article. The following morning a piece of about a thousand words, located on the bottom corner of the travel section, titled "Paleolithic Skull Found in Kilimanjaro," was published. A small photo was included—a featureless Quinton Dudley holding the skull in his left hand. He received no phone calls until the third day following the publication of the article.

Mr. Umberto Icar. who was affiliated with the Foley Auction House, said he would like to see the skull, and perhaps with the skull's owner's O-K auction off the skull to the highest bidder. Quinton became furious. A slew of profanity which ended on "incipient leech" escaped Quinton Dudley's mouth, and he hung up. He really could not believe he had just said all of that to Mr. Umberto Icar. He needed a drink. He went to RJ

Samson's house and rang the doorbell. RJ answered and let him in the house.

"What's bothering you, man?" said RJ.

"I got a call from a Mr. Umberto Icar, who is affiliated with Foley Auction House, and he wants me to sell the skull to the highest bidder. It infuriated me."

"Come in. Let's get us a drink." RJ poured two glasses of scotch.

Quinton was sitting on the living room sofa. The Samson's house was well decorated—the upholstery was purple and there were white angular sculptures on the wall and looked unnatural. Quinton did not like the style choice. In fact, he was rather put off by it and noticed he was more irritated than ever. He needed a drink bad. RJ gave him the glass of scotch and Quinton took it down in two sips.

"Better?" RJ said.

Quinton shook his head.

"Maybe this skull is getting to you," RJ said. "Maybe you should auction off the skull."

Quinton was fuming and turned toward RJ. "It's my skull," he said, his voice raised.

"Don't raise your voice, Quinton."

"I'll raise my voice if I want to."

"Maybe you should auction off the skull to the highest bidder."

Quinton was red and furious. "Finders keepers, losers fucking weepers."

RJ set down his drink and said, "Watch your mouth, you deprecating sonofabitch."

Quinton got up from the purple couch and RJ got up from the armchair. Quinton advanced toward RJ and struck him in the sweet spot on the chin, and RJ's eyes rolled back so Quinton saw the white undersides of his eyes. RJ went down. Quinton left the Samson house and went home. He spoke nothing of the exchange to Annalise, went to bed, and woke up disoriented and confused.

Ten o'clock, the doorbell rang. Quinton expected it to be RJ or the NYPD, who would take him to jail for battery. Instead, a man dressed in a black jacket, with short cropped hair stood at the door. "I'm Mr. Umberto Icar," said the man. "I'm affiliated with Foley Auction House. I'd like to talk to you about your find while in the Tanzania, Kilimanjaro Region. I feel you can get quite a purse for that find and I'd like to see it."

Quinton was bewildered and in disbelief. He slammed the door in Mr. Umberto Icar's face. The doorbell rang. Quinton opened it.

"I'd like to discuss the skull, Mr. Dudley, if that's okay with you."

"Get your damned grimy parasite feet off my property before I chop you up," Quinton said, and he slammed the door once more in Mr. Umberto Icar's face. The doorbell did not ring a third time. Quinton went into the kitchen and Annalise was flipping through a magazine. "People are all over my ass in regards to that skull," he said.

Without looking up, she said, "Maybe you should get rid of it."

Quinton gagged. "It's my skull," he said, and he went outside and watched the oak trees shed their leaves on the mossy stone table. It was hysteria. People were trying to get him to sell the skull, the best, the most archaic thing Quinton had ever been a part of. It was not just RJ. It was Mr. Umberto Icar, and now it was Annalise, too. It was hysteria and Quinton found it hard to breathe. He did not speak to anybody for the remainder of the day. When the night came, he and Annalise went to bed and Quinton made an advance on her, which she accepted. Soon, he was on top of her and he, nearing his peak, found himself hating his wife; Quinton, without any forethought, tagged her mouth hard at the same time as he arrived. Annalise began to cry and shriek. Quinton was delirious.

"Why?" she asked. "Why, Quinton, did you hit me?"

He spoke through the slurred ideas rambling in his head. "It was the skull," he said. "It was the skull. It must have been the skull." The fury and hatred had left him. He sat derelict on the edge of the bed, Annalise crying into her pillow. "It was the skull."

Between sobs, Annalise said, "I want to leave you."

"No, don't leave me. Don't."

"You need to get rid of that thing. You need to get rid of that thing as soon as possible."

Quinton knew she was right. He got up from the bed, put on his briefs and a white tee-shirt, and went down to the living room. The pond at the park? The sewer? Bury it in the Earth? It seemed as though in the short time period between arriving back home and now, the skull had taken an almost omnipotent control over him. He looked at the void-like eyes and the jagged bones of the cranium and the jutting zygomatic and mandible bones, knew he was looking at an invasive and unwelcome cognizance, and decided he was going back to Tanzania. He was not going to rid himself of this skull anywhere near him, not within fifty square miles, not within the United States. He went to his computer and booked a flight to Kilimanjaro International Airport for the following morning. Quinton packed his bags, but the clothes in the suitcase were not for him to wear. The return flight departed six hours following his arrival. The tee-shirts, underwear, and pair of shorts were to conceal the skull. Quinton got into bed and before long was asleep.

Quinton had awoken with his bag packed, and the skull wrapped in clothing was in the bag. Annalise was already out of bed and, in all likelihood, having her ritual glass of orange juice on the patio. The anger had subsided. Somewhere, Quinton rejected the previous night's entanglement; but, he knew it had happened. Annalise was more resilient than she knew. Quinton Dudley brushed his teeth, walked outside, and found Annalise sitting on the patio with one leg over the other. She was drinking orange juice.

"I'll be leaving in two hours," said Quinton.

She looked up at him and Quintin saw she had a fat lip. "Don't miss your flight."

"How's the orange juice?" Quinton said.

"Stings." Her foot jittered.

He could only hope she would still be here when he got home. Quinton Dudley went back inside and ate two slices of toast. He drank a cup of coffee and Annalise came inside, put her flaxen hair up into a bun which exposed her small pink ears and sterling silver earrings. She, too, had a cup of coffee. Her mouth was a plum and Quinton was unable to fathom how hard he had struck her. Annalise wriggled her nose, and as she went to the sink to wash her hands, Quinton remarked to himself, even atop the feeling he had gotten when he first apprehended the skull, the knowledge he was going to rid himself of it within the next forty-eight hours was more acute. He was not spending a minute longer in Tanzania than needed.

He boarded his flight and arrived in Tanzania at ten o'clock A.M., local time. He collected his bag and went to the car rental kiosk. He was on the road toward Kilimanjaro Region and Mount Kilimanjaro with the hour. The paradisiac park gaped, and the grasslands shimmered in the distance. Quinton parked the rented

BMW and approached the trail, which went to the summit of the mountain. He had the skull in his backpack and he followed the trail until he reached the section of trail off of which he had diverged four days ago. He remembered the area well. There was no mistaking the overgrowth and narrow passage between the trail, which tourists were supposed to follow, and the crevasse which led down into a rocky ditch. The mouth of the cave inside of which Quinton had found the Paleolithic skull was small and located in the rocky ditch. Quinton descended into the ditch. The mouth of the cave was at his feet. He entered the cave. It was odd and humid inside the cave, as Quinton remembered. He did not want to spend more time here than he had to. He removed the skull from his backpack and placed it in the uneven cave wall. He zipped up his bag and made for his rental, shimmying up the rocky ditch, and then descending back down the mountain. The climb was not easy. It had taken ninety minutes to ascend the mountain to the section of trail which diverged into the ditch and ninety minutes to descend to the base of the mountain. It had taken an hour to get the rental car and an hour to arrive at Kilimanjaro National Park. He had an hour remaining to get to the airport, return the rental, check his bag, and board the plane. He was cutting it close. Quinton sped down the two lane road towards the freeway and Kilimanjaro International Airport. He returned the car and took the bus to the terminal where he checked his bag, and he went through security as the plane was boarding. He ran through the terminal. They were calling his name over the intercom system— "Quinton Dudley, your plane is now boarding. Quinton Dudley, your plane is now boarding"—and Quinton, the doors about to close, got his boarding pass scanned by the ornate Air Tanzania employee; he boarded the aircraft!

Traditional Tanzania in the form of a familiar montage was viewed by an unnerved and exhausted Quinton Dudley. The aircraft soared Westward through the troposphere. Quinton did not watch movies; he did not play games on the screen. He sat and replayed the events of the past four days in memory and felt sheer abhorrence. He did not speak, though the man beside him attempted to start a conversation. He wanted to go home, kiss his wife, and rest. The aircraft landed and the passengers de-boarded systematic. Quinton waited until he was the last one to de-board. When he did, he made his way over the linoleum floor to immigration. The line was lengthy, but in twenty minutes Quinton Dudley was talking to a man behind a plexiglass window who asked him if he had anything to declare.

Nothing to declare," he said, and this time he was not lying.

Occipital Circus

Phil Gorman looked through the microscope, observing Brownian motion. The atoms ricocheted off of each other. There was complete disorder. Every time Gorman observed the phenomenon, he was brought back to his sound belief chaos reigned supreme. He believed chaos theory was the closest form of creationism there was. He did not believe in god, only in the figurative ideas such as charity, considered as Holy, and science, considered as blasphemous. For the latter, he was resentful. Here they were, trying to find the connection and the source, which bridged god and the human, and scientists all over the world were called heathens. For that, he was spiteful; and as he looked deeper into the microscope, he mused he had found just about all that was left—miasmic constellations of atoms, ions, and molecules, bounding and rebounding off one another, in what was complete and utter disarray, and he marveled at its conception.

The working day was nearing a close, men and women in white lab coats scurrying here and there, collecting notebooks full of notes, petri dishes of viruses, and vials of dye. Tonight, he was visiting the circus, the tent out on Forty-ninth street, which bordered the train tracks and had the omnipresent scent of kettle corn and cotton candy. He was going alone, sure; he had not anybody waiting for him at his apartment—he lived alone, and he had not had a girlfriend in some years—but it did not deter him from the enthralling notion: the zanies, the jesters, the big cats. He was a chemist by day, but at night, when the sun went down, he became a connoisseur of strangeness, movies like Georges Méliès' 1902 film, *A Trip to the Moon*, and his ever-growing collection of Dali reprints, like *The Persistence of Memory* and *Swans Reflecting Elephants* and *The Great Masturbator*. Often, he would close his eyes and think what it would be like to create something enigmatic. The alcohol would hit him, and he would drift, wanton, through the scape of delight.

He was terse and uncomfortable. Everybody knew it. Nobody invited him out to gatherings. He did not mind. It was the sole notion sociability was an illusion, people put on a certain façade when around camaraderie and, home, lent themselves to entire new philosophies. Gorman knew he did it—he acted resolute at work—but when he got home, he scared himself, it was so nonpareil.

Changing, once home, into a green button-down shirt and khakis, he hurried himself into readiness. The circus started at eight o'clock—it was seven-thirty—and presently, he was off, on the road, towards Forty-ninth and the circus.

This was going to be the third time this week he drove all the way out to Forty-ninth street, all for the same reason—the aerialist, one in particular, a girl, of about his age, with blonde hair in a bun and a spandex jumpsuit. Phil Gorman thought he was in love. He had gone to the Monday show and noticed this girl, whom he had never before seen—they must have picked her up in the recent weeks—and, again, to the Wednesday show. The Friday show was said to be something different. The circus brought in big cats for the finale during the Friday night showing. Gorman liked seeing the big cats roar and lash out their claws, while they were being whipped, or just feigning being whipped. He liked seeing the big cats jump through hula hoops. Chewing on his ritual kettle corn, he marveled, much like marveling at the Brownian motion phenomenon, these jungle cats, who had been captured and brought into captivity. Perhaps it was cruel. Perhaps it was slavery, but, Phil Gorman liked it, cruel as it may have been. He pulled into the gravel parking lot and pulled into a spot furthest back from the circus tent. His windows were rolled down and he heard the gravel crunching beneath the tires. He always liked the sound. It made the hairs on his neck stand up much like Pablo Picasso's *Accordionist* made the hairs on the back of his neck stand up the first time he had seen it.

Gorman felt a part of his mental being—the gaseousness and the liquidity and the solidarity, the states of matter and the evening—slip into diaspora. He was no longer Phil Gorman, chemist and eccentric. Now, he was a part of the circus, an integral cog in the machine, which chewed up and spit out heady, perturbed circus goers; for, without the audience there would be no circus. Having gravitated into the concessions tent, he noticed more people than usual. It was the Friday showing, after all; and he acquired a paper bag of kettle corn and made his way into the main tent, which breathed hot air and smelled of hay and mist.

Walking into the circus, a shrill cry heard, Gorman noticed a jester giving out vouchers to children, for their next visits. The bleachers, which surrounded center ring, shuttered as Gorman mounted and across them walked to the upper-most level. The first time he had come to the circus had been with his mother, in 1972. It was not the same circus. (The circus to which they had gone was located further westwards and was rather dismal.) She was long gone, had died of pneumonia back in the 90s and, really, Gorman missed her very little. She had been good to him, but how good can a mother be, when the boy is just starting to experiment with psychotropics and reading books like Freud's *Interpretation of Dreams* and Fredrick Nietzsche's *The Anti-Christ*?

He remembered, while sitting on the bleachers waiting for the show to commence, listening to folk music and his mother telling him to, "Turn that music down before things get ugly!" He could still hear Dylan's voice. "The only thing I knew how to do/Was to keep on keepin' on/Like a bird that flew—"

People had filtered in beside and beneath him, and then the tympani rolled, and cymbals crashed, and horns blared. "Ladies and Gentlemen! It is my pleasure, as Sir Wilfred Crew, to lead you on this exceptional journey through the fantastic, the supreme, the mysterious, the awe-inspiring, the jaw dropping spectacle that is Occipital Circus! Come with me, and you'll find the impossible, the improbable, the mysterious! Come with me, and you'll see the extravagant, the hilarious, the barbaric!" The lights turned off, and with another tympani roll and cymbal crash and horns, the spotlights turned on to five or six zanies, riding unicycles, juggling bowling pins. The horns kept on playing this up-beat, piercing, and synchronized music, which kept up with the zanies. Phil Gorman watched with intensity. He was anxious to see the aerialists, the one in particular. The zanies all crashed into one another and made a dog pile. Ropes dropped from the overhead platform. Women twisted down and, with deftness, climbed up, twisting and swinging back and forth. It was all so captivating. Children were watching, parents were watching, couples who came to the circus for a little good fun and hilarity were watching, and so was Phil Gorman, who took not one second for granted. He loved the zanies' make up, the rope-climbing women's legs—the zanies had gotten back on their unicycles and were cycling around center ring, jugging—and he loved the horns, which blared, and also the tympani, which rolled. How did they do it, these stunts which left him incredulous? There must be destiny if they can perform stunts which break the seeming laws of physics. Somebody must be pulling the strings, a puppet master, leading all men and women, performers and audience alike, to this place on this Friday night, as if they were marionettes. Gorman had given up. He had forgotten about his kettle corn and was staring, transfixed, at the aerialists when they came out. They swung back and forth, exchanging hands, trusting one another with their very lives. (There was no net should they fall.) Phil Gorman saw her, standing on the platform, and then with deftness she swung out to release her own bar and to catch another aerialist's hands, before jumping onto the other platform, which was across the way. It was for certain. Phil Gorman was in love. He forgot to breathe. He forgot to blink, and he was sure, from way up there, she, with her blue eyes, looked his way. Yes, Phil Gorman was in love.

The big cats came out, looking tired and estranged, hopeless. They took to acting for the crowd, jumping through hoops, with the notion in their minds treats followed their performance, the big cats, which, he was sure, were trained to act wild, but really were not. The big cat nearest him looked like something out of a painting, as if it belonged with the plethora of high-detailed graffiti closer-by his workplace, which was in the city. The big cat roared, and it was like a punch in the ribs, the roar so deep it rattled bones.

Coming to fruition was a knowledge, in Phil Gorman, a sureness, which could not have been kept at bay. It was chaotic and pedantic. All theories and all thoughts, all notions and all the

songs and paintings and all the films Phil Gorman had ever heard or seen, collected and were transparent and singular. Painted skin, centric versus peripheral knowledge, the zanies and the harlequin jesters in their chequered suits and bells, the dangling ropes from a central beam, which went straight over center ring, the red and blue and yellow and purple spandex outfits people like his favorite aerialist wore, every other night at eight o'clock P.M., to entertain wayward folks like himself—atoms, ions, molecules—bouncing and recoiling off each other in what was pure and utter calamity, the freezing over of Hell, the contrabass thoughts and the proverbial tympani, rolling and rolling, were as the epitome of organized delirium; and Phil Gorman, the man and the chemist, saw with his own eyes a semantic cleft in reality and in life which ceased the mind's chatter—gray matter and the synaptic phrases, by which the brain with itself communicated, in its paradoxical and hypocritical ways, the malleus bone hammering away at temporal precision, a note and a meaning skewed, all elements in a microscope, magnified to an uncanny and frightening organism, a dancing organism, and an organism in its own right, sovereign and elastic and supple, like the minds of people and of atoms, whom lived, and lived until there was absolution.

sovereign and elastic and supple, like the minds of people and of atoms, whom lived, and lived until there was absolution.

To Die in Brazil

Cletus Tumlin, for four hours, had been sitting in a wicker chair. He had not blinked in the past sixty seconds. There was no sensation in his arms or legs, and in many instances throughout the past four hours he was not able to see, a glimpse of a white void blotting out all which was surrounding him. Cletus Tumlin sat before a wall, which was torn in its wallpaper down the middle. In three seconds, the wallpaper would be decorated with gray matter.

It was instinctual, the way the conception of finality entered Cletus Tumlin's head—an oblong and haphazard birthing and simultaneous betrayal of his time in Brazil and of his time in Nashville, Tennessee. It was a composite acceptance of his end and of his meagre understanding of the divide between the living and the dead, existence and the extinct. Weightless in his hands was the device with which he was to exact his punctual and perfect exit—a single barrel shotgun, the medium between all Cletus had ever dreamed and dissected. Not one hundred miles distant was the beginning of the rainforest. Its dense and humid atmosphere grew only more dense and humid the further one traversed Westwards. Cletus had been to the rainforest many times as a researcher—he even fancied donning himself a scientist—of the Batrachian species, a rather well-developed species of amphibian, most especial in South America, as well as other amphibious and reptilian species. Even in Nashville, where Cletus had been born, the undeniable fixation, almost obsession, with fauna was evident; and he had contrived an insatiable hunger for knowledge regarding the animal kingdom. A pond had been behind the house in Nashville with a host of Batrachians. One could call it an infestation.

Cletus had decided, at seventeen years of age, that he would attend the University and study biology, and then move to a locale more fertile, virile and provocative; Brazil had in its domain a man, Cletus Tomlin, the summer of his twenty fifth birthday, and Cletus, steadfast, became a likable and noticeable personality in the research center in which he worked, and, too, had even been raised in status to supervisor of the laboratory. The home, in which he lived, was small and was not comfortable. It grew too warm in the evenings and, lying in bed, Cletus many times threw off the bed sheet and lay in his boxer shorts. It was the same as in Nashville—an impoverished homestead; but, there was, here in Brazil, an endlessness which compelled Cletus something close to an intellectual savvy. The people around Cletus, too, lived in shanties, Brazilians and indigenous, whom Cletus was not; nobody gave him a hard time, this Caucasian male, with spectacles. As was routine, Cletus, morning after morning, went outside into the backyard and waved to his neighbor, who was often watering the garden or feeding the chickens.

298

Cletus, too, had chickens, and in the morning time he went to the chicken coop and retrieved an egg for breakfast. This was the factor that sold the home, and Cletus, though thriving with skimpiness, went into his kitchen and turned on the gas stove and chopped up a quarter of an onion, poured a spot of oil in the pan, and friend the eggs over the onion. He, then, put away his fork, knife, and plate and went to the laboratory and studied the habits of Batrachians and similar species, which abounded in his psyche as a paradisiac locale.

On the wicker chair, Cletus Tumlin fumbled with the notion of the beyond. It seemed rather stark, insufficient, and incohesive, this monstrous idea of finality. The idea cloyed to him, as per the recent comprehension of his inferiority, his minuteness in regards to ecology. Cletus Tumlin thought of the oscillations in the surface of a pond, and thought humanity was quite similar. In effect, the oscillations grew wider and reached greater distances. That made much sense to Cletus. What did not was the significance of such species, such as himself, with the ability to create theories, which were unproved but ideal, and the inability to apprehend what actuality occurred in regard to the complexity of the ecosphere. The notion and the incomprehension, too, oscillated throughout Cletus Tumlin.

Instead of going to the laboratory, this day he went to a house he had not visited in months. It was the home of his girlfriend, or if she was not his girlfriend, she was a friend. Cletus had stopped visiting her when the thought entered his head, the thought about the forfeit of knowledge. Cletus walked through the chain link fence, up to the girl's house, and then knocked on the door. When she answered, she invited him in and gave him a glass of water.

Cletus watched the water swish and change. "Anna, it's good to see you," he said, knowing in full this was the last time he would in fact see her.

"And you," she said. "What has been keeping you away?"

"Work," he said. That was the first time he lied to Anna. In fact, he had been wallowing in bed, nights upon nights. "I've been busy."

"All has been well here," Anna said.

Cletus took a sip of water. The surface of the water dropped an inch and a half. They spoke of nothing for many minutes until Cletus said what he had intended to say upon arriving at Anna's house. "I've decided nature and its study is no longer for me. I'd have better luck studying the supernatural."

"To some there is no difference," Anna said.

Cletus finished his glass of water and put it on the glass coffee table. "I have to go," he said.

"So soon?" she said.

"So soon," Cletus said, halfway out the door, and in minutes he was at his next destination, the house of an associate, named Gerald Usther, beside whom Cletus had been researching his whole time while in Brazil. "Mr. Usther," Cletus said, upon seeing Gerald Usther sitting on his front patio.

"Mr. Cletus Tumlin, can I get you a drink?"

"Thanks, but no thanks," Cletus said, and sat on the seat beside a table, which was beside Usther.

"You weren't at the lab today," Usther said. "I was afraid."

"No need. All is well."

"Good, good." He took a drink of what seemed to be hard liquor. "Good thing you're the supervisor."

To that Cletus said nothing. He had something else he wanted to talk about. "Why do we study nature, Gerald?" he asked.

"It needs to be studied. That's what the scientific method is for. Nature is the perfect subject for the scientific method."

Cletus disagreed. He said, "We collect facts and then we come up with theories, theory after theory. It's as if all the data is used and minimized. The data is being voided by opinion."

"Let the philosophers think about that and lets you and me do the data collecting. There's no need analyze the scientific method."

"We study the most finite details imaginable— mutations, biological variations. It's futile and senseless."

"What do you suggest we do? Let the mutations and variations occur without recording them? That's insolent, Cletus."

"It seems to me fruitless."

"Where are you going with this?" said Usther. "Is this why you came here?"

"Nature and its study is endless. There is no need to study it from our paltry perspective."

"It's all that we've got," Usther said. "You think you can fathom another way?"

Cletus Tumlin rose from his seat and said, "Good bye, old friend," and went home. He opened the coat closet door, upon arrival, and withdrew the single barrel medium of deliverance, cocked it, and sat on the wicker chair. Heliconia flower, its ten pink and green buds; a saturated rubber tree; orchids, cognizant; cacao nuts, large and pink; the giant water lily, which floated on the sublets of the Amazon River, seven feet in diameter; Bromeliads and Venus fly traps; fibrous and adventitious taproots, dissolving minerals, exponential and breaching the soil; epidermal growths, feathers and hairs, distinctive outer coverings, plumage and keratin; the chitinous skeletons and antennæ of the Ectognatha; Lepidoptera, with their inky, delicate wings; Anthophiles, pollenating flora and creating honey and beeswax; Coccnellidæ, red and black and fluttering, always finding their way onto bare knees; pharaoh, black garden, and carpenter ants; strata atop strata of sedimentary, metamorphic, and igneous rock; basalt, obsidian, paridontite, marble, quartzite, slate, coal, rock salt, limestone, sandstone; fingerprints; the ulnar loop, coming from the pinky side of the hand; the whorl, a spiral pattern; the radial loop, coming from the thumb side of the hand; the arch; the double loop, two loops going in two directions; reptilia, turtles, Crocodilus, snakes, lizards, tuataras, and all their extinct relatives, with bony plates and scales; beryl, quartz, agate, ametrine, and coral; hard, shiny, malleable, fusible, ductile metals, capable of electrical and thermal conductivity; caves formed in karst, limestone, dolomite, gypsum, an acidic tinge; sinkholes, stalagmites and stalactites; soil, loam, clay, and silt—all these naturalistic phenomena had Cletus Tumlin musing on what held it all together.

Dressing the wall behind him, small and shrinking into nothingness, Cletus Tumlin coagulated with the wicker. Housed within the wicker, the colloquy solidified into unreality. He had been condemned, his splattered brain on the wall behind him; he was the material and the wicker. He was the glue.

<u>Stories' Original Publications</u>

"Creighton" *The J.J. Outré Review Volume I, Issue 4*
"A Philosopher's Lexis" *Detectives of the Fantastic III*
"Fire!" *Siren's Call Death In All Its Glory!*
"Occipital Circus" *Danse Macabre*
"The Auk" *Dark Gothic Resurrected Magazine* July 2017
The Phrenologist (HellBound Books)

About Your Author

Anders M. Svenning was born in New York. His work has appeared in many magazines. He has a few books. *50 States Poetry* (Pansophic Press), *Verdant Grounds, Subtle Boundaries*(Adelaide Books) are two books, which have been released, and he has forthcoming pieces, too, *We Are Inmate #881129* (Wild Dreams Publishing), *Otus in Betulaceae* (Adelaide Books), *Life After Schizophrenia* (Scarlet Leaf Publishing).

<u>Other HellBound Books Titles</u>
<u>Available at: www.hellboundbookspublishing.com</u>

Southern House

Filled with copious amounts of black humor, Gerri R. Gray's first published novel is an offbeat adventure story that could be described as One Flew over the Cuckoo's Nest meets Thelma and Louise.

Flashback to 1974. Farika is a lovely young woman who wakes up one day to find herself a patient in a bizarre New York City psychiatric asylum. She has no idea who she is, and possesses no memories of where she came from nor how she got there.

Fearing for her life after being attacked by a berserk girl with over one hundred personalities and a vicious nurse with sadistic intentions, the frightened amnesiac teams up with an audacious lesbian with a comically unbalanced mind, and together they attempt a daring escape.

But little do they know that a long strange journey into an even more insane world filled with a multitude of perilous predicaments and off-kilter individuals are waiting for them on the outside. Farika's weird reality crumbles when she finally discovers who, and what, she really is!

Graveyard Girls

A delicious collection of horrific tales and darkest poetry from the cream of the crop, all lovingly compiled by the incomparable Gerri R Gray! Nestling between the covers of this formidable tome are twenty-six of the very best lady authors writing on the horror scene today!

These tales of terror are guaranteed to chill your very soul and awaken you in the dead of the night with fear-sweat clinging to your every pore and your heart pounding hard and heavy in your labored breast…

Featuring stories from: Xtina Marie, MW Brown, Rebecca Kolodziej, Anya Lee, Barbara Jacobson, Gerri R Gray, Christina Bergling, Julia Benally, Olga Werby, Kelly Glover, Lee Franklin, Linda M. Crate, Vanessa Hawkins, P. Alanna Roethle, J. Snow, Evelyn Eve, Serena Daniels, S.E. Davis, Anya Lee, Sam Hill, J.C. Raye, Donna J.W. Munroe, R.J. Murray, C. Bailey-Bacchus, Varonica Chaney and Marian Finch.

Blood and Kisses

The definitive short story collecting from James H Longmore - an eclectic mix of dark horror, bizarro and Twilight-Zone style tales of the downright disturbing.

Welcome to the long awaited collection from the writer of horror novels *'Pede* and *Tenebrion*; a foreword by Richard Chizmar (co-author of *Gwendy's Button Box* and author of *A Long December*), 18 short stories, 5 flash fiction and even a poem - all skin-crawling, soul-shredding tales of terror, of the darkest things that skulk amongst the night's inky shadows, and of the everyday gone horribly awry.

Discover the alternative implication of technology becoming self-aware, enjoy the acquaintance of a charismatic new pastor who promises his flock a brand new place in which to worship his God, and spend a little time in the company of a nice young man who is inexorably caught up in his home town's terrible secret. Then there is Cupid's revelation that personally he has never experienced love, yet we discover that very emotion alive and not so well amongst the ruins of a post zombie apocalypse world, and we bear witness to a childhood innocence forever destroyed in a war-torn city. There is more, Dear Reader, much, much more; for within these pages we have devils, demons and ghosts, lycanthropes and demi-gods, all rubbing nefarious shoulders with vilest of Hell's offspring who have slithered from the netherworld to doff their caps and wish us all the sweetest of dreams…

Shopping List

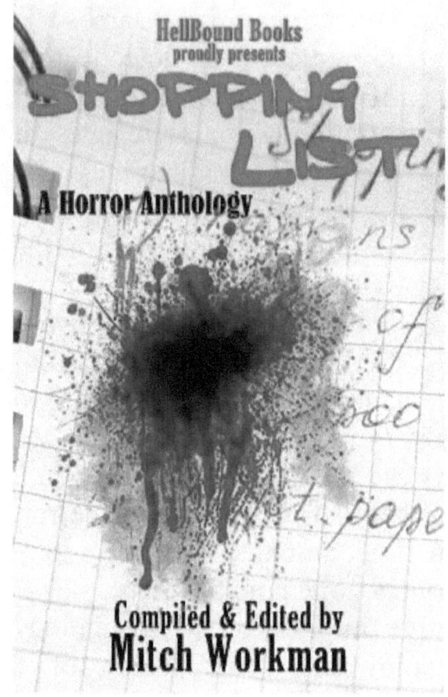

A simply superlative collection of spine-tingling horror from the very best minds in the business!

We decided upon the shopping list theme for this particular volume as an antithesis to those wildly successful writers (they know who they are) of whom it is often said *'we would read their damned shopping list if they published it!'*

Well, we have given twenty-one of the hottest authors in the independent horror scene the unique opportunity to have their own shopping lists read by you - along with their most terrifying tales of course!

Stories of gut-wrenching terror from:
Kathy Dinisi, Robert Over, Christopher O'Halloran, Eric W. Burgin, Russ Gartz, Mark Slada, Jeff Baker, Tim Miller, Nick Swain,JC Raye, Jovan Jones, Ben Stevens, David F. Gray, Brandon Cracraft, M.S. Swift, Kevin Holton, David Owain Hughes, Bertram Allan Mullin, Jeff C. Stevenson, Sebastian Crow and S.E. Rise

The Big Book of Bootleg Horror Volume 4

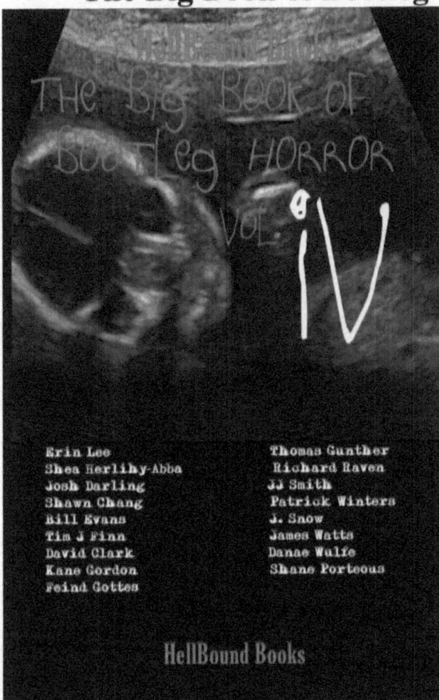

Welcome to Volume Four of our best-selling horror anthology, featuring tales of terror and dark, slithering things to chill the marrow and keep even the most resolute of horror fans awake in the small hours of the night when the inherently evil and deliciously malevolent come out to explore our earthly realm.

Featuring:
Erin Lee, Thomas Gunther, Sheah Herlihy-Abba, Richard Raven, Josh Darling, JJ Smith, Shawn Chang, Patrick winters, Bill Evans, J. Snow, Tim J. Finn, James Watts, David Clark, Danae Wulfe, Kane Gordon, Shane Porteous, and the ever-present Feind Gottes.

Another superlative gathering of the dark and disturbing from some of the best independent authors writing today...

Anders M. Svenning

**A HellBound Books LLC
Publication**

http://www.hellboundbookspublishing.com